"GO INSIDE, ELISABETH," LUKE TOLD HER pushing her gently toward the house. "Get into the shower before you catch a cold."

She turned to face him. "You're not coming inside?"

He nodded at the men coming up the beach. "I'll go see what they want."

"I can wait," she said.

He wanted her away before she noticed both men were carrying guns. "I don't want them to see you like this, honey. Please go inside."

"See me like what?"

"Your lips are swollen and a little red because I kissed you harder than I should have. And you've got a look in your eyes that's making me so hard I can barely walk." He kissed her quickly, then sent her away. "And your hair's so wild and tangled, as if you've been rolling in the sand with your lover. I don't want anyone to see you like that except me."

"We're not lovers," she whispered.

His gaze seared her. "We will be, Elisabeth. Sooner

A sp   "I think
it shoul

WHAT ARE *LOVESWEPT* ROMANCES?

They are stories of true romance and touching emotion. We believe those two very important ingredients are constants in our highly sensual and very believable stories in the LOVESWEPT line. Our goal is to give you, the reader, stories of consistently high quality that may sometimes make you laugh, sometimes make you cry, but are always fresh and creative and contain many delightful surprises within their pages.

Most romance fans read an enormous number of books. Those they truly love, they keep. Others may be traded with friends and soon forgotten. We hope that each LOVESWEPT romance will be a treasure—a "keeper." We will always try to publish

LOVE STORIES YOU'LL NEVER FORGET
BY AUTHORS YOU'LL ALWAYS REMEMBER

The Editors

DANGEROUS LOVE

VICTORIA LEIGH

BANTAM BOOKS
NEW YORK · TORONTO · LONDON · SYDNEY · AUCKLAND

DANGEROUS LOVE
A Bantam Book / April 1994

If you would be interested in receiving protective vinyl covers for your
Loveswept books, please write to this address for information:

Loveswept
Bantam Books
P.O. Box 985
Hicksville, NY 11802

ISBN 0-553-44447-6

Published simultaneously in the United States and Canada

Bantam Books are published by Bantam Books, a division of Bantam Doubleday Dell Publishing Group, Inc. Its trademark, consisting of the words
"Bantam Books" and the portrayal of a rooster, is Registered in U.S. Patent
and Trademark Office and in other countries. Marca Registrada. Bantam
Books, 1540 Broadway, New York, New York 10036.

PRINTED IN THE UNITED STATES OF AMERICA

OPM   0 9 8 7 6 5 4 3 2 1

DANGEROUS
LOVE

PROLOGUE

Luke Sinclair leaned back in the leather armchair and stared at the man across the desk from him. "She needs to be told, Wyatt," he said. "Not knowing about Curtis could get her killed."

"It's your job to keep that from happening."

Wyatt Conner's cold, steely gaze sliced the air between them. Luke leveled his own icy stare to remind Wyatt he was not intimidated. "I'll have a better chance of keeping her alive if she cooperates."

"No, dammit!" Wyatt's open palm slammed flat on his desk, dislodging the phone from its cradle. Muttering obscenities of the sort that Luke didn't often hear from his normally controlled employer, Wyatt replaced the phone with a crash. "If I tell Elisabeth that I'm sending my chief of security to keep her safe from the man who kidnapped her six years ago, she'll turn into a basket case so fast, your head will spin."

"She deserves to know Curtis has escaped from prison. Keeping her shielded will only make it harder to protect her." Luke steepled his long fingers and regarded Wyatt with a determined gaze. "Your sister is twenty-seven, Wyatt. She's old enough to know what's going on."

"I know Elisabeth, Luke. You don't. Curtis about destroyed her the first time around. She can't handle this." His fingers drummed restlessly on the polished wood surface of his desk. "I don't want her to have to."

Almost against his will, Luke's gaze followed Wyatt's to the silver-framed photograph at the corner of the desk. The woman in the photo was exquisite, beautiful in a way that reminded Luke of the rising sun. He remembered the first time he'd seen the photograph, how the breath had been sucked from his lungs, leaving him winded and speechless until his pounding heart had finally forced him to take a breath for the sake of his own continued existence.

That had been four years ago. He'd learned control since then, finding it easier to avoid looking at the photo at all, masking his expression when he couldn't resist.

Gritting his teeth against the thought—no, the *knowledge*!—that she was in danger, he stared at the photo and tried to see the crippling vulnerability Wyatt was convinced was there. Long blond hair fell in wind-blown curls around Elisabeth's shoulders. Dark-blue eyes laughed out at him from a delicately molded face that was both vibrant and healthy. She was a small woman, almost dwarfed by the Doberman that stood on its hind legs to lick her cheek.

The photo had been taken on the rugged beach of Elisabeth's island home in the Puget Sound, the channel of water that divided Washington State from Canada. Quincy Island was halfway around the world from Wyatt's Singapore office, yet Luke could almost feel the brush of her laughter.

He doubted she'd have reason to laugh once he

explained why he'd come to her. Shifting in his chair, he stretched his long legs out in front of him as he studied his boss. Wyatt Conner rarely let his emotions show, and this was one of those times. The lines that creased his face had deepened, and his jaw was so tightly clenched, Luke could see the muscles twitch in protest.

He looked worried. But then, he had a lot to worry about.

There must have been many times over the years when Wyatt had worried about his sister, whom he'd cared for since their parents had died. The couple had been washed overboard during a storm while on a pleasure cruise between Singapore and Java, Wyatt had once told him. Wyatt had been in his late twenties, making his own way through the corporate maze of hotels and miscellaneous properties his parents had acquired over the years. He'd decided to keep Elisabeth with him in Singapore; his only other choice had been to send her to an aunt in South Carolina whom neither of them had ever met.

From what he'd learned about Elisabeth, Luke figured she would have left Wyatt only if he'd tied her up and shipped her UPS. "Elisabeth knows you'll never let anything happen to her, Wyatt."

Wyatt snorted his disagreement. "Just like I didn't let anything happen to her six years ago?"

"That wasn't your fault. I've read all the files, and even you have to admit that you couldn't have prevented Curtis from getting to her." Wyatt's wealth and prominence made him a natural target for terrorists, kidnappers, and other riffraff. Their quest for easy money was as much a fact of life in this part of the world as it was in Italy, South America, or any of the Arab states. Wyatt had taken what precautions he could with his life and that of his sister, but sometimes precautions just weren't enough.

Elisabeth had been too young to fully appreciate the dangers. Too protected perhaps. Too naive.

Luke blew out a long breath. "It's my understanding that once Elisabeth turned nineteen, she paid very little attention to her big brother's advice about who she should date."

"I should have had Curtis investigated more thoroughly—"

"But Elisabeth wouldn't allow you to do anything more than a surface check on any of her dates," Luke finished for him. "Curtis's association with that Libyan terrorist group was hidden so deep, you'd never have found it. There was very little you could do once they'd targeted you to finance their little games."

Luke had known when he came to work for Wyatt that his new boss was one of the most powerful men on the Pacific Rim—which was what had intrigued him in the first place. After a varied career that ranged from a stint with the Navy SEAL to a dozen or so years with an ultrasecret U.S. intelligence organization, Luke had been primed for action and intrigue. Wyatt provided both—without the bureaucratic nonsense that plagued government employment at every level. Being responsible for the security of Wyatt's extensive holdings, not to mention his personal life, was a challenge Luke hadn't been able to resist.

And after four years, keeping Elisabeth safe was not so much a part of his job as it was part of his life.

Wyatt pulled his gaze from the photo. "They hurt my sister for money. *My* money. I have trouble living with that."

"They would have found another way if they were

determined enough. Elisabeth just happened to be available." Luke swallowed the disgust he felt at the easy words, but over twenty years' experience in his field had taught him that emotion was a costly adjunct. "They saw kidnapping Elisabeth as the most expedient way to get your attention—not to mention a few of your millions. The only way you could have prevented it was to keep Elisabeth a virtual prisoner yourself."

"Instead I let her become their prisoner." Wyatt spun his chair to face the large window that overlooked the twinkling lights of the bay.

"But you got her back," Luke reminded him. "Without giving in to their demands."

"And put Curtis away for life, or so I thought." He swung back around and leveled a demanding stare on Luke. "Is she any better off today? Stuck on that island in the middle of nowhere because she's too frightened to leave? So afraid of strangers that anyone new to the island sends her scurrying indoors until you've had them vetted all the way back to kindergarten?"

"You haven't paid attention to her file lately if you think she's that insecure. McCain's reports over the past few years give a different picture from the one you're painting." Luke referred to the man on his staff who was responsible for the on-site inspection and maintenance of Elisabeth's security system. McCain's reports had evolved over the years from a curt, almost painful depiction of a frightened young woman to a detailed accounting of how Elisabeth was learning to cope with her fears. A positive accounting, Luke firmly believed, of a woman who was getting on with her life. Luke should know. He'd all but memorized the file his office kept on the boss's sister. "From what McCain says, Elisabeth seems quite well adjusted."

"As long as she doesn't leave the island."

"Perhaps it's time for her to do just that." Luke leaned forward, ready to make his proposal. "If I tell her Curtis is loose and could conceivably have learned about her hideaway, I'm certain she'll be amenable to me taking her off the island."

"I don't want her frightened—"

"For God's sake, Wyatt!" Luke exploded. "What do you think is going to happen if Curtis finds her on Quincy Island?"

"He won't."

"How can you be so damned sure?"

"I have to be," Wyatt said, his voice a dead calm. "I cannot allow her to be hurt again. That's why I'm sending you. If Curtis gets past me, I know you'll keep Elisabeth safe—and in the dark."

"You're tying my hands." Luke ran his fingers through the short dark hair at the back of his head. "Protecting her on that island without telling her anything will be nearly impossible."

"Tell her you're doing a complete overhaul of the security system. She won't have any reason to doubt you. God knows she's complained often enough over the past four years about how the local wildlife sets off your alarms. She says it scares her half to death when the alarm goes off and she doesn't know why."

Luke's gut twisted at the thought of Elisabeth scared, but logic told him that frightened was better than vulnerable when it came to guarding against the kind of men who had kidnapped her. "If she didn't complain in the two years before I came, it's because the security system was hardly adequate. At least now you know she's as secure as technology can make her."

Wyatt raised an eyebrow mockingly. "She claims she was perfectly safe before."

"You don't believe that any more than I do. A troop of Cub Scouts could have penetrated that excuse for a security system and she wouldn't have known until she smelled the hot dogs cooking." He shrugged. "There's nothing I can do if a rabbit jumps across an infrared beam. She has to expect a few false alarms if the net is working properly."

"I suspect that dog of hers is more of a culprit than she admits."

Luke silently agreed. "It's not going to be easy to pretend to overhaul a system that's already as efficient as we can make it. What's she going to say if I'm there longer than a week? There's nothing in her file that indicates she's stupid, Wyatt."

Wyatt leaned back in his chair and waited a long moment before speaking. "This isn't like you, Luke."

"What? Arguing?" He gave a short laugh. "Hell, Wyatt, we argue all the time—especially when you're trying to do the job you hired me to do."

"That's not what I meant." Wyatt picked up a sleek brass letter opener and held the tip against the middle finger of his other hand. "As my chief of security, you've overseen Elisabeth's protection for four years now. Not once during that time have you suggested we include her in the decision making."

"It didn't occur to me she'd be interested in the merits of pressure pads versus sonic sensors."

"You've never even been to the island," Wyatt continued as though he hadn't heard him. "The closest you've gotten to Elisabeth is that file your office maintains on her."

"By the time you hired me, she already knew McCain. I saw no reason to intrude any further on her privacy."

"Not to mention that you were afraid you'd scare her to death."

"There's that." Luke didn't have to look in a mirror to know what Wyatt was talking about. He'd lived with his size and rough looks all his life. At six feet four inches, two hundred and forty pounds, few men could equal him in size and even fewer could match him in strength. Wyatt came close. He was a couple of inches shorter, and the matter of which man was stronger was as yet untested.

Luke knew it wasn't his size that would frighten Elisabeth. It was his face, where years of harsh realities had been etched in uncompromising detail. Strength, violence, and bruising survival were what he saw when he bothered to look beyond the bristles he shaved twice daily.

He held Wyatt's questioning gaze stoically. "McCain is a lot easier to look at."

"A lot of women find that mug of yours irresistible," Wyatt drawled.

"It's not my face they're wanting," Luke returned, a disparaging grin edging his mouth. "It's the danger they sense that makes them hot." He thought ahead to the impending meeting with Elisabeth and wondered if a bag over his head would cushion the shock.

"Elisabeth needs your strength, Luke. Even if she's afraid of it."

Luke sighed and let his head drop back on the cushioned chair, his gaze narrowing on Wyatt. "You'll keep me informed on the chase?" Wyatt was leading a hand-picked team that would track and, if things went as planned, recapture Curtis.

"Through Sloane," Wyatt confirmed, referring to Elisabeth's nearest neighbor. Matt Sloane, an artist who thrived on the island's remote privacy, had arrived on Quincy Island with his wife and son just weeks before Elisabeth had moved into her own home. He was also on Wyatt's payroll, a little fact that had thus far escaped Elisabeth's attention. She'd been told he was simply a neighbor who would come to her rescue if the need arose. Someone she could call if she got scared, living all alone as she insisted on doing.

In the ensuing silence Luke examined Wyatt's plan for flaws. Outside of its being structured precisely the opposite of what he would have done were he given any choice in the matter, he couldn't find anything worth discussing. He looked across the desk to find Wyatt studying him.

"I've seen the way you look at her picture, Luke. More to the point, I've seen the way you *don't* look at it."

Wyatt's softly spoken comment was a surprise Luke didn't like, and he pretended not to understand. "What the hell does that mean?"

"You care for her," Wyatt said, his expression carefully blank. "I thought you should know I noticed."

Luke watched Wyatt, wondering just how far into his soul the other man had seen, holding his silence in lieu of saying something totally stupid—something like "You're wrong." They both knew better.

Wyatt continued, aiming his observations from a different perspective. "She'll never come to care for you in return, you know. Elisabeth needs a gentle man."

"You're saying I'm not gentle?" Luke tried to make it sound like a joke.

Wyatt didn't laugh. "You're the roughest man I've ever known."

"Sure you're not talking about yourself, Wyatt? Even your friends claim you give a new meaning to ruthless." Luke wasn't prepared to talk with Wyatt about his sister.

He couldn't imagine a time when he would be.

"I know what I'm talking about, Luke. You're rough, rugged, and entirely capable. And there's not another man I'd trust with Elisabeth's life." Wyatt threw the letter opener down on the blotter. "That doesn't mean I think you belong with Elisabeth."

Luke forced a lopsided grin. "Not to worry, boss. On that point I happen to agree with you. Elisabeth deserves better."

"Not better. Different."

"Gentle," Luke said.

Wyatt nodded. "Gentle. She's fragile, Luke. Do your best not to frighten her. She'll fall apart."

Luke's grin widened. "She wouldn't dare. Not with me watching. She's got too much of her brother in her to let anyone see her cower."

The telephone on Wyatt's desk rang. He picked it up, listened a moment, then made a few terse comments before hanging up. "The plane is ready. I've instructed the pilot to stay with the Lear in Seattle in case you need to hustle Elisabeth out of there in a hurry."

"What will you use if your plane is grounded in Seattle?" Luke asked as he stood and shook the hand Wyatt offered.

"I've already leased a couple of other jets to take care of the team." Wyatt checked his watch and walked with Luke to the door. "Remember, Luke, I don't want her told."

Luke shook his head. "I'll decide when I get there—"

"That's not what I said."

"If she's as fragile as you seem to think, I'll keep it

from her as long as I can. That's the best I can promise you." He went to open the door but wasn't surprised when Wyatt flattened his hand against it.

Wyatt's gaze hardened. "I've fired men for less."

A grin pushed at the corner of Luke's mouth. "I know. I've watched."

Wyatt shook his head and sighed. "You're the best man for the job, Luke. I'd rather not have to send someone else."

"I'm going to the island, Wyatt, whether or not I'm on your payroll."

"Why?" Wyatt's eyes narrowed in suspicion. "I thought we agreed you're the wrong man for my sister."

Luke exhaled a long, frustrated breath. "We did." He put his hand on the doorknob and turned it, forcing Wyatt to back up or get serious about stopping him. If he could.

Their friendship wasn't worth the risk finding out whether Wyatt could stop him. He hoped Wyatt agreed.

He did. His boss reluctantly took a step back, and Luke was through the door and halfway through the outer office, heading for the elevator, before Wyatt spoke again.

"Why, Luke? Why are you going to Quincy Island?"

Luke hesitated and glanced at Wyatt's secretary, Sheila, who was pretending she didn't notice either of the two men towering over her desk. "Damned if I know, Wyatt."

Not waiting for Wyatt's reaction, he turned and punched the button for the elevator. Wyatt stared after him for a moment, then returned to his own office.

Neither man was there when Sheila lifted the phone on her desk and made a very long-distance call.

ONE

Elisabeth hung up her phone and smiled. "So he's finally coming."

The only other living being within earshot lifted his head at her words and yipped a noncommittal reply. Then he got up from the rug that served as his daybed and padded across the floor to where his mistress sat at the kitchen table. He stuck his warm nose against her open palm and licked her fingers.

Elisabeth laughed and curled her hand around the Doberman's muzzle. "No, Sneakers, I wasn't announcing an early dinner. I was talking about Mr. Sinclair. The great man himself has decided to pay us a call." A frown creased her brow as she considered the possible reasons for Luke Sinclair's visit.

She'd wanted this meeting for nearly all of the four years Sinclair been working for Wyatt—wanted, but hadn't by so much as a whisper said anything to anyone. Had Wyatt known, he would have questioned her reasons. How could she tell him she wanted Luke Sinclair on the island so that she could exact revenge on him for turning her home into a prison? How could she say that to her brother, knowing it would upset him—the same brother who still blamed himself for what happened all those years ago?

No, she couldn't say that. Nor could she confess that she no longer bothered to turn on the high-tech security system that Wyatt considered essential to her safety. But then, he didn't have to live with the unpredictable blast of an alarm—alarms over nothing more than a falling rock or misplaced hippity-hop. Sneakers had set off so many during the first few months after Sinclair's upgraded system had been installed, she'd nearly given up letting him run alone after dark. Even after McCain had fixed all the fixable bugs and glitches, there had still been the problem of remembering to turn the thing off before Sneakers went outside or before she herself stepped out for a breath of air. She'd long since given up hoping that the rabbits and seagulls would wander elsewhere.

But when pretending to be scared to death every time the alarm went off hadn't swayed Wyatt from his insistence that the system was necessary, she'd done the only thing she considered feasible.

She'd switched it off and left it that way.

The fact that the system was only activated for Wyatt's, Sheila's, and McCain's visits was a secret she kept to ensure Wyatt's peace of mind. She knew that if her brother discovered her subterfuge, he would worry more than he already did. About her safety, *her* peace of mind.

Elisabeth was confident that the pieces of her mind were more or less intact and would remain that way as long as she stayed on Quincy Island. Leaving was a step she considered unnecessary, and risky to boot—unnecessary because she was perfectly happy on her island home, risky because there was always the chance she'd make the same mistake in judgment she'd made before. A life of relative seclusion was preferable to living among people she was afraid to trust.

Trusting the wrong person had nearly gotten her killed six years ago. She couldn't believe her instincts were any better now than they had been then.

So she stayed.

In the meantime she'd given up trying to convince Wyatt that her mind was functioning normally, not counting the odd nightmare or two over the years. As long as she refused to leave the island, Wyatt dismissed her protests that Quincy Island was perfectly safe without all the fancy equipment that warned of intruders, miscellaneous rodents, and the occasional misguided seagull. Even with the system turned off, she continued to complain about false alarms on the off chance that Wyatt would reconsider. So far, he hadn't.

So why was Sinclair coming now . . . and why had Wyatt decided it was necessary? Could either of them have guessed her secret? Sheila hadn't had time to tell her anything more than that Sinclair was on his way. That was better than no notice at all. Elisabeth gave thanks for the early-warning system she'd negotiated several years earlier with Wyatt's secretary.

Not even a flicker of guilt assailed her at the subterfuge. Wyatt should have known better than to hire her best friend and not anticipate a little collusion. And while Sheila was less than comfortable with the arrangement, it wasn't as though she was exchanging information with the enemy.

Elisabeth wondered what was so secret that even Wyatt's secretary didn't know about it.

She shrugged off her questions and released Sneakers' muzzle. Sinclair would explain all when he arrived.

Then she'd have a little fun at his expense, revenge for all those alarm-filled nights.

She gave a low, excited laugh and wondered if Sinclair had a sense of humor. McCain hadn't said anything about that particular aspect of his boss's temperament. In fact McCain hadn't told her much more than that Luke Sinclair was big—*very* big.

Luckily McCain wasn't her only source of information regarding Luke Sinclair. Sheila was also a frequent visitor to Quincy Island, bringing with her news of mutual friends, gossip from the island state of Singapore, and wickedly clever vignettes about Wyatt's fleeting relationships with various women. It was like old times when Sheila visited, reminding Elisabeth of when they were teenagers and Wyatt's sex life had been a subject of considerable awe and mirth.

That Sheila had never fallen for Wyatt had been a mystery to Elisabeth for years, and she'd finally broached the subject during Sheila's most recent visit to Quincy Island. Sheila had laughed and shaken her head, saying something about the absurdity of sacrificing friendship for an affair that didn't stand a hope of lasting beyond a few weeks. Friendship aside, she liked her job too much to trade it for a brief time with a man she didn't love.

She'd then launched into an outrageous account of a red-headed tobacco heiress who had recently pursued Wyatt with such vigor, he'd been forced to flee to his New Zealand hotel-and-casino complex until the woman had finally left Singapore. Unable to imagine her brother running from anyone or anything, Elisabeth had refused to believe the story until Wyatt had confirmed it with his own version of events during his next visit.

Sinclair's arrival on the scene four years earlier should have been an intriguing addition to Sheila's repertoire.

All Elisabeth had been able to get out of her best friend, though, was that Sinclair was "big, polite, and reserved. Intimidating. A man I wouldn't want to get on the wrong side of."

When Elisabeth had asked if that meant Sheila was afraid of him, she'd denied it, then made the comment that had piqued Elisabeth's interest. "Luke Sinclair is interesting in a way that makes me conscious of the difference between men and women." Elisabeth had pressed for an explanation, but Sheila had just shaken her head and said it wasn't something that could be explained. Sinclair had to be experienced.

Elisabeth had been strangely relieved when Sheila had segued into a discussion of the new man in her life. Clearly Sinclair was interesting but not a man Sheila was interested in. A difference Elisabeth noticed and noted.

In the four years since, Elisabeth had learned little else about Sinclair. Not even Wyatt had contributed much, although that was mostly Elisabeth's fault in not daring to ask. She preferred to keep her secrets . . . well, secret. Like her disuse of the security system, her curiosity about Luke Sinclair was definitely a secret.

Luke Sinclair is interesting in a way that makes me conscious of the difference between men and women. Sheila's words lingered on the outside edge of Elisabeth's consciousness, coming to the forefront of her thoughts with a frequency that both intrigued and annoyed her.

Big, reserved, and interesting. Sense of humor, questionable. Four years later she was about to get a chance to add her own adjectives. She couldn't wait.

Standing up, she decided she'd better worry less about his sense of humor and more about what to feed him. The Doberman followed when she crossed the room to rummage through the freezer, pushing his head between her thighs to sniff at the wonders that were stacked haphazardly on a lower shelf. Elisabeth grabbed at his collar before the dog glued his tongue to the icy interior, reaching with her other hand for a package of steaks. Elbowing the door shut, she threw the meat onto the counter.

Sneakers reared from her grasp, whining plaintively because he'd only just realized there was no kibble forthcoming. He perked up, though, when Elisabeth went to the back door and pulled her jacket from a hook. A tramp along the beach rated high on Sneakers' list of preferred activities. The Doberman was through the door and shooting around the corner of the house toward the water before Elisabeth could stuff her hands into the deep pockets of her all-weather coat.

A smile lit her face as she imagined the meeting between Wyatt's chief of security and her pet attack dog.

She was willing to bet Sneakers would be the more friendly of the two.

A brilliant triangle of white sliced across the edge of her vision. Elisabeth moved the heavy field glasses a fraction and caught the tail end of the sail before it ducked behind the stand of trees that obscured her view of the bay.

Sinclair had arrived. She would have missed him if it hadn't been for that sensation of *knowing* he was there, a feeling that had made her raise the glasses when she'd only just put them down.

"Indulging in fantasy now, are we?" she asked aloud as she searched the choppy seas from the vantage point of her bedroom window. She was fairly sure there wouldn't be another sighting. Unless he changed the tack he was on, Sinclair probably intended to moor the boat several hundred yards down the beach from her dock. There was an older dock there, half rotted but adequate for a tie-up. The only other options were anchoring in rough seas or, even worse, her own dock, which was tricked out with a variety of alarms.

Sinclair's alarms. Sneakers yipped in his sleep, and Elisabeth lowered the glasses. No, Sinclair wouldn't announce his presence abruptly. He'd probably wait down on the beach until she came to walk Sneakers and let her find him. Or he'd go over to Matt Sloane's and call her from there. Turning her back to the window, she let her gaze drift over to the oversized four-poster where Sneakers was catching a late-morning nap.

She thought of the steaks soaking in the datil-pepper marinade and decided a brisk walk was just what Sneakers needed to wake him up.

She couldn't wait to see if Luke Sinclair liked his food spicy. Very spicy.

With Sneakers at her heels, Elisabeth rounded the nest of boulders that screened her private stretch of sand from the old dock, where a sleek twenty-foot sloop was moored. Fighting the cowardly urge to spy on the boat from the cover of one of the larger boulders, she instead came to an abrupt halt within sight of the boat, pretending she'd only just noticed it in case Sinclair was watching. It bobbed erratically on the water, a brilliant slash of yellow and white that was pleasantly anomalous with the gray skies above. The wind whipped caps of froth against its sides, and Elisabeth grimaced as the gusts caught at her hair and slathered it across her face. Brushing it away, she peered more intently toward the boat, waiting for Sinclair to appear. Remembering the shy, nervous type her brother had surely billed her as, she backed up a few paces, trying to look as though she was ready to run.

Sinclair didn't surface to witness her meager acting attempts.

"So how are we supposed to do this now?" she muttered, knowing it would be totally out of character for her to go any closer. She was pondering the solution to that when Sneakers looked up from his investigation of a tidal pool and discovered the sailboat. Incautious as always, the Doberman surged toward the new addition to the coastline at a dead run.

"Sneakers! Come back here!" Either the wind took her words or the dog simply wasn't paying attention, because he didn't even look back. Realizing this was the perfect opportunity to announce her presence without seeming to, Elisabeth was just about to yell at the dog again when a shadow fell across the sand at her feet.

A shadow in the shape of a man. A very large man. Her head jerked toward the shadow's origin even as she jumped a few feet toward the clouds. Tall, burly, and looking at her from behind aviator-style sunglasses, the man made no move to impede her flight. In the split second that she was airborne Elisabeth understood the frustration of the flightless chicken. She wanted to fly away, escape into the skies where it was safe.

Just as for the chicken, it was a no-go.

She knew it was Sinclair before her feet hit the sand. Sinclair, a very big man. A man one wouldn't want for an enemy. McCain hadn't told her any lies. Neither had Sheila.

Luke Sinclair is interesting in a way that makes me conscious of the difference between men and women.

Elisabeth knew now what Sheila had meant, if one could possibly know something without understanding it.

She also knew it was the "interesting" element that had made her jump, not his size—which was formidable, she granted. Even though he now stood at least six feet away, she felt as though he was towering over her. Which put him at least a foot taller than herself. Probably taller than Wyatt, she mused, with shoulders to match. Even beneath the bulky duck-cloth coat, she could discern their broad outline.

If he didn't want her to run, he wouldn't have any trouble stopping her. Elisabeth took a moment to remind herself he was on her side, a simple fact that didn't calm her pounding heart.

She wasn't afraid of him, yet she was afraid.

Sucking in erratic breaths, she crossed her arms beneath her breasts and stared at him, forgetting that the Elisabeth he expected to meet would break and run from a stranger. Forgetting everything except that she wanted to know more about this man who stood silent and immobile under her scrutiny, his hands out of sight in the pockets of the dark-green coat.

He was older than she'd expected. Early forties, she guessed, his short brown hair streaked with gray. The flesh of his face was tanned and pulled taut over features that were almost harshly honest; a nose that had been broken more than once; high, flat cheekbones; and a square jaw. No dimple on this man. In a fluid movement he lifted his hand and pulled off the sunglasses to reveal calm, assessing eyes, eyes a shade of gray that reminded her of rain-filled skies.

"I'm Sinclair," he said. "Luke Sinclair. I work for your brother."

Well, yes, she'd rather assumed that. But he wasn't to know that he was expected. Or welcome—after a fashion. Mustering an expression of disbelief, she backed off another few feet and bit her lip as though she were too afraid to speak.

Sinclair didn't budge. With the sunglasses dangling from one hand, he spoke again, his deep, gravely voice carefully nonthreatening. "Probably the best thing for you to do is go up to the house and call his secretary. Wyatt is traveling, but Sheila will be able to reassure you."

So easily did she trust him that it was all she could do to hold her ground and feign total fright. She thought she heard him mumble something vaguely obscene under his breath, but when he spoke again, it was without a single thread of impatience.

"Elisabeth, I'm not going to hurt you. I'll wait right here until you make the call."

"How do I know you won't follow me?" she whispered, feeling like an idiot.

He looked toward the boat where Sneakers was dancing excitedly on the rotting dock, clearly awaiting someone to welcome him aboard. "Take your dog with you."

Her fears were suddenly real. Wouldn't the real Sinclair know Sneakers wasn't your typical Doberman, that his attack-and-guard skills were essentially nonexistent? It didn't take a conscious decision for her to back off several more feet, but the look of frustration on the man's face stopped her.

Pushing long fingers through his hair, he kicked a broken shell at his feet before suddenly raising his head, revealing a wicked gleam in his eyes. "If you keep Sneakers with you, at least I'll be safe from him. We both know that animal will lick me to death if I get too close to you."

Her fears evaporated. "I should take him for your sake?" she asked, a smile threatening the corners of her mouth.

"And yours." Sinclair put his glasses back on, leaving her to wonder whether that spark of mischief had flared into something more. "He might not be the best protection in the world, but at least he'll warn you if I follow."

Or he might not. Elisabeth was never too sure how much Sneakers knew about what went on in the world around him. Uncrossing her arms, she stuffed her hands into her pockets and tried to appear as though she might be prepared to make the call. "It's the middle of the night in Singapore. Sheila will be at home asleep."

"It's your choice, Elisabeth. I don't have any other way to establish my credentials with you."

You could try asking me who I think you are, she returned silently. Aloud she said, "I'll leave Sneakers with you. Once he realizes you're here, he won't come with me anyway."

Sinclair's eyes narrowed in surprise. "I thought he wasn't trained well enough to guard and hold a man."

She couldn't help her grin. "Not in the conventional sense." Glancing over her shoulder, she shouted for the dog. To her pleasant surprise he bounded off the dock and sped toward her, landing in a spray of sand at her feet. She reached down and stroked his sleek neck. "Sneakers, meet your new playmate."

Sneakers and Sinclair regarded each other with interest—Sinclair's expression tinged with disgust, Sneakers' with enthusiasm.

"Sneakers," she said clearly, "play."

"Play? What do you mean—" The rest of Sinclair's words were lost as Sneakers launched himself across the gap between the two humans. Elisabeth stayed just long enough to notice Sneakers didn't manage to knock Sinclair over on his first assault. Confident, though, that Sinclair wouldn't last long on his feet, she turned and ran toward the house, slowing to a walk when she was out of sight of the frolicking duo.

She hoped Sinclair enjoyed this little playtime. She knew Sneakers would.

Elisabeth still hadn't asked him why he'd come.

Luke followed her through the back door, raising the duffel bag he'd brought from the boat so that Sneakers could nudge ahead in line. With every movement he made, Luke felt as though he were engulfed in a fine shower of sand, so he was careful not to make many. He'd given up trying to brush it off, dig it out, or otherwise get rid of it. It filled his hair, his pockets, and everywhere else it shouldn't be, thanks to Sneakers' idea of play. The animal hadn't been satisfied until he'd managed to knock Luke to the ground for a prolonged wrestling match. Unable to use tactics that might have injured the dog—Elisabeth would probably have objected—Luke had been forced to play along, filling his clothes with sand and the stink of seaweed long past the time when enough was enough.

It had taken Elisabeth forever to return to the beach.

Luke was trying to figure out how he'd get the sand out of his ears as she led the way into the kitchen. Following her lead, he shrugged out of his coat and left it on a hook behind the door, wishing Sneakers would quit dancing around his legs. It made him nervous.

Pet or not, Dobermans weren't supposed to be so damned friendly.

"I'll have a meal ready in about thirty minutes," Elisabeth said, crossing to the counter where preparations were in progress. "Go ahead and explore the house. If you're anything like McCain, you won't relax until you know everything is in order."

He already knew everything was in order. Sloane had met him at the dock just minutes before Elisabeth's arrival with a report on the status quo. Except for the in-house systems, all was as expected. He could wait to inspect the house until Elisabeth had time to show him around.

He didn't want her to feel like he was invading her privacy. Besides, the need for urgency had lessened somewhat when Sloane had passed on a report from Wyatt that had placed Curtis at the Bangkok airport six hours ago. Just a sighting, but a reliable one that had put Wyatt's team in motion.

Luke looked around the spacious family-style kitchen with its large Formica-topped table and abundance of modern appliances. It was a warm room, friendly, and almost as big as his entire apartment back in Singapore. His gaze returned to Elisabeth, who was studiously chopping a stalk of celery, her long hair drifting forward across her shoulders. She was everything he'd expected her to be, more or less.

She was prettier than her picture. Not in the knock-'em-dead sense, but more real, vibrant. Textures, he supposed. The photo hadn't done justice to the silky sheen of her hair, the delicate glow of her skin. And her eyes. Dark blue, he'd thought. He hadn't realized they would be a blue unlike any he'd ever seen, shifting in the light, with her mood, her emotions.

She was dressed much the same as she'd been in the photo, in a long-sleeved chambray shirt that brushed her slight curves without calling attention to them, jeans with a belt that circled a waist so small, he knew he could easily span it with his hands. Her movements were as casual as her clothes—except when she looked at him and remembered she wasn't alone. Then she seemed to freeze, her systems on full alert as she evaluated the threat he posed. As a result he'd done everything he knew to appear as nonthreatening as possible, clear down to speaking in a deliberately calm voice and keeping a reasonable distance between them. His efforts had been rewarded when he'd caught her studying him with curiosity, not fear.

Even so, she was every bit as nervous as Wyatt had prepared him to expect. Yet there was something behind that obvious show of fear on the beach, something he couldn't quite put his finger on.

Something to do with the way she'd sicced her dog on him.

She looked up and caught him staring at her, and a blush rose to her cheeks when he didn't look away.

But then neither did she. Not until Sneakers broke the silence with a demanding bark. Elisabeth spoke sharply to the dog, who was still circling Luke's legs. "Go to bed, Sneakers." She waggled the knife in the direction of the door. "And don't you dare shake that sand all over my kitchen. I'll brush you later."

The Doberman gave Luke's hand a farewell slurp, then wandered over to the door and fell in a heap on the braided rug. He was asleep before Luke could count to three.

When he looked back at Elisabeth, she was still holding the knife poised in midair. "Go ahead and look around," she said. "I really don't mind."

"I'd rather have a shower." He resisted the impulse to shake his head in a Sneakers-like attempt to rid himself of another layer of sand.

Her brows drew together in bewilderment. "You're a mess." She sounded surprised.

This from the woman who'd made him play with her dog in the sand. "So is Sneakers."

He followed her gaze to the rug where Sneakers snored in his sleep. She nodded slowly, clearly adding two and two. Luke could have sworn she only that moment remembered how she'd left them rolling in the sand. And there was something about the way she was still holding the knife aloft, almost as though she'd forgotten about it.

He was concerned about her short-term memory.

She looked back at him and smiled brightly. "Then I guess you'd better get cleaned up."

"I'll feel better about leaving you alone if you put that knife down."

"Excuse me?" she said, staring at him incomprehensibly.

"The knife. You're holding it like it's an extension of your hand. I'd hate to imagine what would happen if you used that hand to scratch an itch."

She looked at the length of steel as though wondering what it was doing in her hand, then lowered it to the chopping block. "I knew I was holding it," she said, her expression daring him to disagree.

He didn't. At least, not out loud.

She went back to chopping vegetables. "You'll have to use my bathroom. The guest room has a separate hot-water tank that I keep switched off when I'm alone here. Since I didn't know you were coming . . ." Her words trailed off as she raised her head, her expression puzzled and a little nervous. "Why *have* you come?"

Luke damned Wyatt's edict about not telling her anything that might possibly frighten her. But until he knew whether or not she was strong enough to handle the news, he decided to keep Curtis's status to himself.

The frightened woman on the beach would probably faint if she knew Curtis had escaped. The vaguely distracted woman with the knife might have forgotten who Curtis was.

He lied. "There's a new alarm system I want to try out here. McCain was off on another assignment, so I came myself."

"Another system?" A flicker of annoyance crossed her features before she bowed her head and proceeded to make confetti out of a carrot. "I don't suppose you've come up with something that doesn't go off every time I breathe, have you?"

His gaze narrowed on her. "I wasn't aware the alarms went off that frequently," he said slowly, wondering why Sloane or McCain hadn't mentioned this. Though a few false alarms were to be expected, they were annoying at the best of times. Living alone as she did must make them even more trying. He didn't blame her for being a touch irritated.

"They don't," she said. "Not if I remember to stay away from the windows and doors when the system's on." She finished shredding the carrot and went to work on a piece of celery, giving it similar treatment. "And if the local wildlife manages to avoid the infrared beams, I get to sleep through the night."

Luke was beginning to sense a slight exaggeration in

her tone. "According to McCain, it doesn't happen more than every four to six weeks."

She looked up at him, then seemed to remember something, because the next thing he knew, she was shaking her head and laughing softly. "I'd never disagree with McCain. Never mind, though. I'm sure the new system you're here to install will be far superior to anything that went before."

He knew he wasn't imagining the sarcasm. "I'll see what I can do about adjusting for your wildlife. Maybe a mildly electrified trip wire or fence will discourage them."

She looked horrified. "Don't even think it! What if Sneakers ran into it?"

"Sneakers shouldn't be wandering that far from you."

She clenched her jaw and lowered her gaze to the pile of minced celery. "Sneakers doesn't always think before he dashes off. Dogs have been known to chase a rabbit or two. In any case I won't have it. Try to put something so barbaric on my property and I'll—" She shuddered, obviously unclear just how far she'd go to stop him.

Luke figured she'd go pretty far. "Don't worry about it. It was only a thought."

She seemed to accept that, because she changed the subject. "Why didn't you call before you came? McCain always calls."

Because Wyatt wouldn't let me. Luke gritted his teeth and lied again. "It was too early when I left Annacortes. I planned to call from Orcas Island, but it was fogged in and I didn't stop."

Her head jerked up, and he couldn't miss the stark disbelief in her eyes. She knew he was lying, and she knew he knew that she knew. Full circle. He waited for her to call him on it, demand the truth.

When she lowered her lashes and began wielding the knife in abrupt motions, he understood something about Elisabeth he hadn't known before.

She didn't want the truth.

He felt . . . disappointed.

Without looking at him again, Elisabeth told Luke where he'd find fresh towels, said she assumed he'd studied the blueprints and could find his own way, then went into the pantry so that he wouldn't see the frustration in her expression.

The confusion.

The anger.

Sinclair had been on the island for an hour and she still didn't have a clue what had brought him. Or why he hadn't called her. The installation of a new security system would have been believable if McCain hadn't mentioned just last month that the system in place outclassed everything else on the market. And as far as Sinclair's excuses for not calling, she simply didn't believe them.

She didn't believe *him*.

Randomly choosing a can of sliced pineapple in case he was still in the kitchen, she left the pantry. A sigh of relief escaped her at the discovery that both Sinclair and his duffel bag were absent.

Going over to the sink, she put the plug in the drain and started washing lettuce. It was bad enough when Sheila wouldn't tell her what was going on, but to have Sinclair stonewall her questions put a dangerous edge on her temper.

Not to mention this strange ability he had to make her forget what she was doing or why she was doing it. Staring down at the sinkful of lettuce, she wished she'd written down what else they were having for dinner. For the life of her, she couldn't remember.

TWO

Sinclair came to dinner smelling of her lavender-scented shampoo and soap. Successfully curbing her smile, Elisabeth offered him a glass of wine. He refused, so she quickly turned to pull the steaks from the broiler before any of a variety of lavender-scented jokes left her lips. The hot spices of the datil pepper conquered the air, giving her an excuse for the suppressed tears of laughter.

He didn't buy it. Closing the distance between them, he reached around her shoulders to shut the oven door. "What are you laughing at?"

What, not who. She still had a chance. Biting the inside of her cheek, she swallowed a giggle and tilted back her head so that she could see his fierce countenance. "Nothing, Sinclair. I must have soaked these steaks longer than I should. Peppers are like onions; the fumes tend to make you cry."

He looked down at the tray in her hands. "What kind of peppers?"

"Datil. I order them out of New Mexico."

His expression was devoid of suspicion. "They're hot, I assume."

"A little."

He held her gaze for a moment longer, then shuttered his own and said he was glad dinner was ready. He was hungry after the long trip.

Disappointed, almost, that he'd been so easily diverted, she sidestepped him and served the steaks onto plates. Sinclair followed her to the table, surprising her when he pulled out her chair.

Big, gullible, and polite. She was beginning to wonder what Wyatt saw in Sinclair that she hadn't yet discovered. He took the chair in front of the place she'd set on the other side of the table, then waited for her to start eating before picking up his fork. She was thinking that the little game she'd fashioned to make him crazy might go entirely over his head when he spoke.

"If McCain didn't leave some plain soap in the guest room, you'll just have to get used to it."

Well, she hadn't seriously believed Wyatt would employ a gullible security chief. She batted her lashes and grit her teeth to keep from laughing. "Get used to what, Sinclair?"

He harrumphed and went back to eating, the extremely spicy steak causing him no apparent discomfort. Elisabeth dug into her own food, her appetite whetted by the challenge inherent in his silence.

It was a silence that she found strangely exciting.

When they were both finished eating, she asked about her brother. "You said Wyatt was traveling. Any chance he might drop by here?"

Sinclair appeared to consider his answer. "Last I heard, he had some business to take care of in Bangkok."

She pushed her plate aside. "Did you come straight from Singapore, or is this just one of many stops?"

He shrugged. "This is the only thing on my agenda for now. Once Wyatt finishes up that business in Bangkok, I imagine he'll find something else for me to do."

"And how long do you think it will take?"

His gaze narrowed. "What?"

Something about the way he was looking at her made Elisabeth wonder if they were talking about the same thing. "What you're going to do here. You said something about a new system?"

He seemed to relax, almost as though the answer she'd given him was both welcome and unexpected. "A week, maybe more. I hope you don't mind the company."

She didn't. A week fit in perfectly with her plans. By the time it was over, Sinclair would know who was boss. Elisabeth smiled and rose from the table. She couldn't wait to get started.

"I'm sure you're tired after that long trip. Why don't you prowl around the house while I do the dishes."

He leaned back in his chair and cocked his head. "You don't mind? I would have thought you wouldn't like to have a stranger roaming around."

She avoided his gaze by beginning to clear the table. "Of course I don't mind. After six years of having McCain wandering through here, I'm finally used to it. And besides—" She bit off what she was about to say, thinking thoughts that were annoyingly uncomfortable. Thoughts about Sinclair and how glad she was that he was there. Sinclair, a man she hardly knew. Just a man, the way McCain was just a man.

But so very, very different. She'd almost told him as much. Impatient with her unpredictable mouth, she turned on the water in the sink and began rinsing the dishes.

"Besides what, Elisabeth?"

He was standing so close behind her, she nearly jumped. Plunging her hands into the water, she decided to finish what she'd started to say. More or less. There wasn't any sense in telling him all of it.

"I don't mind you wandering through here, Sinclair, because I suppose I trust you."

He leaned against the counter, his hip just inches from the sink where she was soaking her hands—not washing dishes, because she didn't trust herself to mess with china and glass. Folding his arms across his chest, he waited until she looked up at him.

"Because Wyatt sent me?" he asked in a voice so gentle, she couldn't believe it had come out of this big, rough-looking man.

She found she couldn't look away from his gaze, which was equally gentle, and knew she had to answer that question with total honesty. "If Wyatt hadn't sent you, we wouldn't even be having this conversation, Sinclair."

He stared at her for a long time, so long that she began to wonder if he realized he was doing it. When he finally spoke, it was to say something so totally unexpected that she couldn't hide the surprise in her gasp.

"Call me Luke, Elisabeth. I've waited a long time to hear you say my name."

She said the first thing that came into her head. "How long?"

"Four years." Then, when his gaze had become so tactile that the gentleness in it almost squeezed a sigh from deep inside her, he asked her again. "Say my name, Elisabeth."

She bit her lip and grinned. "Sinclair."

He grinned back, the first time she'd seen him do that, and shook his head. "The other one."

Shyness overwhelmed her, a kind of shyness she hadn't felt in years. Ducking her head, she made busy motions with her hands in the water. He didn't move.

"Luke Sinclair," she said, glancing up at him in time to see the satisfaction flicker in his eyes. "I'm beginning to think you and McCain don't have very much in common."

"Because he's easier to look at?"

Elisabeth thought about the younger man and realized Sinclair must be referring to McCain's looks—looks she'd always considered on the bland side. Then she studied the man who towered over her, saw a face filled with character and life, eyes that hid any and all emotion behind shields of gray.

She wondered how surprised he'd be to know which man she found the more interesting.

She realized she must have been wandering in her thoughts for quite a while when he repeated his question. His voice held a harsh note, as though he knew the answer and needed the reality of hearing it from her. "Tell me, Elisabeth. Why are McCain and I so unalike?"

She grinned again. "McCain doesn't have a first name."

Elisabeth shot straight up in bed, her heart pounding as she stared wild-eyed into the darkness. At first she didn't know what had thrown her awake—literally *thrown*, not anything like the gentle pull of a normal awakening. Sneakers too. The dog was on all fours, his body bridging her legs as he defended her from the unseen threat. Elisabeth fought to control her fears, thinking—absurdly—that she hadn't seen Sneakers that alert in years. Then she heard it again, the bliplike alarm that was fixed just behind the headboard of her bed.

The security system had been breached.

She smiled.

Throwing off dog and covers, she scrambled out of bed and paused to squint at the clock. Eleven-forty. Sinclair hadn't gone to bed after all. Shaking her head, she wondered why the alarm had nearly scared her half to death when she'd known it was going to go off— sooner or later. Probably because it had been years since she'd last been awakened by it. A simple lack of conditioning. For Sneakers too. He was prancing around her bed like an excited pup, growling and whining in his peculiar expression of doggie confusion. Reaching around the bedpost, Elisabeth shut off the alarm. The resulting silence was good enough for Sneakers, who collapsed back onto the duvet.

Excitement churned in her stomach as she rushed to the window and picked up the binoculars, training them on an outcropping of rocks that marked the path to the beach. The only sensor she'd fiddled with was located at the base of the outcropping. Not even a shadow crossed her field of vision. Given the time it had taken her to awaken and get to the window, Sinclair had probably made it all the way back to the house, hurrying because he'd realized he'd tripped an alarm. He'd want to reassure her before she went ga-ga from fright.

She grinned. He'd also be wondering how in the hell he'd tripped a sensor when he was supposed to know where they all were.

Setting the glasses back down on the windowsill, she hurried toward her chosen hiding place. Not one of the three regulation priest holes that Wyatt had had built into the house. No, Sinclair would look in those first, fully expecting to find her. The drill was for her to get to the closest priest hole, use the phone there to call her nearest neighbor, Matt Sloane, and wait for help. She'd called on Sloane a lot in the first year she lived on Quincy Island, all false alarms of course, but how was she to know? Sloane and his dogs had always been real quick about responding, but never once had the alarm sounded for anything but a stupid accident of nature, such as a squirrel nibbling on the laser or a woodpecker that had become interested in wires better left alone.

She'd tired quickly of the game, but knew that if she was to keep her brother off her back, she had to make a pretense at maintaining a secure environment. After a few inadvertent lessons in electronics from McCain, she had learned how to switch off, modify, and just plain circumvent the security system. To keep Sloane from getting suspicious—Wyatt didn't really believe she didn't know Sloane worked for him, did he?—she arranged a false alarm every few weeks or so, calling him in a near panic, then hiding in the priest hole only seconds before he arrived.

Not tonight, though.

She hated those little closets.

Besides, she had no intention of letting Sloane in on the fun. Her plan to exact revenge on Sinclair was strictly a two-person show.

Two-person and a dog. Grabbing Sneakers' collar, she pulled him off the bed and shoved him into the bathroom, where he curled up on the rug and fell back asleep. Somewhat irked at the dog's total lack of curiosity, she sandwiched herself between the open bathroom door and the wall and looked through the crack. It afforded her a perfect view of the priest hole in her bedroom. Satisfied that she would see Sinclair before he saw her, she forced herself to relax against the cool wall.

She'd tell him she couldn't get the door to the priest hole open, she decided. Which explained what she was doing hiding behind the bathroom door, shivering and afraid. A shudder tore through her as she realized she was shivering in earnest. No robe.

And no time to get one.

But there was time to get a weapon—something to make Sinclair believe the alarm had truly frightened her. She slipped out of her hiding place, reached into the cupboard under the sink for the only weapon she could think of, and was back behind the door before her heart beat twice.

Tightening her grip around the wooden shaft of the toilet plunger, she wondered once again if Sinclair had a sense of humor.

Luke paused just inside the door to punch in the code that would switch off the house's internal alarms, then hurried toward the wide staircase at the end of the entry hall. Moonlight flared through the enormous windows that comprised an entire wall of the living room, pitching irregular shadows across the polished wood floor of the hall. Getting something to cover those windows was on the next day's agenda, he reminded himself as he raced up the stairs in sets of threes and fours. Right after he figured out what had gone wrong outside.

There was not supposed to be an infrared beam where he'd set off the alarm. The pencil-thin, invisible rays from the tiny semiconductor lasers made excellent trip wires, but they had to be staked out along an exact perimeter and aligned perfectly with their sensors. It looked as though the installer, McCain, had screwed up big-time. Luke would decide what he'd do to McCain after he saw just how badly the alarm had unnerved Elisabeth.

Slowing his pace, he crossed the threshold into Elisabeth's room and looked at the bed. A brilliant shaft of moonlight revealed rumpled covers and nothing else. It reassured him that she'd not been too frightened to make her way into the priest hole. And she'd taken the dog with her, he realized as he pivoted on the balls of his feet and headed toward the opposite wall. Grateful he'd taken the time earlier to locate the hidden latch, he was running his fingers across the smooth paneling when a whirlwind erupted from the bathroom. A small white whirlwind capped by a golden veil that shifted and roiled in the moonlight as she raced toward him.

Elisabeth, the whirlwind. A flurry of panic and aggression all wrapped into a package so tiny and fragile, he had trouble believing it. But in the fraction of time during which the surprise of the attack was supplanted by the logic of who was behind it, Luke realized something important.

There was more of her brother in her than he'd let himself hope. A lot more, and it was heading his way.

He ducked and rolled, evading the thing she wielded high above her head. Why had he ever imagined Elisabeth would cower in safety when she was so obviously capable of putting up a fight?

He admired her guts. And he'd make sure she never did anything so unbelievably stupid again.

"Elisabeth!" he called out, rolling to his feet. She whirled and came at him, clearly not hearing him, the oddly shaped weapon slicing through the air. He lifted his forearm to block the blow, shouting her name again, stifling the temptation to simply disarm her and get it over with. He couldn't do that, though, not and leave her with the spirit she'd need if the occasion to defend herself ever rose again.

The weapon bounced off his arm without leaving so much as a dent, and he wondered if she'd pulled the blow at the last moment, recognizing him as he stood motionless in the face of her attack. Motionless and unsmiling, although it was a stretch not to laugh out loud as he recognized the weapon she let fall to her side.

"Sinclair? Is that really you?" Her voice was rusty with the adrenaline of the abortive battle. She backed up several feet, moving toward the bed, silently urging him to turn his face into the moonlight. He complied, somehow mastering his amusement and his admiration for her splendid effort, letting her see the calm mask that would tell her only who he was and nothing more.

The same mask served to hide his reaction to seeing her in a nightgown that was no barrier to the strong moonbeam in which she stood. His laughter gone, he fought against showing another emotion, the one that she provoked with her perfect body—the long, shapely legs that made her seem taller than she was, the gentle flare of her hips and the shadow wedged between them, the full curves of her breasts, high and firm and tenting the nightgown from her body.

He stared at her, telling himself he was waiting for her to speak. In truth he was too stunned by his reaction to break the silence.

He wanted her. Urgently. Like he'd never wanted another woman.

He damned Wyatt for not stopping him from coming to her. What had once been a longing to know her innocence and her laughter had turned into a physical yearning that sprang from the male inside him, the sexual male.

"It's Luke, Elisabeth," he said in the softest voice he could muster. "Not Sinclair."

"Luke." Her mouth rounded over his name, and he thought a smile flickered in her eyes. She blinked, her lashes a pair of golden fans in the moonlight. "What happened? I thought someone—"

He held up his hand, silencing her questions, her fears. "I tripped a sensor when I was outside. McCain must have omitted changing its location on the plan."

"What were you doing outside?" She dropped the toilet plunger to the floor and crossed her arms under her breasts. "I thought you'd gone to bed."

His molars nearly cracked under the pressure of his clenched jaw as he attempted to keep his libido under control. But he couldn't stop looking at her, seeing the press of her breasts against the thin cotton nightgown and the effect of the night's chill on her nipples. They were taut and distended, and he wished more than anything that she'd put on a robe before he totally lost it. He had lost enough control already, what with the pulsing hardness that crowded his zipper, the thin film of sweat that had broken out on his skin beneath the sweater and jeans.

He cleared his throat and lifted his gaze to hers. "I couldn't sleep, so I went for a walk."

"You nearly scared me to death. It's been ages since I've been awakened by the alarm like that."

"I came back as quickly as I could. I didn't want you to be frightened any longer than necessary." He shot her a sharp glance. "Why weren't you inside the priest hole?" He thought he detected a show of nerves as she gulped and avoided his gaze.

"My hands were shaking too badly to open it."

If she'd wanted to make him feel like pond scum, she'd succeeded. Thrusting his hands into his back pockets, he took a deep breath and tried to think of something to say that would make up for it. He couldn't, so he just stood there, letting her get used to the reality of his responsibility for her protection, needing her to get used to him. To trust him.

Her life might soon depend upon it.

And because her safety came first, before anything else, he would have to ignore the fires that were raging inside him, passions she stirred without so much as a touch.

His gaze went to her mouth and he imagined, just for a moment, what it would be like to feel her lips under his, her tongue in his mouth, filling him with her taste—all hot and spicy and exciting.

Wyatt would kill him if he so much as laid a hand on her. Luke didn't have to wonder if it would be worth it. He knew it would. But he also knew better than to indulge in that particular fantasy. Elisabeth needed a man totally unlike himself, a man who knew how to be gentle.

A steady throbbing in the vicinity of his crotch reminded him that it was also his job to ensure that she didn't have to worry about fending off sexual advances when none were welcome. Belatedly realizing that he wasn't exactly hiding the physical signs from her, he slowly pulled his hands from his pockets. She was too wound up to notice the effect she was having on him, though, he guessed. She didn't look as if she was ready to jump and run.

She looked a bit sleepy, with her eyelids low over her eyes, her mouth curved around silent words that he imagined she didn't even know she was saying.

He wondered what was on her mind.

Elisabeth forced even breaths through her parted lips, trying not to show that she understood Luke's excitement . . . or thought she did. With her gaze riveted on the V-neck of his sweater, she wondered if she did understand. It had been such a long time since a man had looked at her with fire in his eyes that at first she hadn't been certain it was passion she was seeing. But when he'd pushed his hands into his pockets, the material of his jeans had stretched across a distinctive bulge that even she couldn't mistake.

He wanted her. The knowledge filled her with a wistful longing, prodding a responding need deep inside that she'd long ago imagined dead and buried. Not that she'd consciously put her sexual reactions aside; it was more a case of lifestyle. Living essentially as a hermit, she had no opportunities to meet men who were not already attached to other females. Or men closer to her age than Sloane's teenage son or the octogenarian fisherman who lived on the far side of the island. She was sobered by the humiliating thought that Luke was, for all intents and purposes, the first available man she'd met in the past six years—except for McCain, and he didn't count.

A man of Luke's obvious sensuality would have women falling all over him, she mused, and in no small numbers. Women who were sophisticated and gorgeous and confident of their own ability to give pleasure. Elisabeth was none of those things. Her limited sexual encounters had certainly not prepared her for a man of Luke's experience.

She knew he was experienced as she knew the sun must eventually rise. Just as he must know she wasn't. Experienced, that is.

For the first time in her life she wished she was something she wasn't.

A man like Sinclair had bigger fish to fry.

A man like Luke wouldn't find sport in near-virgin waters.

She *hated* thinking in metaphors.

The silence between them stretched and lingered as she fought the inner battle of needs and wants, a skirmish of fantasies and realities—all without lowering her eyes below his belt to do a reality check on her rampant imagination.

In the end there were no answers, only truths. By the time she lifted her gaze to meet Luke's, she decided she must have been mistaken in what she'd seen outlined beneath the taut fabric of his jeans. It must have been something else, a trick of the night's shadows perhaps. She didn't think Wyatt would be stupid enough to hire someone who carried a gun in his front pocket.

"Elisabeth?"

His voice was husky and soft, an almost physical caress that she wanted to wrap around her. She nodded, incapable of any of the comebacks she'd planned when this game had still been a game.

"You should probably get back into bed." He backed off a few feet, leaving without leaving.

She wasn't ready for that yet. "I can't sleep. My nerves are still a bit jangled." He winced, and she didn't feel any of the satisfaction she'd so looked forward to.

"I didn't come here to frighten you," he said, shifting so that the moonlight missed the harsh angles of his face, almost as though he was hiding something he knew she didn't want to see. "It won't happen again."

She was surprised to feel a smile tugging at her mouth. "You shouldn't promise what you can't deliver." Not that it was something in his control, but still, his arrogance could stand a little softening.

"Neither should you." He grabbed her robe from where it hung on the post at the end of the bed and tossed it to her. "Put this on."

She stared at the thick chenille wrap in her hand, then lifted her gaze to his shadowed face. "I don't remember promising anything."

"No, probably not." He sounded resigned as he turned his back to her and headed out the door. "I'll put some milk on for chocolate. Meet me in the kitchen."

He was gone before she could figure out what he thought she had promised. She pushed her arms into the robe, then pulled the belt tight around her waist and went into the bathroom to wake Sneakers. Reaching down, she punched the sound-asleep dog in the stomach. "Get up, Sneakers. Luke is making us a snack."

The Doberman's ears pricked at the word *snack*. He scrambled up from the rug, nearly flattening Elisabeth as he surged past her and through the door.

She followed him at a more sedate pace, puzzling over what Luke had thought she'd promised.

"When does the ferry arrive with your supplies?"

Elisabeth blinked at Luke across the rim of her cup. "Two days. I don't think we'll starve before then."

He shook his head. "It's not starving I'm worried about. It's those damned windows in the living room. I want to order black-out curtains."

"Excuse me?"

She heard a low growl that didn't come from Sneakers, who was chewing contentedly on the bone Luke had retrieved from the scraps of their dinner. Trying not to look surprised when she realized the sound had emanated from the man seated across the table, Elisabeth just smiled.

"Those windows are a security risk," he said. "Anyone walking past can see nearly everything that happens on the ground floor." He took a sip of the chocolate and stared at her. "I want them covered."

She bit the inside of her cheek to keep from laughing. How was Luke to know she and Wyatt had already had this discussion . . . and Wyatt had lost. She wouldn't live in a prison, she'd told her brother when the house was still in the design stages. Covering the windows would make it feel like one.

She'd had enough of that once already.

Wyatt had given in because she'd refused to listen to his arguments. Or because his responsibility for having been the cause of her captivity had still been eating at him. The twinge of guilt she'd felt at using that particular argument had been stifled by her need for open spaces and light. No more prisons, not for her.

Obviously Wyatt hadn't passed along word of that defeat to Luke. Somehow, though, she wasn't in the mood to discuss prisons or her captivity with Luke. Not tonight, when she felt more alive than she'd felt in years.

Tonight, when she felt safe and feminine and excited by the challenge of outwitting this too-somber man who didn't even know he was being challenged.

She grinned and tried a logical argument. "Sinclair, nobody *ever* just wanders past here. That's the advantage of living on an island. Trust me on this one."

Sneakers apparently lost interest in his bone, because he left it beneath the sink—he hadn't quite mastered opening the cabinet where the waste basket was located—then curled up beneath the table, closer to Luke than to

Elisabeth. She knew because she was used to Sneakers' habit of sleeping on her feet, and now she could barely feel the nudge of his body against her toes.

The Doberman had never curled up anywhere in McCain's vicinity. She noted the behavior as she waited for Luke's response, confident he'd see the error of his ways.

Luke put his mug down and flattened his hands on the table. She couldn't help but notice that he wasn't grinning back at her.

"I want them covered immediately. I'll try to arrange for a helicopter to drop something off tomorrow. We can just nail up some lengths of dark fabric or whatever until you can get someone out here to do a prettier job. In the meantime I want you to stay out of the living room."

It occurred to Elisabeth that she might have a fight on her hands. Not one that she wouldn't eventually win of course. She could always call Wyatt and get him to override whatever Sinclair did that she didn't approve. But it was a fight nevertheless. Lacing her fingers around the mug, she met his steely gaze . . . and wondered how she'd ever imagined passion in that cold, hard stare. "You've known ever since you came to work for Wyatt that those windows were uncovered. Why all the fuss now?"

Luke nearly told her then, about Curtis. Her reaction to the alarm had been good; excited and nervous without an undue measure of panic. He was almost certain she'd be able to handle the news. Almost certain, but not one hundred percent. The discrepancy stopped him. He met her gaze, hoping she'd chalk up his hesitation to something other than skirting the truth. "But I didn't know, Elisabeth. I assumed Wyatt, if no one else, would have seen the need. It's not like him to make such an obvious mistake."

Elisabeth almost laughed at his bewildered expression. "Wyatt has spent enough time here with me to know what I said is true. Besides, how could anyone be out there, watching or anything else? What with all the mantraps you've laid outside, not even a squirrel has a chance of sneaking up on me."

"All the same, we'll cover the windows."

"With bars?"

"Curtains will do."

Her smile faded under the piercing measure of his stare. He wasn't going to budge from his position, she realized. Not a single inch, no matter which argument she used. There was only one thing left to say. Unsmiling, she stared back at him. "No curtains, Sinclair. If I have to get Wyatt to tell you that, I'll do it."

A muscle twitched in his jaw, the only sign he'd heard her. Then he got up from the table and reached for the phone that hung on the wall beside her. He punched in a series of numbers, then leaned against the wall to wait.

Confusion made her slightly wary. "What are you doing?"

"Calling Sheila. It might take a while, but she'll be able to get through to Wyatt." His voice was flat, devoid of expression. Still she could tell there was anger in him, a hostility that hovered around him. It didn't frighten her, though, because she somehow knew that it wasn't directed at her.

She listened as the connection was made and Luke did what he'd said he'd do, keeping his conversation with Sheila direct and to the point before hanging up. He took his mug to the sink and rinsed it under the tap. "Sheila said Wyatt had just called her a few minutes ago from Kuala Lumpur. It shouldn't be a problem getting back in touch with him." He propped his hips against the sink and folded his arms, looking at her in that same expressionless way that made her realize this was all business to him.

Nothing personal at all.

"I thought Wyatt was in Bangkok," she said, distracted by this detail.

"He was. I imagine his business there is finished."

"Do you have any idea what it was about? I wasn't aware he had any properties there."

Luke moved his head a bare fraction in a negative response. "Wyatt doesn't share everything. I do security for him, that's all."

Elisabeth was willing to bet there was more between her brother and Luke than what he admitted. She also knew she'd never find out unless he was disposed to tell her. Clearly he wasn't.

For a moment she almost hoped Wyatt would come down firmly on Luke's side. Luke wasn't going to like it when he lost this one. Even though his devotion to his job was the bane of her existence, she knew he would take it as a professional affront when Wyatt sided with her.

The game she'd begun that night was a personal vendetta, designed to undermine his invasion of her privacy. The windows, however, had nothing to do with her game.

The "I won't live in a prison" argument had worked with Wyatt. She had no real reason to believe it wouldn't work with this man, who obviously felt very strongly about keeping her safe. And sane. The speed with which he'd come to her room after the alarm sounded proved he didn't want her frightened. From her seat at the table she studied him without any of the self-consciousness she'd felt earlier. She wanted to know his strengths, just where he drew the line between the things he could control and those he couldn't. Or wouldn't. The question was whether she could use the truth, her aversion to being shut in, and succeed in diverting him from forcing this change on her.

Even then she knew, somehow *knew*, it was useless to pursue her arguments. Nothing she said would change things. Luke would do what he needed to do, with or without her permission. Or Wyatt's. The phone rang as she grappled with the realization that Luke's will was nothing to be trifled with.

Instead of going to answer it, Luke stayed where he was. "Go ahead, Elisabeth. Take your best shot."

The phone rang a second time. "Thanks, but I don't need to plead my side. Wyatt knows me well enough not to change his mind on this." But then, this wasn't up to Wyatt, was it?

Luke stared at her through the third ring, then crossed to answer the phone, holding her gaze as he spoke to Wyatt. Elisabeth had to give him credit for not beating around the bush. Luke's end of the conversation went straight from "Sinclair here" to "The windows in the living room need to be covered. Elisabeth disagrees."

His expressionless stare didn't change as he listened to Wyatt. She imagined, hoped, and prayed her brother was adequately explaining just why Luke wouldn't win this one. She gave him an encouraging smile, hinting that she wouldn't lord her victory over him, but knowing deep in her soul that she'd lost before the contest had begun. Luke ignored her overture, speaking in monosyllables before holding the phone out to her.

"Wyatt wants to speak with you."

She knew, then, that she had lost. Not because there was victory in the cool gaze he leveled on her. Nor because Wyatt had just called her two days earlier, and why would he want to talk with her now unless it was to confirm something she didn't want to hear?

No, she knew she'd lost because Luke wouldn't fight battles without winning, not even meaningless ones like this one over stupid curtains. He'd been sure he would win before he'd even picked up the phone. And she'd been foolish enough to ignore her understanding of the man . . . a man she knew so little, so well.

Luke Sinclair wasn't a man who lost.

She shook her head, hiding her defeat behind the dignity of a gracious surrender. "You wouldn't lie to me, Sinclair. Your point, it seems. Although I think you're both crazy to imagine that after six years a set of curtains will make me any more safe than I already am." She waggled her fingers at the phone, her expression mutinous. "I'm not in the mood to argue with Wyatt too. I've lost enough tonight."

"You haven't lost anything," Luke said, then muttered a few words into the phone before slamming it back onto its wall hook. He yanked a chair away from the table and turned it so that he could straddle it and still face her. "Beefing up your security isn't going to hurt you."

It'll just drive me crazy, she said to herself as she rose from the table and walked toward the hall. "Have it your way, Sinclair. I'm not going to waste any more sleep arguing with you tonight."

"Understand something, Elisabeth. You can call me Luke or Sinclair or son of a bitch—that's up to you. But it's not going to change the way things work around here. It will be easier if you accept that now."

His words slammed into her back, making her turn and look at the man who was now the total professional. He watched her with a caution she could almost feel, his arms folded across the back of the chair, his cool gaze entreating a measure of understanding she didn't want to summon.

"What things?" She deliberately refrained from using either name.

"The things I have to do. The changes that need to be made. They'll happen with or without your consent." He hesitated, then finished in the same even voice as he stood and pushed the chair aside. "Your brother hired me to watch over you, to ensure your security. I intend to do it the best way I know how."

"So why did it take you four years to come?" The words were out before she could stop them. Appalled, she held her breath and prayed he wouldn't answer that.

A flash of humor blended with curiosity in his expression. "You never asked."

"I didn't this time either." She took a deep breath and let it out slowly, feeling ridiculously disappointed and relieved at the same time. And exhausted. For all her questions he had answers. Responses that filled a void, whether or not they were accurate. She believed him about the windows, although that didn't mean she had to like it. As for why it had taken four years to visit . . . Well, not having an invitation was probably a polite way of saying he'd been too busy in the more important corners of Wyatt's empire.

The bigger question still hadn't been answered. "You still haven't told me why, Sinclair."

He gave her the same blank, shuttered look he'd given her earlier. "The windows? I already told you. You're too exposed without coverings of some sort."

"No, that's not what I meant." A coldness she hadn't felt in years gathered at the pit of her stomach. "Why have you come to Quincy Island now? And what's happened that Wyatt would go against my wishes about the windows?"

He stared at her for a moment that was filled with hesitation and, finally, decision. Before she could analyze either, he turned and bent to pick up a towel that had slipped from the counter. "Because he knew I'd quit if I didn't get my way. I told him when I signed on that I couldn't do this job without his cooperation."

Recalling his confidence when speaking with Wyatt, she believed him.

"It never occurred to me," she said, "that Wyatt would sacrifice my peace of mind at the suggestion of an employee." A low blow, she knew, but she wasn't in the mood to mince words.

"Then you didn't think, Elisabeth." He rose and faced her, his previous lack of expression unchanged even as Sneakers belly-crawled from beneath the table to settle within rubbing distance of Luke's feet. "Wyatt cares more for you than he does for anyone else in his world. And whatever else you want to believe, I'm not getting any kicks in having to do this to you. I've read your file. I know this isn't going to be an easy adjustment."

"I hate being closed in."

"I know." He pushed his hands into his back pockets. "You've been somewhat claustrophobic most of your life. But Wyatt says you've learned to deal with it."

"By not feeling closed in any longer than I have to. Covering those windows will make that room feel like a prison."

"Then stay out of the living room at night. The rest of the house isn't as vulnerable; the windows are high enough that you can move around pretty much without being seen from outside."

"That's your best offer?" she asked.

He nodded. "It'll be just another habit to get into, Elisabeth. No worse than learning to sit in the priest holes. Wyatt says you've been able to do that without much trouble."

Not a good argument, she silently disputed. She hadn't been in a priest hole for more than sixty seconds in years. Of course she couldn't tell him that.

Gritting her teeth in frustration, she turned and walked quickly down the hall. She was surprised when Sneakers rushed to catch up with her; she'd thought he was still dead asleep at the great man's feet. Fine, she thought as she stomped up the staircase. So now they'd get curtains or drapes or whatever.

It didn't mean she had to use them once Sinclair left.

THREE

Elisabeth's alarm clock bleeped a weak signal just minutes past five the next morning. It took long seconds before she remembered why she'd set it, then several more before she managed to shut it off. Even though she'd taken the precaution of turning the alarm down to its lowest setting, the bleeping tone seemed blatantly loud, a flagrant disregard for the still silence of dawn. Worried that Sinclair might have heard it from where he slept in the guest room at the other end of the house, she waited ten minutes with the covers up to her chin and the body of a slumbering dog draped across her thighs. If he came to investigate, she'd tell Luke she was getting up for an early-morning jog.

He didn't have to know she never jogged. Walking was her thing, not running. She was still trying to figure out if she could fake a quarter mile or so when she realized there were no sounds of stirring from the room at the end of the hall. Clearly he hadn't heard the alarm clock.

Now, if Sneakers would just cooperate. Pushing the covers down to her waist, Elisabeth tickled the Doberman under his chin, softly, the way that was guaranteed to drive him crazy.

Crazy and awake. In seconds Sneakers was dancing in circles on the bed, a confused look on his face that meant he couldn't figure out why he was awake when the sun was hardly up yet. She threw off the remaining covers and attacked the dog in discreet silence, finding all his ticklish spots as he nipped at her fingers. It was a familiar game they played, albeit at an odd time of day.

Sneakers wasn't known to be an early riser. In fact Elisabeth had trained him soon in his residence on the island that getting up before she rolled out around seven was a sure way to set off alarms as he let himself out through the doggie door. She'd been amazed at how easily Sneakers had learned the habit of sleeping late— later sometimes than Elisabeth herself. Not that it was a factor anymore, now that she lived with the alarm system switched off. Unless Wyatt or McCain were visiting of course. Then she was grateful Sneakers had learned to sleep in, late enough for her to sneak downstairs and shut the thing off before the dog figured out it was time to get up and blasted through his door.

Elisabeth knew Sinclair would have reset the alarms before going to bed.

But Sneakers wouldn't know that.

Convinced the Doberman was wide awake, she made the motions of getting out of bed, going so far as to reach for her robe. Sneakers went tearing out the bedroom door and down the stairs. Jumping back into bed, she dragged the covers up to her nose and waited, her heart thudding in anticipation.

Seconds later it happened.

Luke had been awake for ten minutes, trying to figure out what had nudged him from sleep, when the first alarm sounded. His gut tightening in reaction to the unexpected, he rolled out of bed, pulled on jeans, and grabbed his gun, all in one smooth movement, but not before the second alarm went off. Without stopping to switch off either alarm, he ran barefoot down the hall to Elisabeth's room.

She was halfway out of bed, her face flushed from sleep, her eyes wide with fear. "What is—"

"I don't know. Probably nothing," he added, calculating the distance from Bangkok and knowing that Curtis couldn't possibly be there yet. But it might be someone in Curtis's employ. He gestured toward the priest hole, grabbing her robe and tossing it to her. "Turn off the alarm. I'll be back as soon as I can." Then, remembering that she'd been incapable of opening the priest hole just hours ago, he paused to slide the panel open. He didn't wait to see if she minded him. It never occurred to him she wouldn't.

Still, when the alarms were abruptly silenced, he felt a sense of relief that she wasn't too frightened to follow orders.

Descending to the ground floor in quick, silent movements, he cautiously made his way toward the front door where the security panel was located. He didn't figure anyone was actually inside, given the order in which the alarms had sounded. When he'd refined the system right after going to work for Wyatt, he'd assigned different-sounding alarms to the inside and outside sensors. The two he'd just heard were pressure plates next to doors or windows, followed by the infrared array outside. In that order.

Someone leaving, not coming in. Someone, or something.

He had his suspicions, but he was careful all the

same, studying the shapes and shadows emerging in the early light of dawn and finding nothing out of place. He flipped open the panel's door, his gaze narrowing on the blinking light that pinpointed the location of the breach.

The back door, where the doggie door was cut. It made sense. Luke tried to remember if he'd seen the dog in Elisabeth's room, but couldn't. Still, that didn't mean the lazy animal hadn't been hidden in the covers of her bed.

He couldn't afford to take anything for granted, not when Elisabeth's safety was at risk. Moving with quiet caution, he retraced his steps down the wide hallway, pausing at the entrance to the kitchen. He flicked the safety off the gun and had made just two steps across the shining black-and-white-checkered linoleum, when a shiny, wet nose poked through the doggie door, followed by the slightly damp body that belonged to that nose.

Sneakers, clearly no slouch when it came to noticing a change in his environment, yipped with delight and scrambled to meet the second early riser of the day. Luke barely had time to reset the safety on his gun before the Doberman was on him, slathering his bare chest with kisses that Luke figured were meant to show Sneakers' pleasure in seeing him.

The pleasure wasn't mutual. Stifling an urge to throttle the animal, Luke shoved the giant paws away and turned to head back upstairs. To tell Elisabeth her stupid dog had set off the alarm . . . and to shower off the residue of Sneakers's licking frenzy.

He couldn't figure out why McCain had never mentioned Sneakers' setting off the alarm. Or why Elisabeth hadn't asked that the system be modified to preclude such an event.

Or what had awakened him in the first place.

———❧————————————❧———

Elisabeth broke the last egg into the bowl, thinking that perhaps she'd been a tad precipitous in telling Luke they'd make it until Wednesday without fresh supplies. Oh well, she sighed, whipping the eggs before pouring them into the skillet. Eggs and toast this morning, frozen bagels the next, and, if she could find where she'd stashed them, homemade cinnamon rolls after that.

If that wasn't good enough for Luke Sinclair, then perhaps he'd learn to call before dropping in.

A smile twitched at the corners of her mouth as she relived in vivid detail the disgust on Luke's face when he'd returned from rousting their intruder, Sneakers trotting blithely along at his side as though nothing untoward had occurred.

Luke's expression had darkened even further when he'd discovered Elisabeth wasn't in the priest hole but cowering under the thick quilt, her eyes saucer round and filled with terror—she'd practiced that look in the mirror when he'd gone downstairs. Obviously she'd practiced well, because his anger had evaporated in his haste to reassure her. Her act had been so good that he hadn't even asked why she'd not done as ordered, although she could pretty much assume the subject was shelved, not forgotten.

The difficult part had come when she'd realized he was less fully dressed than she'd noticed earlier, his jeans only half zipped. A wedge of dark hair arrowed down from his waist in an intimate invitation to see more than she imagined he intended. He caught her startled gaze, though, and casually pulled up the zipper before reaching behind himself to lose the other thing that had caught her stare—his gun. It had disappeared when his hands came back into view, probably tucked into the waistband of his jeans. That solved the question of whether or not he carried it in his front pocket.

Not that she'd really given that theory any credence.

Sneakers was lucky Luke hadn't shot him, she mused, making appropriate responses to Luke's words of reassurance. Perhaps next time she'd take more care in assuring neither she nor Sneakers provided a likely target. Not that she imagined Luke was trigger happy, but after the series of false alarms with which she planned to interrupt his sleep over the next few nights, he might be weary enough to shoot at anything that moved.

So went her thoughts, none of which served to help her avoid noticing the magnificent expanse of sleek, bare chest and shoulders so broad and powerful, she would have been intimidated had she not known he would never use his strength against her.

A strength she found strangely intoxicating.

Sneakers had suddenly tired of being ignored about that point. He'd leapt onto the bed and tried to resume their game of feint and tickle, the distraction snapping her thoughts back to reality. Thankfully Luke had only seemed relieved she wasn't totally unnerved by the alarm. He'd suggested that she try to sleep for a couple more hours, then agreed to meet her in the kitchen for breakfast when she'd said she couldn't possibly close her eyes, not after all that excitement.

Stirring a touch of milk into the eggs, Elisabeth could only hope she'd soon get used to having Luke around, before he noticed her fascination with his body. *His gorgeous body*, she corrected herself, humming as she turned off the flame under the eggs and covered the pan. Luke wasn't sculpted in the Mr. Universe sense, but he was powerful in a way a muscleman could never be. There was a subtlety in him, something inherent in his makeup that said that no matter how big he was, his strength was from within, his size incidental.

And she'd known him less than a day. A mocking laugh escaped her lips, a reprimand to her rampant imagination. "That's what comes from living alone," she said aloud, turning aside to pour juice into the glasses. "An unbridled imagination for company."

"What is so unbridled about your imagination, Elisabeth?"

She came close, very close, to dropping the pitcher. Setting it on the counter, she turned and discovered Luke standing just inside the door, his hair wet from the shower, a V-neck sweater topping dark jeans that fit snugly across his muscled thighs. Dragging her gaze up to his face, she had to admit he looked surprisingly bright-eyed and bushy-tailed for a man who hadn't gotten much sleep.

She wished she looked that good.

"Your imagination, Elisabeth?" he prodded, crossing the room to pick up the glasses and set them on the table. "You were going to explain what's unbridled about it."

"No I wasn't." She lifted a single shoulder in teasing defiance, then turned to scrape the eggs onto plates. Setting those and a stack of toast on the table, she took her place and tried her best to look innocent. "You were eavesdropping on a private conversation, Sinclair. Since I'm not going to fill in the blanks, you're just going to have to make do with your own fantasies."

"We're talking fantasies here?" A smile curved his lips, his cool eyes assessing her from across the table.

"Considering the night's events, I'm surprised you've got the energy for anything so . . . strenuous."

"You have *strenuous* fantasies?" She couldn't even begin to imagine what prompted her to pursue this line of conversation, except that it was more fun than she'd had in years. She didn't even care if her eggs were getting cold.

"I'll tell you about my fantasies if you'll tell me about your unbridled imagination," he countered, staring pointedly at her plate.

She took the hint and picked up her fork, giving him the signal to begin eating. He dug into the scrambled eggs with an enthusiasm that made her think he'd forgotten he'd dropped a challenge. One that she certainly had no intention of taking up, but a challenge nevertheless. She watched him eat for a few minutes until she realized her stomach was making hungry noises. Her first taste awakened further interest in the meal, and soon she quit trying to decide what she would say if he reissued the challenge.

Almost quit, because she'd rather not be caught unprepared if the subject came up again. She was thinking about strenuous fantasies when he finished eating and shoved his plate aside. Reaching for the green-pepper jelly, she spread some on a piece of toast as Luke suspiciously studied the hand-printed label. When she suggested he try some, she wasn't surprised when he declined on the grounds that he'd already finished.

"Does Sneakers do that often?" he asked.

"Do what?"

"Set off the alarm." Luke got up from the table and poured two cups of coffee from the fancy drip coffee maker on the counter. Setting the mugs between them, he sat down and slid his chair back from the table just as Sneakers wandered over for a quick pet.

Elisabeth rubbed two fingers between the dog's ears, wondering how to answer Luke without telling an outright lie. "Sneakers usually sleeps as long as I do," she said, pushing the dog's head off her lap. His brown eyes were staring up at her as though it was her fault the alarm had nearly scared a year's growth out of him. "I can't imagine what made him want to go out so early this morning. It must have been all the excitement of last night."

"It was my impression that Sneakers didn't even notice the excitement. He slept through most of it."

Elisabeth snuck a bit of egg from her plate and popped it into Sneakers' mouth, a reward for a job well done. "I'm sure he knew it was a false alarm."

"He's not much of a guard dog," Luke said, his gaze thoughtful as he looked at her across the rim of his mug. "I've never understood why you worked so hard to subvert his training."

"I didn't subvert anything. Sneakers was never cut out to be a guard dog. I just encouraged his natural instincts to surface." Actually it had been much easier said than done, but Elisabeth didn't think that was the point. Sinclair probably wouldn't appreciate hearing the painstaking efforts it had taken to gentle the Doberman. She grinned and snuck another piece of egg below the table, where greedy teeth nabbed it from her fingers.

"Given the circumstances," Luke said, "I would imagine you'd feel safer with the protection a well-trained Doberman can give you."

Honestly, she mused with a degree of exasperation, Sinclair was like a dog with a bone—an image that pushed her mouth into a smile she was incapable of hiding.

Instead of sharing her thoughts with him, she mumbled something about dishes and a walk for Sneakers, then left the table before Luke could object.

She was fighting a losing battle against all-out laughter when he said, "I'll do the lunch dishes. Right now I'm going to make arrangements for the windows. Then I'll see what I can do to modify the alarm around Sneakers's door. The last thing we need is another night like the last one."

As if he had a choice.

With an arrogance that reminded Elisabeth of her brother, Luke called a business contact Wyatt used in Seattle, totally disregarding the early hour. He arranged for bolts of dark material to be delivered later that day, although Elisabeth pointed out that the extravagant order could easily enshroud the entire house. He ignored her, just as he ignored her suggestion that the project could wait until Wednesday, when the ferry made its weekly trip to the island. Instead he arranged for the helicopter Wyatt used when he visited to drop off the cloth.

Just to complicate things, Elisabeth asked him to include eggs, lettuce, and fresh crab in the order. No sense in having to wait for Wednesday, she reasoned, as long as the helicopter was already coming. They might as well take advantage of it.

Luke added her list to his, although she knew very well he thought groceries didn't deserve to come airmail. He even managed not to growl at her when she interrupted him again with a request for anchovy paste and fresh Parmesan. She wanted to make a Caesar salad, she said as he put the man on hold and stared at her in patent disbelief. It was touch and go for a moment, Luke staring at her with a look that said he was assessing her desire for salad versus the possibility that she was making the curtain delivery as difficult as she could, and Elisabeth holding his stare with as innocent an expression as she could manage.

She couldn't help the tiny smile of victory when he went ahead and ordered the anchovy paste and Parmesan, a smile that she knew he noticed. She'd intended him to notice. The game was broadening from its original charter to challenging Luke at every step, instead of just over security matters.

It wouldn't have been any fun if he didn't at least suspect something was going on that was out of his control. She knew better than to believe she'd get away with her sabotage of the security system for long, but defying him on the little things might divert his attention for a while, give her an edge.

She thought about adding a request for sourdough bread, but one look at the stubborn set of his shoulders made her decide that what she had in the freezer would do very nicely.

She wanted to challenge him, not annoy him to death.

After taking a final gulp of coffee, she backed out of the kitchen door, herding Sneakers along for his morning romp. The sky was overcast and moody, and she was buttoning her coat when she turned to find Sinclair on her heels. He'd already put on the aviator sunglasses. She couldn't help kidding him about them.

"Take a look at the sky, Sinclair. Unless those glasses are part of the security guard uniform, I doubt you'll need them." She turned to lead the way down the path to the beach, hiding a smirk as she passed the laser she'd tripped him up with earlier.

"They're more habit than anything. And they're not so much dark as they are protective against UV rays. My eyes have been fairly sensitive to the sun since the last time I went skiing."

As the path widened onto the beach, she felt him move alongside her. "Skiing in Singapore? Things *have* changed!"

He chuckled, shooting her a sideways glance. "Not that much. I was in Colorado over Christmas. My sunglasses broke—"

"The first time you fell?" she interrupted, delighted by the image of Sinclair floundering facedown on the slopes. "Catch an edge, did you?"

"Sorry to disappoint you, but it was more a case of getting run over by a class of four-year-old pygmies who had escaped from their teacher." He put his hand beneath her elbow as they came to a cluster of boulders blocking their passage.

A very polite security chief. Elisabeth smiled, thinking that big and polite was a lovely combination in a man. She was delighted he really wasn't as gullible as she'd feared last night . . . as long as he fell for at least another night's worth of her tricks. A little gullible was okay in a man.

"So the pygmies broke your glasses?" she asked when they'd cleared the boulder field. She wished he hadn't felt it necessary to drop his hand.

"Yeah, though I guess I'm lucky they were skiing without poles. Getting my eyes a little sunburned is better than getting one poked out."

Elisabeth laughed with him, thinking how nice it was to have someone to walk with who didn't continually demand she toss a stick long distances. Sneakers was overjoyed at the company, too, particularly when he discovered Luke could throw much farther than Elisabeth ever managed.

A mile up the beach and back the threesome climbed boulders that blocked their way, walked on the solid, wet sand when they could, and trudged through the deep, dry stuff when they couldn't. They didn't talk much, except to praise Sneakers for finding the stick, chastise him for rolling in the surf, and admonish him to keep his mucky paws to himself. Elisabeth thought of asking Luke more about himself, such as if he had family in Colorado, but decided to save that for mealtime, a diversion that would keep the conversation from straying too close to unbridled imaginations and strenuous fantasies.

Even so, she couldn't help but be disappointed that he hadn't pursued the provocative dialogue. Stealing glances at the somber man who walked beside her, she couldn't imagine how he'd ever loosened up enough to tease her.

For that matter she couldn't imagine herself responding so easily. So eagerly.

They were nearing the path to the house just as she admitted to finding Luke Sinclair entirely more complex than she'd ever envisioned. More interesting, and exhilarating in ways she understood but had never truly experienced.

Nothing in her life measured up to the excitement this one man aroused in her. That particular thought left her feeling nervous and flushed and just a touch stupid, because this was a man she hardly knew. As he hardly knew her.

Her imagination was racing along from unbridled to wild with no stops along the way for a dose of reason.

A slight pressure on her arm brought her to a stop. She looked up at him and smiled, thinking that not even her budding interest in Luke as a man would save him from the planned games with his security system. He said something about checking on his boat, then loped off down the beach, Sneakers following without questioning his right to go.

Elisabeth watched man and dog until they were out of sight, then hurried to the side of the house to rig a surprise for the coming night.

Within minutes of returning to the house Luke got busy with the doggie door.

"I assume," he said, "that if I fix this so that Sneakers can go out early, he knows enough to avoid the infrared motion detectors outside."

Elisabeth nodded. "He's never set those off before. I've always figured there was something about them that made them more obvious to dogs than to humans."

"Probably something to do with being at eye level." Luke pulled up the linoleum by the kitchen door, then repositioned the sensor plate off center so that it would still respond to the pressure of a person walking in through the door. He left the area directly in front of the doggie door unprotected, though not without thinking it through. The last thing he wanted was to leave the entrance vulnerable. Therefore it made perfect sense to Luke when he asked Elisabeth to try to crawl through the small opening.

She glanced up from the cookbook she was reading, and he couldn't help noticing how the sapphire sweater she wore deepened the color of her eyes. "Never," she said in a firm voice, then returned her attention to the book.

He didn't intend to take no for an answer. "I need to

know it's not any bigger than it looks, Elisabeth. I figure if you can get through it, I'll have to lay the pressure pads back down where they were or make the door smaller or something. We can't take the chance of anyone breaking into the house this way."

"Forget it, Sinclair. I'm not in the mood for crawling around on my hands and knees. Besides, I bruise easily." She put a marker in the cookbook and pushed it aside, her gaze lifting to meet his. "Why don't you just measure it?"

"Because that's not good enough."

"So crawl through the hole yourself." She grinned when she said it.

"We both know I can't. What we don't know is if a smaller person could." He crossed to the table and flattened his palms on its shiny surface, then leaned forward to narrow the gap between them to a mere half dozen inches. "Do I have to call Wyatt and get him to make you do it?"

She laughed. "Even you don't have enough nerve to call Wyatt for this!"

"I will if you make me." A smile finally cracked his face as he, too, pictured Wyatt's reaction. "Come on, Elisabeth. Do it or I'll have to put the pressure plates back where they were. I'm sure you don't want the alarm going off every time Sneakers needs to go."

Not that it was a problem, but Elisabeth decided it would be more in character if she gave in to the need for security. It was bad enough that she'd almost blown it the night before when she'd gone into that short diatribe about alarms that went off too often and for no good reason. Now wasn't the time to get on her soapbox about his stupid system.

And so, grumbling all the way because there were

some things she couldn't help, she went outside to the small porch, waited until Sinclair closed the door, then crouched down and stuck her head through the flap. Then her arms and part of her shoulders . . . which was when she got stuck, trying to angle her shoulders through what was really a very tiny space.

Luke hunkered down just inches from her nose and pulled the flap off her head, twining his fingers in her hair to hold it off her face. "You didn't get very far. Are you sure you're trying, Squirt?"

"Squirt?"

"Mm-hm, although you're obviously too big for this job. I guess it's safe to say no one is going to break in through Sneakers' door."

Resting a forearm on Luke's thigh, which just happened to be in the right place at the right time, Elisabeth turned her head and glared at him as he brought his own head down to her level to check out the situation. "I've done my bit, Sinclair. Now it's your turn. Get me out of here, or I'll put so many anchovies in your salad tonight, you'll be up drinking water until dawn."

"You don't mess around when you threaten someone, do you?" he murmured, trying to wedge a finger between her shoulder and the door. "Can you try moving sideways?"

"I'm stuck, Sinclair. That means I can't move. Get it?"

He rubbed his chin as he considered the problem. "Hold on, now, Elisabeth. I've got to figure out the best way to approach this."

"Now you take time to think," she muttered, then banged her forehead against his knee in frustration. Sneakers appeared from wherever he'd been napping and slathered her face with his characteristic token of support.

"Sneakers! Go 'way!" She tried to talk without letting her tongue touch her lips, which were wet with doggie slurp.

"He's just trying to help. Maybe if we grease you with—"

"Sinclair, I'm sure there's a simple way out of here," she said, false patience dripping from every word. "Find it now or die. And keep Sneakers away from me. I'm not in the mood for him right now."

"It's taking both hands just to keep your hair off the floor," he murmured as he diligently restacked the blond pile. "Maybe I should braid it—"

"Sinclair! This isn't funny!" She could have sworn he was gagging on a laugh, but she couldn't prove it. Her view of him was pretty much limited to his thighs—a fact which would have aroused all sorts of interesting thoughts had she not been wedged in a pet door with her breasts flattened painfully against her chest.

"Are you bigger on top or on bottom?"

"Excuse me?"

"Do your hips measure bigger or smaller than your breasts?"

"Don't you dare use the word *measure* around me." She lifted her head again, twisting so that she could catch the look on his face. If he was smiling, she'd bite him. She couldn't quite see, though, and collapsed back onto his thigh, deciding it had been a close call. Her erstwhile pillow was as hard as steel. Her teeth would likely have broken if she'd bitten him.

"I just wondered," he went on, "if it would be easier to pull you through forward, or if you should ease out backward. If your hips are bigger than your breasts—"

"My breasts will be permanently flattened if you

don't do something in the next sixty seconds," she interrupted.

"We certainly can't have that," he murmured, edging his finger down past her shoulder.

She snapped at the finger that was verging on intimate ground, and her teeth closed on a mouthful of air as Luke pulled the digit safely out of range. "Trust me, Sinclair. If your finger gets stuck in here with me, I'll tell Sneakers to chew it off."

The dog responded to attention with a delighted lick that skated from her chin to her forehead.

"Personally I think Sneakers would rather lick than chew." Luke elbowed the dog aside. "Why don't you try backing out?"

"Because I can't get any traction, that's why!"

"Then I'll just have to pull you. May I have my thigh back?"

Elisabeth muttered an Indonesian curse that would have appalled him if he'd understood, and propped herself up with her hands. Her breasts squished more forcibly against the door in the awkward position. She watched as Sinclair's booted feet headed across the kitchen. "Where are you going, Sinclair? You can't just walk off and leave me!"

The boots turned and faced her. "You're stuck in the door, Elisabeth. Unless you want me to open it with you swinging like a dead cat across the floor, I thought it would be prudent to take the long way around." The boots turned and left her with a burning desire to stick *him* through the doggie door and watch him squirm.

A dead cat? She was adding wicked embellishments to her game of making Sinclair crazy with the alarms when she felt a hand settle on her bottom, then slide around to her hip. By the time her other hip was similarly covered, she was no longer thinking about retribution.

She was thinking how right it felt to have him touch her when he began to pull. Gently—although she couldn't imagine how he managed that—and steadily Luke pulled her back through the door that was meant for beast, not human. She felt the constricting pressure against her breasts lessen as his hands moved forward, steadying her shoulders, pulling her hair out of the way lest it be caught by the swinging flap.

Then she was on her feet, standing only because he'd helped her, swaying a little as the blood rushed from her head to her feet and back again. He held her carefully, delicately, with one hand at her waist. The other tilted her chin upward so that she didn't have any choice but to look at him.

"You okay?" His thumb stroked the side of her face, and he studied her with a seriousness that made her knees weak.

"Mm-hm." *Not breathing regularly, but otherwise intact,* she thought, and wondered if he could tell. He must have noticed something, though, because his smile suddenly slipped into a memory as he bent his head.

Down, until their noses were almost touching. Down, until her focus was lost in the pools of gray that held her mesmerized. Down, until his lips almost touched hers . . . which was when she panicked.

Tilting her head back in a limited retreat, she swallowed and said, "You don't want to do this, Sinclair."

"I don't?" Long fingers threaded into her hair, warming her scalp, stilling her backward flight.

"Nuh-uh. These are the same lips Sneakers slobbered all over. You'll get dog cooties."

He cocked his head and regarded her seriously. "Is that the only reason you don't want me to kiss you?"

She couldn't tell a lie. "Unless you want to talk about the normal stuff, like us barely knowing each other, why you want to kiss me, me not knowing what I'm doing here. Things like that."

"I don't." He bent his head again, this time not giving her a chance to evade him. He brushed his lips across hers, then settled his mouth on hers.

The kiss was warm and hard and unlike anything she'd ever experienced . . . and over before she got used to it. But she knew she'd learned something, even with her thoughts ascramble and her heart beating a thousand times faster than normal.

She'd learned she would never get used to it. But she wanted the chance to try, even though it was a pipe dream to imagine Luke would ever come back to her island for anything more than his job.

"Such serious thoughts, Squirt." He rubbed his fingers against her scalp, then let her go and put his hand on the doorknob. "It was only a kiss."

"Probably not one of your better decisions, Sinclair," she said, walking into the house on legs that were noticeably wobbly. She crossed to the table and resumed her place in front of the cookbook, looking down because to look up would be to let him see she was thinking very seriously indeed. "You know I've been on this island for six years. It follows that I'm not used to being around men. Kissing means more to me than to the women you're used to."

"Good. I like knowing it means something."

"But I don't know if I liked it because it's you or because you're male and available," she groused.

"I'm not in the habit of taking advantage of people—"

"I think I'd know if you were taking advantage of me," he murmured.

"Maybe not then," she admitted. "But you should probably take it into consideration before doing it again. If you do it again. Or plan to." She quit before her rambling tongue got totally out of control.

Silence stretched between them until she realized he was waiting for her to look at him. She lifted her head, surprised to find his smile had been replaced by a look that was somber and just a little angry.

"McCain is male and available," he said softly. "Did you kiss him?"

"McCain?" she said, incapable of hiding her reaction to the absurd suggestion. "Of course I didn't. Not that he ever tried, mind you. Why, he doesn't even have a first name!"

His features relaxed, and she felt herself relax along with him.

"Squirt?"

She frowned. "Don't call me that, Sinclair."

"I've got a name besides Sinclair. It would please me if you used it once in a while." He grabbed his coat from the hook by the door and pulled it on.

"Where are you going?"

"To see Sloane. Wyatt asked me to thank him for keeping an eye on you."

More probably Sinclair was going to update Sloane on what he'd done thus far to her security system, she mused, then remembered the unfinished business between them. "I thought we were discussing why you shouldn't kiss me."

He shook his head. "What I said before still goes."

She was having trouble keeping up. "What did you say before?"

He turned and opened the door, then looked at her over his shoulder. "I said I didn't want to talk about it, Elisabeth."

She almost asked why, but he left before she could get the words out. "Just as well," she said to Sneakers who ambled across the room to chew on the tassel of her shoe. "If he doesn't want to talk about it, he certainly isn't going to tell me why."

She yanked her shoe away from the Doberman's mouth, and wondered when Sinclair was coming back. However long it was, she'd need every second of it to slow her heart to a normal beat.

His kiss had meant something to her, something she wanted to remember for a very long time.

FOUR

Luke took his time returning from his meeting with Matt Sloane, detouring past the helipad that was on the inland reaches of Elisabeth's property. Sloane had already assured him the pad was cleared and ready, but Luke needed the time to think . . . to decide what he was going to do now that he'd made what probably ranked as the biggest mistake of his life.

He'd kissed her. What's more, he knew it was going to happen again. Nothing on earth could keep him from exploring the sweet magic of her lips. He accepted that truth even as he acknowledged the dangers of that simple, exotic act. Could he, he wondered, keep from taking the kiss too far? It wasn't a question he'd had to ask himself before, with other women. He'd never once lost the ability to control himself with a woman. If a kiss was followed by sex, it was because they both wanted it—before the kiss, not because of it.

Luke didn't lie to himself by imagining he didn't want to make love with Elisabeth. The fact was that he couldn't allow it to happen. With Elisabeth, kissing was dangerous.

Danger had never seemed so sweet, so inviting.

Ducking beneath low branches, Luke walked easily across ground that was littered inches deep with pine needles until he reached the helipad at the center of a small clearing. As Sloane had said, it was ready for the afternoon's delivery. It was one of his son Todd's jobs, clearing the pad of sticks and other rubble created by the surrounding trees. The sixteen-year-old boy was also charged with keeping the *H* white-washed for easy visibility, a task Luke noted he did well.

Satisfied, he returned to the forest and made his way toward the water, thinking it wouldn't hurt to go check the boat again as long as he was down this far. Not that he expected trouble. Wyatt had called Sloane with the message that Curtis had contacted one of his associates from his preprison days, an associate who was only too happy to take Wyatt's money in exchange for information. Curtis had asked for help in getting out of Kuala Lumpur; Wyatt was heavy on his trail.

As long as Curtis was still on the other side of the world, Luke felt he could breathe a bit easier. Not much, though, because if Curtis wanted to and had the money to pay for it, he could get someone else to do his dirty work. But both Luke and Wyatt were of the opinion that Curtis would want to do the job himself, particularly as there hadn't been a single threat over the past six years when Curtis had been locked up but not necessarily incommunicado. He could have easily arranged for something nasty to happen to Elisabeth on Quincy Island, if he knew where she was.

Luke had to assume he knew, just as he had to assume Curtis wouldn't go to ground without taking his best shot at Elisabeth. According to everything he'd learned about the man, revenge against Wyatt—the man who

had personally turned him over to the authorities—
would come before any other concern, even at the risk
of his own freedom.

Which was why Luke hadn't left Elisabeth totally
alone. Todd Sloane was currently helping her mount a
needlepoint canvas on its frame—an excuse to be with
her that really wasn't an excuse, because the boy had
promised to do it earlier in the week. When Luke had
arrived at the Sloane cottage, Todd had shaken the hand
Luke offered, then shrugged into his coat and bounded
off the porch, informing Luke of where he was going
and why Elisabeth wouldn't think it odd. Halfway across
the lawn, Todd had turned and said he planned to stick
around Elisabeth's until Luke returned.

Luke had been reassured by the maturity he hadn't
expected to find in a boy his age. Todd was very much
like his dad, he'd realized, and not just physically. Both
were blond, blue-eyed, and broad-shouldered, and the
teenager already topped his father's height of about five
feet ten inches. Todd still had a ways to go, however,
before he attained Matt's solid frame.

In the reports both McCain and Matt had submitted
over the years, there had been occasional references to
Todd and the friendship that had developed between
the boy and Elisabeth. The relationship had facilitated
Matt's job of looking after Elisabeth while taking
nothing from the sincere affection between the two.
Through Todd, Matt was able to report to Wyatt that
Elisabeth was well, happy, and otherwise safe without
having to intrude on her privacy any more than was
normal for a neighbor. And as Todd got his education
from books, his parents' tutoring, and occasional brief
excursions to a private mainland academy geared for the
exceptionally bright student, he was almost always on

the island. He could keep Elisabeth company when she wanted, help with chores around the house when she asked.

Watching the young man disappear into the forest, Luke had made a mental note to discuss Todd with Wyatt when he returned to Singapore. While the boy was only sixteen, he would soon be ready for college, and Luke knew Wyatt would want to get involved.

Jenny Sloane, Matt's pretty, quiet-spoken wife, had been politely unobtrusive as Matt and Luke exchanged information. It wasn't until Luke was ready to leave that she'd come forward to ask if he and Elisabeth were coming for dinner the following night, a weekly appointment, it seemed. Luke had declined, then left Matt to remind his wife why it wasn't a good idea for Elisabeth to be outside, especially after dark.

At least Matt could tell Jenny the truth, Luke reflected as he shouldered his way past a stand of saplings. In Elisabeth's case he'd have to rely on lies and subterfuge to keep her indoors. An animal of the small, furry sort flicked its tail as it dove down a burrow at the base of a tree, making Luke wonder if that was how Elisabeth would react if he had to tell her about Curtis before Wyatt got his hands on him. Would she want to find a hole of her own and dive into it for the duration?

He couldn't imagine that the woman who'd attacked him with a toilet plunger would find hiding a viable alternative. The memory of her fierce offensive brought a smile to his lips. No, he couldn't picture Elisabeth cowering while others determined the course events would follow. Even frightened half out of her wits, she had attacked him. Boldly. Foolishly.

And surprisingly, because Matt's reports revealed a different pattern. Over the years the alarms had sounded dozens of times—although with much less frequency now than in the early years. Each time Matt had responded to Elisabeth's call, he'd found her in one or another of the priest holes, waiting for his all-clear.

Unlike the two occasions Luke had thus far experienced. While he believed her excuse of not being able to open the door to the hiding place last night, it didn't explain why she'd failed to get into the priest hole that morning.

Luke was puzzled but not unduly concerned over the inconsistency in her behavior. The thing he needed to worry about, he told himself, was finding a way to look as though he was remodeling the security system while not doing anything to it beyond checking for any remaining discrepancies between the plans and the actual layout.

Coming to a halt amid the trees that lined the shore, he searched the open landscape for footprints or other signs of man's passage along the wet sand. When all he saw were his earlier tracks muddled by those of the Doberman, he left the camouflage of the trees and walked to the boat. Stepping carefully along the dock, he could only hope the half-rotted timbers would last the week. Tying the boat up in front of Elisabeth's wasn't an option. If Curtis did surface on the island, he wouldn't likely associate Luke's boat with Elisabeth, thus giving them an added edge for escape if it was needed. The sailboat, along with Matt's speedboat, were last resorts, though.

If Curtis got that close, Luke knew it would be more efficient to take him out rather than run from him. More efficient and infinitely preferable, because with Curtis permanently out of the picture, Elisabeth would be able to stay on her island in peace—if that was what she really wanted.

Luke wanted so much more for her.

Elisabeth took advantage of Luke's absence to get some work done, spurred as much by Todd's arrival as by her own need to keep busy. The boy sat Indian-style on the Aubusson rug that protected the wood floor from the two sofas and assortment of comfortable chairs scattered throughout the living room. Using a heavy-duty stapler, he mounted the new canvas on its wooden frame as she put the finishing touches on a delicate petit-point eyeglass case. Curled up in a murky blotch of sunshine, Sneakers slept undisturbed by the loud click and bang of the staple gun.

After snipping off a last thread with tiny scissors, Elisabeth set the finished project aside and dragged her working stand from behind the wing chair. Todd helped her tighten the wing nuts that held the frame in place on the stand, then moved it in front of her sewing chair.

"This one looks big enough to take you a couple years," he said. "Think you'll have it done before I go to college?"

"Months, not years. Otherwise someone's going to be disappointed for Christmas." She settled herself in the small swivel tub chair, then tilted the frame toward the meager daylight that fell over her shoulder. "Even so, you'll still be leaving for college long before I'm ready for you to go. Who is going to fix these canvases for me when you're gone?"

Todd grinned, perching on the edge of the facing sofa. "If you'd admit a staple gun isn't really a gun, you'd be able to do them yourself."

"It's got a trigger, Todd," she said, looking up from her lap where she was sorting the threads into a dark-to-light rainbow. "It shoots, can be aimed—if you're good—and leaves holes when you pull out the staple. It sounds an awful lot like a gun to me."

"So think of it as a tool. Like a hammer."

"I have better luck with hammers. My brother taught me how to use one when we made a birdhouse the summer I was eight." She smiled at the memory as she returned to sorting through the colors and comparing them to the canvas. Estimates of square inches per color were checked against what she'd been sent. She paused to scribble a note to order another shade of yellow, and set aside two greens that she wouldn't need.

"Guns are tools too," Todd said, a somber inflection in his voice. "A gun can keep you from getting hurt."

She sighed, and lifted her lashes to find his solemn gaze on her. "Only if you're willing to use it, Todd," she said quietly. "Only if you're willing to kill. Otherwise it's useless."

"A gun doesn't have to kill," he argued. "Like any tool, it has to be used properly, and that requires training."

"You sound like my brother. Wyatt nearly had apoplexy when I refused to have a gun in the house." She sighed again, in frustration, knowing better than to inform the boy she could hit a target with reasonable accuracy. A paper target.

Human targets were another story. "Todd, it's not as though we haven't had this argument before. When will you get it through your head that I won't . . . I *can't* use a gun?" Not on something that walked and breathed.

A grin lightened his expression. "Just checking, Elisabeth. I've always figured there was hope you'd change your mind."

"Why?"

"Because you're not afraid of them," he said, leaning back on the sofa and spreading his long arms across its back. "You see Dad's gun all the time and I've never seen you so much as wince."

"It's not the gun I'm afraid of," she said smartly. "It's the men behind them. And since I have no reason to fear your father, his gun doesn't bother me either."

"But you're afraid of the staple gun," Todd persisted. "You don't even like to pick it up."

She laughed. "That's because it's heavy, Todd! Besides, the first time I used that thing, I shot four staples into the leg of my dining room table. With that kind of control, you should be glad I refuse to use it." She wrinkled her nose, remembering what an idiot she'd felt at having to pluck the staples from the table leg with the pliers. Not only had the leg been permanently maimed, she'd been too chicken to use the staple gun again, worried that a leg of more tender composition might be her next target.

"Dad will always be here when I'm not," Todd pointed out.

As long as Wyatt pays him, Elisabeth added silently, although she really didn't believe he'd leave even if her brother took him off the payroll. Matt was as settled on the island as she was. His days were filled with art—oil painting, to be specific. It was a pastime he'd never been able to explore fully before. He was good, too, and Elisabeth wondered how long it would be before he was "discovered."

"Your dad is soon going to be too famous to worry about manning the staple gun for me," she teased. "Besides, that's not the only reason I'll miss you. Who else will come visit me as often as you do?"

"I could always ask Old Harry to fill in for me. You know he's sweet on you."

Elisabeth groaned. Old Harry lived on the other side of the island and was responsible for maintaining the ferry landing. He was at least eighty, never bathed, and didn't care where he spat the tobacco he chewed. He also thought he was God's gift to women, a claim seriously disputed by Elisabeth and Miss Eleanor Croome—the only other single woman on the island. Elisabeth saw Old Harry on a regular basis, thanks to the fact that her supplies were delivered by the ferry once a week. Every Wednesday she drove the two miles across the island, loaded her groceries and mail into the back of her truck, and told Old Harry that no, she really didn't want to go to Seattle with him for the weekend.

In six years she'd never even hinted she might one day accept his invitation.

In six years he'd never quit asking.

Miss Eleanor Croome, a widow of indeterminate age, had recently suggested to Harry that he quit propositioning her, or she'd get the authorities to stop him. Harry had reminded her there were no authorities on Quincy Island.

And besides, he'd added, if she didn't like his propositions, then why did she come to the ferry every week?

At that point Miss Eleanor had realized there was no winning with Harry. As she'd told Elisabeth, it was easier simply to pick up her groceries and try to ignore the old reprobate.

The battle lines having been drawn, Elisabeth had recently found her weekly trips to meet the ferry more interesting than before. It was fascinating to watch the two feint and jab, although neither would admit that things were any different now than before. Miss Eleanor wasn't doing a very good job of ignoring Harry, just as he wasn't easily disposed to being ignored.

Elisabeth figured an explosion was imminent.

"Old Harry has more important things to do than hike all the way over here," she finally said, hoping she was right. "You'll have to find a better substitute if you think I'm going to let you go anywhere."

"Mom will probably come over more often, but you know how hard it is to get her out of the house." He shook his head. "Then again, maybe not."

Elisabeth laughed. "Your mother just likes being at home, Todd. With your dad. Besides, I see her every week at dinner. For a lot of people, that's as much socializing as they can stand. Speaking of dinner—"

Luke's deep voice interrupted her. "Jenny asked me to tell you she wants to give it a miss this week. Something about being worn out from her trip to Seattle last weekend."

He was standing at the entrance to the living room, one shoulder propped against the end of the bookshelves that ran along the wall. She could only guess how long he'd been standing there, because her attention had been divided between the threads on her lap and Todd. Not long, she finally decided, since as surely as she could breathe, she could feel him . . . his presence.

She would have known if he'd been there for longer than a few seconds.

She dragged her gaze from Luke's casual pose and focused on the younger man. "Todd, you didn't tell me your mother wasn't feeling well."

Todd rose from the deep cushions of the sofa without any seeming effort and shook his head. "She's not sick, just tired. Dad says she shopped nonstop for the two days they were in Seattle." He bent down and retrieved the staple gun from where he'd left it on the rug. "Should I put this back with all the other guns?"

She nodded, grinning. "And don't forget the safety lock. Every time I poke around in that drawer, I'm certain I'll come away with holes in my fingers."

"You have a gun drawer?" Luke asked sharply.

"Doesn't everyone?" she said, hiding her amusement as Luke narrowed his gaze on Todd.

"Wyatt told me you refused to keep a gun here."

Todd chuckled and crossed to the antique mahogany library desk that stood against the wall just inside the entrance to the room. He pulled open the long, flat drawer and put the tool inside, then stepped back so that Luke could see the contents.

Elisabeth couldn't resist detailing the inventory. "There's a staple gun, squirt gun—"

Luke interrupted, swinging his gaze to meet hers. "I thought you were talking real guns."

"Those *are* real guns," she insisted. "There's also a glue gun, a caulking gun—"

"You keep a caulking gun inside the house?"

"Only when it's loaded," she deadpanned. "If I leave it in the garage, the squirrels chew off the pointed end."

"No guns with bullets?" he asked.

She shook her head. "No guns with bullets."

Luke looked at her thoughtfully as Todd slid the drawer shut and went back to the sofa for his coat. "Call me when you decide where you want that dogwood moved, Elisabeth. Mom says we should get it done before much longer if we're going to do it at all this year. It will need most of the summer to get settled in."

"I will, Todd. Maybe next week." She smiled as he shrugged into his coat. "And thanks for doing the frame for me."

"No problem. See ya."

He walked away in that loose-limbed way growing boys have of moving, like colts who are just beginning to understand their strength. Elisabeth watched as he paused a few steps from Luke and mumbled something she didn't catch before heading down the hall toward the kitchen.

"What did he say?" She pulled the frame closer, avoiding Luke's stare as she draped the colors across the top of the frame.

"Nothing important. What are you doing?" He walked across the room toward her, his steps as silent on the hardwood as they were when he reached the Aubusson. He circled around behind her, stopping to look at the canvas from an angle that didn't block her light.

It took an effort to keep from looking behind to see how close he stood. "It's a new canvas. I do needlepoint for a living."

His chuckle made nerve gremlins race up her spine. "I know that you do needlepoint for a shop in Seattle, Elisabeth. And that you also finish work other people have done, such as that glasses case over there."

She couldn't resist twisting her head to look at him. "So why did you ask?"

"I'm just curious about what you're doing now. Trying to decide where to start?" He moved to sit in a nearby wing chair, crossing his long legs at the ankle as he leaned back.

"No, I'm sorting colors to be sure I have enough of everything," she said, returning her focus to the job at hand. "The shop is usually pretty good at sending what I need, but it saves a lot of time in the long run if I check before I get started. Especially on a project this size. I'd hate to have to rip out anything. The profit margin in this business is low enough as it is."

"Why would you have to rip out anything?" He leaned forward and snagged a length of wool from the frame. A tiny gold label dangled from it, and he squinted to see what was written on it. "Number Eight-ninety-one. Doesn't that tell you what to reorder?"

"In theory yes. But then I run the risk of getting a different dye lot. And if it doesn't match . . ." She let her words trail off, reaching for the length of wool Luke held out to her. Their fingers brushed as he laid it across her palm, the wool still warm from his touch, her skin burning from the same.

"If it doesn't match, you rip it out," he said, leaning back again. "I see your point."

Elisabeth just nodded, incapable of putting into words anything that resembled the subject at hand. Rattled, she thought. Not a sensation she remembered feeling before, but definitely apropos as far as describing her reaction to him. Rattled and breathless.

It probably had something to do with the position of the planets. Miss Eleanor was always trying to convince her that human feelings and emotions had more to do with the stars than was generally credited. For the first time Elisabeth wondered if Miss Eleanor could possibly be right.

Either that or she was attracted to Luke Sinclair in a way that resembled nothing she'd ever experienced. Elisabeth wasn't certain that the stars weren't a safer explanation.

"Elisabeth?"

"Hmm?" She wondered if they could try that kiss again, the one he'd planted on her that morning when she'd been too worried about taking advantage of him.

"Is there any profit in this?" he asked.

"In what?" In the stars? Kissing? A profit in kissing? What on earth was he talking about?

He waved a hand toward the canvas. "In needlepoint. It seems that spending several months on something that size would make it a very expensive product."

She felt her face warm with self-conscious relief. Twining her fingers in the length of wool, she concentrated on a logical response to his logical question. "For doing complete projects like this, you're right. If I were to charge what it was worth, only the very rich could afford it. But if I just did finish work like that glasses case, I'd probably be able to totally support myself . . . although not quite in this style." She looked past him, studying the photos and books that lined the floor-to-ceiling shelves, the artwork that reflected her taste in soft colors and shapes. Her heart warmed as her gaze touched the familiar things that made this house her home.

"You're saying that working your fingers to the bone won't keep this place up?" he teased.

"Not hardly." She tossed the wool onto the frame. "Let's get some lunch. I'm starved."

Right on cue Sneakers lifted his head and barked once, then raced out of the room toward the kitchen.

"He knows the word *lunch*?" Luke stood and pushed the needlepoint stand aside so that Elisabeth could get up.

"For a dog he's got a remarkable vocabulary." She slid her hand into Luke's and let him pull her from the low chair, enjoying the encompassing warmth of his grasp for an extra second before pulling away. "I'd warn you about a couple of the more important words, but that wouldn't be as much fun."

"Fun for whom?"

She grinned.

He scowled. "If they're anything like *play*, I'm not sure I want to know."

"They're even better."

As promised, Luke did the dishes, then got some tools from the garage and tucked the linoleum in front of the door back into place. Then he began rigging a complicated circuit that he said would control the infrared sensor array outside the back door, turning it off when Sneakers left and back on when he returned. While he explained that, Elisabeth forced herself to pretend indifference, although she was secretly impressed by his handiwork.

She left him to it, returning to the living room to get to work on the new canvas. Before sitting down, she opened a cabinet attached to the bookshelves that concealed a sophisticated sound system. She pushed a cartridge into the CD player, then adjusted the volume a touch downward as the first notes of a modern rock opera nearly blasted her across the room. With the music still loud enough to block most any other sound, she settled into her chair, tucking her feet beneath her as she pulled the needlework stand close. After a moment's debate she set aside the more colorful wools in favor of the soft ecru she would use on the background. Threading the needle, she made the first stitch of many, many thousands.

A few minutes later Luke appeared in the hall with his coat bunched in one hand and Sneakers at his heels. He waited until she clicked off the music with the remote before attempting to speak. "It was nice of you to turn that up so that I could hear it all the way in the kitchen."

She grinned. "My pleasure."

"I was being facetious," he growled.

"Sorry." She shrugged a half-hearted apology, then dragged her gaze back to the canvas and poked her needle in what she hoped was a logical place. "I'm not used to having other people around, especially when I'm working."

"You always work with it so loud?"

"Mm-hm. It's the only way to block out the woodpeckers."

"What woodpeckers?"

She looked up from the tiny orchid petal she'd been outlining. "The ones that are trying to eat their way through the south wall. They wait until I'm working, then start drilling. It drives me nuts."

"Ignoring them won't make them go away."

"Neither does throwing things at them." She wound a piece of thread around the base of the needle without taking her eyes off Luke. "And even if I had a gun, I couldn't shoot them. The wildlife people frown on stuff like that."

He leveled a disbelieving stare on her, then shook his head. "I'm going to be outside for a while. Is it okay for Sneakers to come with me?"

"In case you haven't figured it out yet, Sneakers goes exactly where he wants to go."

"As long as the system is off, that's not a problem." Luke held up a sheaf of papers. "I'll be checking the plans against what's really out there. Just in case McCain forgot to record any other changes."

She smiled brightly, pleased she'd not messed with any of the lasers earlier that morning when she'd fixed the other trap at the side window. "I'm sure McCain didn't forget anything else." She ducked a twinge of guilt, reminding herself that Sinclair would discover the truth before McCain got himself fired.

"He'd better not. I don't employ fools."

Luke and Sneakers left before Elisabeth could summon up an argument on McCain's behalf that wouldn't give away her own machinations. Lowering her gaze to her work, she decided it would be best to fix the laser by the beach path when Luke went to meet the helicopter.

She'd fix it so that even a ground squirrel couldn't get past.

Luke spent most of the afternoon working, although Sneakers was convinced it was a game they were playing. Each time Luke stopped to adjust, move, or just confirm the location of the dozens of lasers, Sneakers danced ahead, waiting with ill-concealed excitement for a stick to come flying through the air. Luke never threw a stick, or anything else for that matter, but Sneakers never quit anticipating that magic moment.

When Luke found the laser that he'd triggered the night before, he swore a string of curses aimed at McCain that somehow encouraged the Doberman's noisy enthusiasm. The constant barking grating on his nerves, Luke switched his verbal target from McCain to Sneakers. The dog leap joyfully toward him, delighted by the attention. Luke's growl of frustration was answered by Sneakers' overwhelming excitement.

And so went their afternoon, Luke trying to get the job done before the lack of sleep made him careless, Sneakers forgiving Luke's occasional barks of temper with lavish slurps of his tongue. By the time the job was finished, though, man and dog had come to a working agreement. Luke had promised to take Sneakers for a walk before dinner if the Doberman quit licking his ear. The bribe was effective, although Luke was fairly convinced Sneakers quit licking his ear from lack of interest rather than any understanding of upcoming treats.

The pulsing rotors of the helicopter filtered into his consciousness just as he was making the final adjustment. Leaving his tools on the front porch, Luke headed toward the helipad. He moved stiffly at first, his muscles tight from the precision work he'd been doing for the past hours. Stretching as he walked, he wondered if there would be time for a nap before dinner—after Sneakers' promised walk naturally. He'd need a nap, because he planned to work outside again after dark. He had completed the realignment of the lasers. Now it was time for a practical test. In the dark—with the alarms silenced of course—he could use special goggles to check each beam. It was either that or use the Christmas-tree-light method: Turn on the system and run from laser to laser until he found the one or two that set off the alarm. Effective, but noisy . . . not to mention somewhat unprofessional.

Luke arrived at the landing pad just as the helicopter was setting down. With Sneakers keeping a prudent watch from behind the trunk of a massive fir tree, he ducked under the still-turning rotor blades and helped the pilot unload. Scant minutes later he stood beside Sneakers and waited until the helicopter was aloft and skimming across the tops of the trees before hefting the packages into his arms. Heading back to the house, Luke did his best to keep the heavy bolts of cloth from smashing the lettuce. Sneakers helped by not tripping him.

In the kitchen he piled the packages on the table and shucked his jacket. When Elisabeth failed to appear, he sorted through the groceries and put them away, tossing into the sink the blocks of dry ice that had been used for temporary refrigeration. She probably didn't want to leave her work, he figured, although he was surprised because the house had been miraculously silent since he'd returned. Thinking that perhaps she was too involved in what she was doing to get up and change the CD, he decided he'd offer to do it for her. While he was at it, he could broach the subject of covering the windows. He wanted to get it done before dark, before he took his nap. Or walked Sneakers. Time was getting short, he realized. Leaving the bolts of cloth on the kitchen table, he walked down the hall to the living room.

"Elisabeth, I put the food in the refrigerator. . . ." His words trailed into silence as he reached the doorway and discovered that he'd been mistaken in a very important assumption.

Elisabeth wasn't too involved in her work to get up and put away groceries or reload the CD player.

She wasn't even there.

FIVE

Luke searched the house, then called Matt Sloane with instructions to search the south stretch of beachfront and the woods surrounding the helipad. He would go north where he and Elisabeth had walked that morning, then move inland toward the road and work backward. With Todd helping, the men figured they could cover the area and meet back at the house in twenty minutes.

Luke slammed down the phone and headed out the back door, checking his gun before replacing it in the leather holster clipped to his jeans at the small of his back. Twenty minutes, then they'd have to expand the search area if they hadn't found her. Sneakers followed him out and kept pace, his exuberance clearly dampened by Luke's anxiety.

The beach was the most logical place to search, because if Curtis or one of his cronies had managed a snatch, it was almost certain they would have arrived by water. The only other access to the island was by air or the ferry, and the ferry wasn't due until Wednesday. Luke slowed as he neared the treeline rimming the beach, then ran ahead as a quick scan offered nothing unusual.

She couldn't have been gone long. It would have happened when he'd gone to meet the helicopter, because he'd been too close to the house until then for anyone to risk going around him. Ten minutes, maybe fifteen, since he hadn't exactly rushed to put away the groceries.

The high rise of boulders he'd helped her climb that morning slowed him momentarily as he tried to hurry across them without making the unforgivable error of getting hurt in the process.

He couldn't help her if he broke an ankle or leg.

Then he was over and running again, Sneakers at his side, his view of the beach ahead limited by a sharp bend. He didn't swear. He didn't worry if Curtis had hurt Elisabeth, or if she'd made her capture easy or hard.

He concentrated on the various actions that might be open to him when he finally caught up with them. What he would do if they saw him first, or if he saw them. If there were two of them, or ten. What kind of weapons they carried. If they were already on the water, or still on the beach.

If Elisabeth was conscious, if she wasn't.

Luke brutally ignored the emotion engendered by that particular image and slowed his pace, sneaking up on the bend rather than exploding unprepared on the other side. He pulled out the gun and slipped off the safety lock. The Doberman stuck close, slowing to a stealthy pace as he flanked the man beside him. Using a stand of trees as cover, Luke edged around the corner.

Nothing. He broke into a run, his gaze examining the beach for the second time as disappointment fed his growing apprehension. Sneakers hurdled from slow to fast in a single movement, then let out a high-pitched yip as he peeled away from Luke. A flicker of color teased the edge of Luke's vision, a shade of sapphire that contrasted sharply against the green-gray sea in the background. He turned his head toward it and watched as Sneakers sped across the sand toward the waterline, where Elisabeth was straightening from behind a huge piece of gnarled driftwood.

She lifted her hand to wave, and her smile reached for him across the sandy beach. She shouted something Luke couldn't hear at the dog that fairly flew toward her. The breeze brought him her laughter as Sneakers plowed into her, tossing her off her feet with a gentleness Luke could only pray he wasn't imagining. He didn't break stride as he changed direction, tucking his gun away as he ran. His long legs brought him to the woman and dog within seconds. Then he was on his knees beside her, pushing Sneakers away, holding her face between his hands as she laughed up at him. Real laughter, not tears.

"You're okay?" he demanded. A look of surprise flickered in her eyes, followed by something that made his breath catch.

"Of course I'm okay, Luke. Sneakers wouldn't hurt me."

Sneakers. She didn't even know he'd been chasing after her with the assumption he'd have to kill people just to hold her again. Seeing the laughter in her eyes, he was suddenly glad she didn't know.

He took a deep breath, then leaned toward her. Resting his forearms on either side of her head, he lowered his lips to hers and kissed her. *Really* kissed her, with his mouth hard on hers, his tongue taking advantage of her surprise to delve inside. His eyes closed, and he gave himself entirely to blind sensation. She was sweet and warm and alive, so wonderfully alive! His heart thudded hard against his chest, much harder than earlier when he'd been wondering how many men would die before he got her back.

He suddenly realized he was kissing her hard, too hard to tell if she was kissing him in return. Taking, not giving. Taking, because he'd thought he'd lost her and he couldn't live with that. He softened the kiss, gave her a chance to breathe . . . to decide. Then he realized her hands were behind his neck, her fingers threading into his hair, pulling him closer.

"*Harder*," she said, her lips against his. "*More*."

She arched toward him, using her grasp around his neck to lever away from the sand. He could feel the slight pressure of her breasts against him, teasing . . . promising. Then all conscious thought fled as her tongue stroked boldly along his. He quit worrying about too hard and taking. Using his body, he crowded her back down until she was flat against the sand, then threw a leg over her thighs to keep her there. He savored the softness of her breasts beneath him and the taste of her as he plundered her mouth again and again.

Above the rhythmic lapping of nearby waves, he could hear her soft, passionate moans as he left her mouth to explore the creamy skin of her throat. Another sound intruded, the whine of a dog too long ignored. Luke didn't care if Sneakers' feelings were hurt, but that slight distraction opened the door to remembering it all.

Matt and Todd Sloane were still looking for Elisabeth. He had to find them first, before Elisabeth figured out they were searching for her.

He captured a tiny moan from her lips, then stole a last taste of her mouth before lifting away from her warm, soft body, bracing himself once again on his forearms. He waited until her eyelids fluttered open before speaking. "You scared me. I thought you were . . . hurt," he said after a brief hesitation.

Elisabeth stared up at the man who had kissed the breath out of her. "You two have a great act. Sneakers knocks me down and you hold me there."

A smile kicked up one corner of his mouth. "Would you rather it was the other way around?"

Dropping her hands from his neck, she shook her head. "I think it worked pretty well this way." She tried to keep in mind what he'd said earlier about kissing and not wanting to discuss it. "Are you sure you're not paying me back for letting Sneakers play with you yesterday?"

His gaze sharpened on hers. "I'm not sure about anything, Elisabeth. Certainly not about this."

"This?" *As in "kiss"?* she wondered, shivering as the breeze filled the space between them.

"About us. I think we've got to make some decisions before things get out of hand." His gaze filled with a kind of wanting that she recognized as a reflection of her own.

"And I thought you didn't want to talk about it."

"That was before."

"Before what?" she whispered. Her heart resumed that same mad pace from moments ago, when he'd kissed her as though it was a prelude to a more intimate joining.

"Before I realized how fragile my control is around you." He abruptly rolled to his feet, pulling her up after him. Turning her to face the opposite direction, he brushed sand from her back, butt, and thighs, then tried to shake it from her hair.

She took over that job, bending from the waist to briskly rub her scalp, taking longer than necessary because she needed the extra seconds to compose herself. Luke had made it uncompromisingly clear that he desired her. Lying beneath him in the sand, she hadn't been so overwhelmed by his kisses that she hadn't noticed the hard length of his erection pressed against her thigh. That awareness had triggered a response in her unlike anything she'd ever known, a sensation of soaring that somehow blended with that of coming home.

In his arms she'd felt at once safe and free.

There was an attraction between them, and something more. And she knew that whatever she felt for Luke, it was being returned in full measure. Unless he could come up with some variables she hadn't considered, it wasn't any more complicated than that. She rubbed her scalp harder, stalling as she considered how to best tell him there were no decisions left to make.

She'd already made hers.

When she finally stood upright, she could feel the deep flush of blood that had raced to her head. Luke was looking at her with a strangely grim expression. It made her hesitate, suddenly unsure, where she'd so recently been filled with the confidence of knowing he wanted her. After a long moment he held out his hand and waited until she slid her palm against his. They started walking back toward the house, and she had to work to keep up with Luke's long stride.

"Any particular reason we're in such a hurry?" she asked after a hundred yards of the half-trotting, half-skipping step she was forced to do.

"I forgot to put the groceries away."

"They'll keep. The helicopter hasn't been gone all that long."

"I don't want to take a chance on the crab. If it gets warm, it'll spoil." He slowed marginally, though, and checked his watch. "Besides, you need to wash your hair."

"It's not an emergency, Sinclair," she replied, a little piqued at how easily he reverted to the mundane details of life. "Sneakers is always knocking me over. I spend half my life washing sand out of my hair." A shiver lashed at her spine as the late-afternoon chill assaulted her, a surprise because their quick pace should have kept her warm.

Luke muttered something she was sure she didn't want to hear, then put his arm around her shoulders and pulled her against his side—all without slowing down.

Sneakers chose that moment to try to trip her. She stumbled and would have fallen had Luke not tightened his hold on her. He pulled her more tightly into his side, splaying his fingers just above her waist to give her added balance as he continued to walk toward the house.

A shiver of a different sort shook her as every nerve in her body became aware of the hand that pressed against her just below her breasts.

"What were you doing out on the beach without a coat, Squirt?"

"It was warmer when I started." *And you weren't holding me then, Sinclair. Don't you realize there are shivers . . . and then there are shivers?* An impatient sigh parted her lips. "What were you and Sneakers doing chasing after me anyway? I thought you had work to do." She glanced up at him, but the effort only served to make her lose her balance again. She slipped an arm around his waist, surprised when her hand brushed over the gun she hadn't realized he was carrying. She just raised her arm a bit, not bothered by the presence of the weapon but thinking Luke was being overly cautious for a quiet place like Quincy Island.

"We weren't chasing you. I'd promised Sneakers a walk. We just happened to go in the same direction."

The lies were beginning to sicken him. The bitter taste of them filled his mouth as he remembered what he'd said to her about decisions.

The only one he had to make was whether he could make love to her amid the lies. Even though one had nothing to do with the other, they both involved trust. Would she ever trust him if the time they shared was steeped in lies?

Luke was agonizing over the questions without answers when he saw Matt and Todd a ways down the beach, heading toward them. He took his arm from Elisabeth's shoulders and shooed her in the direction of the path to the house. "You go on inside, Elisabeth. Take Sneakers with you." He pushed her gently between the shoulder blades when she seemed reluctant to follow orders. "Get into the shower before you catch cold."

She turned to face him, hugging herself in an attempt to ward off the chill. "You're not coming inside?"

He nodded toward the pair coming up the beach. "I'll go see what they want."

"I can wait."

Frustrated because he wanted her away before she noticed both Sloane men were carrying guns, Luke went to her and closed his hands around her forearms. "I don't want them to see you like this, honey. Please go inside."

"See me like what?"

"Your lips are swollen and a little red because I kissed you harder than I should have. And you've got a look in your eyes that's making me so hard, I can barely walk." He kissed her quickly, then set her away. "Not to mention your hair. All wild and tangled like it is, you look like you've been rolling in the sand with your lover. I don't want anyone to see you like that except me."

"We're not lovers."

The whisper barely reached his ears, but he didn't have to hear to know what she meant. "We will be, Elisabeth. Sooner than you think."

A spark of mischief flared in her already heated expression. "I'm thinking it should be very soon, Luke."

A rush of air left him almost light-headed. By the time he'd recovered, she was nearly halfway up the path, Sneakers shuffling along at her heels. He was just about to race after her when he heard sounds that reminded him why he'd sent Elisabeth on ahead. He waited until she had rounded the bend and was out of sight before turning to greet the Sloanes. Both father and son were sweating lightly, but didn't appear overly exerted by the physical demands of running up and down the island.

"She slipped out for a walk while I was meeting the 'copter. Sorry to call you out for nothing."

Todd slipped his gun into his coat pocket. "Can't you confine her to quarters or something? I haven't run that fast in months."

Luke just shook his head. "Not until I tell her everything, *if* I decide to tell her. If that happens, I imagine we'll leave the island until it's safe." He nodded at the pocket where Todd's gun resided, his jaw tightening as he considered what happened when inexperienced people got hold of weapons. "You any good with that?"

"Yes, sir." Todd met his cool stare with a composure that forcibly reminded Luke of the boy's maturity. "I wouldn't carry it if I didn't know what I was doing. Dad made sure of that long before you got here."

"Does Elisabeth know?"

"That I carry this?" Todd shook his head. "She doesn't like guns much. I didn't figure showing it to her was a good idea. Besides, until you called Dad from Singapore, it hasn't been out of the house except for target practice."

Luke studied the boy, who was wiser than most men twice his age, and nodded. "That's okay, then." He turned to Matt, who was watching the exchange with an impassive expression. "Want to come in for a drink? It's the least I can do after this."

"Thanks, but we've got to get back. Jenny lassoed us into helping her can some red-pepper jelly, and we kind of left her in the lurch."

Luke grinned. "Is Jenny the one who got Elisabeth hooked on peppers?"

Matt shook his head. "More like the other way around. Why? Is she trying to fry your taste buds?"

"Trying, but not succeeding. I think she's forgotten how spicy Malaysian food can be."

"Watch out for her beans in habanero sauce," Todd warned. "It'll take the fur right off your tongue."

With that warning the Sloanes turned and left. Luke headed back inside, finding Sneakers in the kitchen, passed out in front of his water bowl. The Doberman lifted his head long enough to acknowledge Luke's presence, then went back to his dreams. Luke locked the back door and pushed a piece of plastic into the grooves of the doggie door, effectively sealing the entrance. Next he went down the hall to the front door. He locked that, too, then flipped open the security panel and activated all alarms except for those on the grounds outside. He'd work on them later, when the darkness enhanced the performance of the night glasses.

In the meantime he could cover the living-room windows. Or take that nap he'd promised himself.

Or he could go upstairs and find out if Elisabeth had meant what she'd said.

Elisabeth stood under the hot, comforting spray of the shower long after the last grain of sand had been washed out of her hair and down the drain. Even then she didn't have an answer to the question she'd been asking herself over and over again.

Why had Luke said he hadn't put the groceries away?

It had amused her at first, when she'd entered the house and discovered the job had been done with his usual efficiency. Even the box and wrappings had been set outside on the porch with the other trash. Shrugging off Luke's memory lapse, she'd picked up Sneakers' water bowl and walked over to the sink to fill it. A block of dry ice had hissed as she spilled a few drops of water on it. Dry ice wasn't something most people dealt with when unpacking groceries. That, if nothing else, should have made an impression upon Luke, enough of one that he would have remembered unpacking the groceries.

It was such a little thing to lie about.

Elisabeth shivered under the stinging spray, then reached for the controls to make the water so hot that steam clouded her vision. It wasn't the lie itself that bothered her. She'd sensed before that he mixed lies with truth, but it hadn't troubled her because she'd felt he was equally uncomfortable with them. She'd actually felt a touch guilty, imagining he somehow knew she wasn't using the security system as designed and was there to prove it. And she'd lied to him, too, yet another reason to keep her silence.

It was that guilt that kept her from pursuing too eagerly why he thought lies were necessary. She'd pretended to believe and in the meantime had come to realize that Luke Sinclair was a man she could trust, whatever his reasons for being there.

She knew that she trusted him, despite the lies. And that trust exposed her to emotions she was finding strangely comfortable. He kissed her, and her body responded as though kissing him back was the most natural thing in the world. He held her close, and she fitted against him with the ease of long practice.

His lies hadn't mattered. This time it was different, though, because this lie made it impossible for her to pretend any longer. Something was wrong, something big enough to bring the great Sinclair all the way from Singapore to Quincy Island at what resembled a dead run. She had calculated the time from Sheila's heads-up call to the moment he'd sailed up to the island, and the numbers had been impressive. It didn't make sense for a man to push himself that hard.

There's a new alarm system I want to try out here. McCain was off on another assignment, so I came myself.

Sure. Just like the groceries jumped out of the box and put themselves away. She took a deep breath and reminded herself of one very important thing: She trusted Luke. Whatever his reasons, he wasn't lying to hurt her.

"Elisabeth?"

Scare her to death, maybe, but not hurt her. Whirling, she flattened herself against the tiles and stared incomprehensibly at the rather large shadow beyond the frosted glass. What was Luke Sinclair doing in her bathroom?

"It's me—Luke. I didn't mean to frighten you."

She found her voice. "Of course it's you. How many other men do I know who would have the nerve to interrupt me in the shower?"

His low chuckle drifted through the steam. "I got tired of waiting for you to come out. How much longer do you think the hot water will last?"

She ignored his question in favor of one of her own. "What do you want, Sinclair? Need to borrow my soap?"

"No."

"Then why?"

"I'm here because I think you invited me." The sound of the shower was the only thing she heard for several long seconds, then he added, "Did you, Elisabeth?"

His form was unmoving through the glass, coming neither closer nor backing away. Elisabeth shivered from a chill that wasn't from cold and wrapped her arms tightly across her chest. Her thoughts went back to the beach, to the moment when he'd promised they would be lovers.

Even she hadn't expected *soon* to come all that quickly.

"Elisabeth?" His voice smoothed to that gentle tone he used when he didn't want her frightened. "I need to know if you want me to stay."

"Stay." The word came out in a rush because she couldn't for the life of her imagine letting him leave, not now.

At first she didn't think he'd heard her, since he didn't move. Then suddenly the shower door was sliding open, and there was only steam between them. Steam and silence. Luke stood barefoot just outside the open door, apparently not caring that the shower spray was hitting him. Beads of water trickled down his bare chest and dampened his jeans. She swallowed nervously as his gaze traveled over her, not feeling self-conscious precisely, but wishing for the earlier comfort of being held and kissed.

His gaze was steady and certain as it met hers. "You're beautiful. I don't think I'll ever forget how you look at this moment."

"I'm nervous." Her teeth chattered in unconscious punctuation.

"Of me?" His knuckles whitened where he gripped the door.

"Of me. That I won't know how to let you go when it's time."

"Then don't think about it, honey." He reached through the driving spray and grabbed her wrist, pulling her across the tiles until she was standing in his embrace. His arms were warm and hard, uncompromising bonds that held her with urgency and comfort.

She was where she belonged.

When he felt her arms slide around his waist, Luke knew it was going to be all right. For now anyway. He shut off the shower, then squeezed Elisabeth lightly in approval. Otherwise he didn't move or hardly even breathe, so afraid was he of going too fast . . . of scaring the woman who had come to him with such incredible honesty.

I won't know how to let you go when it's time. Yes, that was going to be a problem, a far worse problem than she could possibly realize. He knew her well enough to understand how deeply she felt things, how in tune she was with her emotions. She cared about him. He could see it in her eyes, could feel it in the way she kissed him, sharing all of herself without holding anything back. Yes, she cared, and because of that she would find letting him go almost as difficult as it would be for him to leave.

Because he would leave, eventually. When the excuses, real or imagined, were no longer valid. Wyatt had meant it when he'd said Luke wasn't the right man for Elisabeth.

Luke had meant it when he'd agreed.

Nothing had changed . . . except that he was going to make love to the woman who had stolen his heart.

He was going to make love to Elisabeth, and pray that she'd forgive him someday for not being the man she needed.

SIX

Luke looked over the top of her head and into the bathroom mirror, his gaze following his hands as they caressed her back with long, firm strokes. She was so small against him, so incredibly fragile-looking, that he felt the need to reassure her.

"I won't hurt you," he whispered, hoping that by easing her fears, his own would somehow disappear. *I love you*, he said silently against her hair, and knew that was the one thing he couldn't say aloud.

"I know that." Elisabeth opened her mouth against his chest, thinking how ridiculous it was for him to worry about such a thing. Their mating would be nothing less than perfect.

She'd waited too long for him to think otherwise.

"I'll protect you, honey. I care for you too much to take chances."

"You care?" She sighed and wondered how deep that caring went. Her own heart was dangerously close to the line. "How much?"

His next words nudged her heart even closer. "More than I should." He hesitated, then shook his head when she knew he'd been about to add something more. Her curiosity went on full alert, her heart thudding hard in nervous anticipation.

"What aren't you saying, Luke?" She leaned back in his arms and looked up at him.

"It doesn't matter," he said, and attempted to draw her close again.

She resisted. "I think it does matter. Tell me, Luke. Finish what you were going to say."

His eyes blazed with a mixture of frustration and desire, and she knew it was the heat of the moment that forced him to answer her.

His gaze softened, and he said quietly, "How can I tell you that I love you when I know I'll have to leave you one day soon?"

She focused on the first part, ignoring the second because she didn't want to hear it. Her mouth went dry, and she almost wished she hadn't asked. His words came so close to expressing feelings she didn't dare think about. "You love me?" she couldn't resist asking, her voice less strong than it had been just moments ago.

He nodded. "I fell a little in love with you the first time I saw your picture." He grabbed a huge towel and wrapped it around her, tucking the end against the curve of her breast, then urged her to sit in the low chair in front of the vanity. Snagging another towel from the rack, he began drying her hair, his thighs hard against her shoulders, his gaze meeting hers in the mirror that was still fuzzy from the mist.

"I didn't know that," she whispered, lifting her hand to catch his. Their fingers laced, hers trembling, his steady. Neither doubted their right to touch.

A smile lifted one corner of his mouth, and he put her hand down as he resumed working the towel over her hair. "You weren't supposed to know."

"Is that why you finally came to Quincy Island?" It answered a lot of questions, looking at it that way. The vague fears that had bedeviled her for two days suddenly evaporated.

But the tortured steel of his gaze made her realize that life was rarely that simple. "Will you be satisfied if I tell you it's why I couldn't not come?" he asked softly.

"I don't understand."

"I know. It's not fair, is it?" He threw the towel into a corner and leaned past her shoulder to grab her brush. Working carefully, he began untangling the still damp curls.

No, it wasn't fair, she thought. To either of them. Then she remembered what she'd been thinking about earlier, about trust and how even though she'd known he was lying to her, she still trusted him. Now that the lies had stopped, he deserved no less.

"Did Wyatt send you?" she asked, afraid of the answer yet needing the truth.

His hands stilled for a moment as he held her gaze with his own, then he resumed the slow, delicate work. "In a way. But he also tried to stop me from coming."

"Why?"

"Because he knows how I feel about you."

She couldn't help the smile that tickled her lips. "What was he afraid would happen?"

"This." Luke bent down and brushed his mouth across her shoulder, then drew a long finger along the edge of the towel where it clung to her breasts. Her flesh tingled from his touch, his calloused finger a rough contrast against her soft curves. When he straightened, his gaze was intense, almost hungry.

"My brother actually said he didn't want you to make love to me?" That was not the reserved, mind-his-own-business Wyatt she'd grown up with. Outside of the irritating security checks he'd run on her dates, he'd been totally respectful of her privacy.

But then, times change. As do people, she mused.

"Not in so many words," Luke said, "but the message was there."

"Then whatever it was that brought you here can't be all that important." She took a deep breath, then leaned more easily against his thighs. "If Wyatt had time to worry about you and me and the possibilities of anything . . . intimate happening, the big picture can't be all that bad."

"You're not worried?"

"Not anymore. Whatever it is, you'll handle it." She reached up and captured his hand, stilling his movements. "Just one thing, Luke."

"What?"

"Would anything change if you told me right now exactly why you're here?"

He looked at her curiously. "Are you asking if I'll still make love to you . . . or if you'll still want me to?"

"Both."

He dropped the brush onto the vanity and rested his hands on her shoulders, his fingers stretching across the delicate curves and valleys of her collarbone. "Whether or not we make love has nothing to do with why I'm here."

A great relief flooded her senses. Whatever his secrets, they could wait. "Then tell me tomorrow, will you?"

"Tomorrow," he agreed.

She met his gaze in the mirror for a final time. He was absolutely certain of what he was doing, she realized. Of what they were doing.

As was she.

With a nervous fluttering in her stomach that had nothing to do with questions and everything to do with anticipation, she rose from the chair and turned to face him. His hands dropped to his sides, clenching with the fierce emotions she saw in his eyes.

"I don't know if I love you, Luke. Does that matter?"

"I never expected you to." His expression softened. "Do you trust me, honey?"

She nodded. "From the beginning."

"Then that's all that counts." He reached toward her, almost in slow motion, and hooked his fingers in the towel between her breasts. With gentle pressure he pulled her to him. "Love is something we can't control, Elisabeth. I love you. And I know that what we're doing here will result in memories, not ties. Even so, I can't stop myself from wanting this."

"No ties?" she whispered, suddenly unsure of the ground she was standing on.

"No ties. Which is why loving me would be a mistake." With a flick of his wrist, the towel lost its hold and fell to the floor. "I'm the wrong man for you, honey. In the long run. You need to remember that."

"But you said you love me—"

"And I probably always will. That doesn't change what I said. There can't be any ties between us, Elisabeth. Not ever." And with those ominous words he lowered his mouth to hers and swallowed her protests.

Elisabeth allowed Luke that small victory, thinking she could correct him at a more appropriate time. Then she forgot all about words and logic as his hands found her breasts. Sliding her own hands up his chest, she reveled in his touch, his caress, the care he was taking with her. His long fingers circled her breasts, drawing circuitous paths to the very tips, then retreating. Again and again, until he must have gotten the message—her muffled moans, her fingers digging into his neck, whatever—and he found her nipples, rubbing them between his thumb and forefinger lightly, teasingly, then hard, testing her need, her desire.

She wanted him, and that wanting was as unfamiliar to her as were the budding emotions he stirred within her.

For a very short moment self-consciousness reigned. She felt small beside his massive body, inadequate. It worried her . . . until she recognized his groan of discovery that was as honest as the tide. In response she swelled beneath his touch, loving the feel of his hands, the care he took to make her know just how much he valued her.

And so he touched her, carefully at first, then with more confidence as she caught his hands and pressed them closer. The nonsense about his being the wrong man for her faded into insignificance as she discovered the smooth contours of his shoulders, the taut muscles that lay hard as steel beneath her touch. She'd argue with him later, she mused, when she could string three words together. Three rational words.

The only ones that came to mind now were, "Fill my heart."

She knew he wouldn't understand.

Being naked had never been so natural, so important. She shimmied up against him, wrapping her hands around his neck, her calf hooking around his leg. He responded with an urgency that took her breath away, sliding his hands down her back to her fanny, cupping her and lifting her hard against him.

His zipper.

That had to go.

Luke tried to keep tabs on rational thought, but it fled the second he felt her hands at his belt, struggling with the cinch, then pushing it aside to unsnap his jeans. It worried him for a moment, thinking her eagerness might easily draw blood. But she slowed her frantic movements, tugging at his zipper with the needed restraint so that the procedure wouldn't emasculate him.

He shuddered his approval when her fingertips found his hard, pulsing arousal. Then he lifted her into his arms and carried her to her bed, where they could do something useful about the need that was suddenly at flashpoint. Pushing his jeans down his thighs and kicking them away, he followed Elisabeth onto the down-filled covers.

She was hot and soft beneath him, her eyes wide open, her expression eager. With one hand he pushed her thighs apart and settled himself between them, then stole a long, deep, tongue-spiraling kiss. That was as close to making love as he was ready to come at that precise moment. His desire to please her bridled his own haste, and he learned the tastes and textures of her mouth with greedy enthusiasm. When he lifted his head for air, he was extraordinarily pleased to know that he was where he belonged, between her thighs, and that she was as breathless as he. Breathless, but no less eager.

She moved her hips against him, and he pushed her deeper into the bed. "We're going to slow down now, love. Stop wiggling."

"Why?" Her fingers were in his hair, stretching, testing his neck muscles as she tried to pull him down. "If you're taking a time-out to put on a condom, you don't have to. I've been on the pill since I was a teenager."

He smiled. "Nowadays there are health reasons for

using protection. And I know you're on the pill because your cycle is too erratic without it." He kissed away her gasp of outrage, calming her with facts she should have realized he'd possess. "It's in your file, honey. Besides the fact that the pills are sent directly from Singapore, everything the doctor knows is reported in your file."

"That's what I get for having a doctor come here every year instead of me going to his office in Seattle," she grumbled, then sent him a mock scowl. "So, any other reason for you slowing down?" She pulled harder against his neck, a contest of determination versus brawn.

Brawn won. "Because I'm too big for you."

"How do you know?"

He stole a long, wet kiss before replying. "I would have thought that was obvious, honey. I'm somewhat larger than you are. It stands to reason our body parts might have some trouble adjusting."

A mischievous smile lit up her face. "Last I heard, Wyatt's file on me isn't that specific."

He reprimanded her with a stern frown. "I'm talking common sense, Squirt. I don't want to hurt you."

"Then how can you say you're too big when you've no . . . proof?" She slid her hands down his shoulders and back. "Seems like you made me climb through Sneakers' door with a lot less concern for fit."

She threw down the challenge with the same aplomb that she'd sicced her dog on him. Luke couldn't help his laugh . . . in the same way that he couldn't resist her challenge. "You think I should measure first?" he whispered.

She didn't answer, but he really hadn't expected one. Holding her tightly, an arm beneath her shoulders, his gaze pinning her against the pillow, he slid his hand between them, across her belly, finding the nest of tight curls that told him he was near.

The wet heat of her desire didn't surprise him. Elisabeth was too open in her passion not to be totally aroused. Still, he took a moment to revel in it, to coat his fingers in her honeyed welcome and know she was responding to the same need that drove him. Her eyes drifted closed, and he heard her soft sigh as he found the center of her passion. First with one finger, then two, he stroked the core of her, the sheath that would soon stretch around his throbbing erection.

Soon.

Her hips rocked in time to his intimate caress, and he swallowed her tiny cries with his mouth. Reassuring her, taunting her. His thumb found the tiny nub amidst the soft curls, and she reared beneath him, her fingernails sinking into his shoulders, her legs wrapping around his and urging him to get on with it.

She was ready. Slick and smooth and wanting, so incredibly wanting in her passion. So much faster than he'd planned, more intense than he'd ever dreamed.

He guided himself to the entrance of her heat and teased her yet another moment, finding pleasure in her frustration, her cries of demand. Their hearts beat madly against each other as he pushed into her, and he knew it was a memory that would outlast all others . . . a moment in his life that was more vital than anything that had or would ever occur.

And as he slid into her—impossibly easily given the tightness of her sheath—he knew he would never love again this well, this completely.

He would never truly love another woman except for the one in his arms. Elisabeth, who caught her breath as he entered her, who smiled up at him, encouraging, *demanding* he do the right thing.

So he filled her until they were one.

What followed was pure magic. Together they traveled through realms of time and space never before discovered, places where stars burst in glorious shows of light and each moment was as precious and unforgettable as the next. Words of love and passion flew between them, some whispered, some shouted with the joy of their sharing.

Elisabeth saw into his heart and knew the strength of his caring, his love. In return her own passions exploded into a reality of loving she couldn't begin to express. She settled for telling him other truths, confiding her total trust, her feelings of comfort and of coming home. She writhed in his arms, hiding nothing of her desire or excitement.

When he finally pushed her past the edge, into that dimension of exploding sights and sounds, she went eagerly, taking him with her, crying his name because she'd never been there before. His gentle strength surrounded her as his shudders of passion filled her with confidence and satisfaction.

His love warmed her heart, and Elisabeth feel asleep in Luke's arms knowing her life would never again be the same.

With Luke her life was suddenly beginning.

Something cold and damp poked Luke between his shoulder blades. He opened his eyes cautiously, terrified for a split second that it had all been a dream and Elisabeth wasn't really sleeping in his arms. There was no need for concern. She was snuggled close to his chest, her body all warm and soft and yielding, her face slightly flushed, her mouth curved into a smile even in her sleep. He pulled the covers higher across her shoulders, shielding her from the cool air that drifted in through an open window.

A few more minutes of rest, he told himself. Then he'd awaken her and show her just how slowly he could make love to her. His body tightened in anticipation, and he took a deep breath for patience. That was a slightly counterproductive move, because the scent of their lovemaking was still heavy in the air. He smiled, savoring the assault on his senses, remembering each detail of the love they'd shared.

Another sticky nudge against his back reminded him of a third presence. Moving carefully so as not to wake Elisabeth, Luke turned his head and found himself nose to nose with Sneakers. The dog grinned and slopped a giant kiss across his cheek.

Luke glared at him. "Get lost, beast."

Sneakers barked and jumped onto the bed, landing squarely on top of Elisabeth, who came awake with considerably less subtlety than Luke had planned.

She yelped and yanked the covers up to her neck. "Sneakers! Go 'way!"

Luke tried to shift the dog off the bed, but Sneakers was clearly in play mode and didn't get the hint. The Doberman took an edge of the down quilt in his jaws and started to pull. Luke grabbed before giving it any thought, thus giving way to a tug-of-war he'd had no intention of beginning.

A tug-of-war the dog was clearly winning.

"Let go!" Elisabeth dragged at Luke's arm, crouching beside him in seeming unconcern about her nakedness.

Luke wrapped his fist in the material and tugged hard. "He's not minding, Squirt. This is what you get for messing with a trained animal." He got to his knees and pulled hard, fighting the full weight of the dog who had braced his legs against Luke's strength. It was an even contest, one neither male intended to lose. Even if it meant having to replace the quilt.

"No, stupid! I meant you!" Elisabeth fell back against the pillows, hugging herself as gales of laughter overwhelmed her.

"Me?" He let go without warning, a move that sent Sneakers flailing backward off the bed, trapped in the folds of the quilt. Luke stared at Elisabeth, astonishment vying with indignation. "You're calling me stupid?"

Sitting up against the mahogany bedpost, she wiped her eyes with the back of her hand and nodded brightly. "He was only trying to get into bed with me. Us," she added after the barest hesitation. "You shouldn't have invited him if you didn't want him up here."

"I didn't invite him."

"You said, 'Get lost.' That's doggie shorthand for 'Let's play hide-and-seek.'" She laughed at Luke's expression of disbelief. "He was trying to pull off the cover so that we could get up and start the game."

"Then it's your fault." Luke looked torn between growling and laughing. "If you hadn't challenged him over the quilt, I could have gotten rid of him."

Luke glanced down to the bottom of the bed where Sneakers was having no luck finding a way out of the tangle of covers. He grinned at Elisabeth, totally unrepentant. "I got rid of him."

"And pretty much totaled the duvet in the process."

"I'll get you another." He leaned across the expanse of white sheet and dragged her back against him. "That dog spends too much time jumping on you. I'm surprised you can still breathe from all that weight landing on you."

She wound her hands around his neck and smiled up at him. "You weigh a lot more than Sneakers, Sinclair.

And I seem to remember you lying on top of me for a very, very long time."

He rolled her onto her back and resumed the position she spoke of, his thighs cradled between hers, his weight supported by his forearms. "Is this what you're complaining about?" he asked, lowering his chest to rub lightly against her nipples.

She moaned luxuriously and closed her eyes as he rained wet kisses across her shoulders and throat. "Yes, that's exactly what I was complaining about." She rubbed the soles of her feet up and down his calves, then began to move her hips in a slow, even rhythm.

Luke felt himself harden and swell against her. He found the aroused tips of her breasts with his mouth as his hand delved low to the silky temptation between her thighs. She was ready for him, wet and swollen at his first caress.

Forgetting everything about slow and easy, he slid his hard length into her, discovering anew the perfection of how they fit together. She tightened around him, swallowing him whole, urging him with her body to give them both what they wanted.

"*Fast,*" she begged, because she was so close to the edge. Her nails left grooves in his back as she surged against him in response to his quickening pace. "*Harder. I won't break,*" she promised, then threatened to break him if he held back.

He couldn't. Bracing himself on one forearm, he slid his other arm beneath her, pulling her hips tight against him, holding her still for his thrusts. Strong and fast, he plunged into her, his face buried in the crook of her neck, her legs wrapped high around his waist.

He came without warning, shouting his release, exultant because she'd been with him all the way. The shuddering waves of her climax washed over him, the convulsions within her tight sheath continuing long after he collapsed against her. By the count of thirty, he'd found enough strength to roll them both to their sides, a feat he was quite proud of in view of his body's complete surrender to the woman he held close.

His heart was still pumping hard when he opened his eyes to find her staring at him.

"I didn't break," she murmured, brushing her lips across his chin.

He grinned. "I'm not sure I didn't."

"Strength is not always in size." She snuggled against him, her small body slippery with their sweat.

"We probably need a shower." He wasn't sure he could walk that far.

"We need food too. I'm starved. It seems like ages since lunch." She nibbled on his chest, salving the sharp bites of her teeth with her tongue.

Sneakers barked, and they both looked up to find the dog staring at them from atop the covers on the floor. Elisabeth sighed and pulled away, dragging her hair out of her eyes. "Me and my big mouth."

Reluctantly admitting to a slight hunger himself, Luke saw the merit in getting out of bed. "I'll feed the dog, you fix dinner." He rolled onto his back and contemplated the effort it would take to stand. At the moment it didn't sound feasible.

If Sneakers hadn't jumped back onto the bed, he was convinced he wouldn't have made it to his feet. But the dog did jump, and Luke was up and gathering his clothes before second thoughts got the better of him. He paused to drop a kiss on Elisabeth's smiling lips, then headed back to his own room for a quick shower. Alone.

It was understood that showering together wouldn't get anybody fed.

SEVEN

Elisabeth's only regret about dinner was that she couldn't serve that new rice recipe with habanero peppers she'd been studying that morning. While she was sorely tempted, in the end she acknowledged it might be a touch overwhelming for the fresh crab.

Otherwise dinner was wonderful. They ate quickly, using their fingers to tear into the succulent flesh of the crab, the intimacy of the bedroom reprised and amplified as they shared hungry gazes across the kitchen table. Elisabeth had never felt so alive, so utterly aware of herself as a woman. It was an extraordinary feeling, as though she'd happened upon a new dimension and found Luke there, waiting just for her.

Yes, dinner was pretty darned exciting. The food wasn't bad either.

"I didn't expect it to be this way," she said, reaching into the basket for another piece of bread. "Is it always this easy?"

Luke looked at her curiously. "Is what always this easy?"

"Afterward. Sharing a meal and remembering what we just did upstairs. You'd think I'd be self-conscious or nervous or something, but I'm not." She shrugged, then popped a garlic-fried crouton into her mouth. "Guess that only goes to show how little I know about sexual relationships."

Luke almost choked on the salad he was chewing. By the time he recovered, she was looking at him with a distinctly innocent expression on her face. "How little is little?" he asked before he could stop himself.

"A gentleman wouldn't ask," she teased.

"You brought it up." He ripped a piece of bread into shreds as he waited for her answer.

"*Very* little," she conceded with a smile, then asked if he was going to finish the salad or could she have it? He pushed the wooden bowl toward her, then resumed eating his crab because she obviously wasn't in a hurry to tell him the rest. The nerves she'd torched with her casual reference to other lovers recovered a bit as he reminded himself that Elisabeth's past was her own, as was his.

It was just that he didn't like thinking about it.

He wiped the bottom of his salad bowl with a piece of bread, wondering what she'd say next. He didn't have long to wait.

"The only lover I've ever had was out of my bed and among the missing before I'd finished explaining to him that while it had been okay so far, I really couldn't see what the fuss was all about." She sighed and shook her head. "I guess he was too young to know much about it. Is there a magic age when men figure out how to please a woman sexually?"

He stared at her in amazement. "Only once?" he asked, incapable of getting more than those two words out of his mouth. Not that numbers were important, but he'd rather touch that subject than get into a discussion of why some men pleased women and others didn't. He'd save that for a more appropriate time, when he had the energy to follow up on the passion such dialogue would likely ignite.

Besides, he'd just learned something about Elisabeth he hadn't known before. Something Wyatt hadn't known either.

Curtis hadn't sexually assaulted her.

In the aftermath of her kidnapping, Wyatt had been determined to let her have her way about everything—up to and including her reluctance to discuss what had happened to her in those weeks of captivity. Experience had taught Luke that the more they knew about her ordeal, the better equipped they'd be to help her in the recovery process. Upon taking over security for Wyatt, he had twice sent a man to visit Curtis and the other three men who'd gone to prison for their part in Elisabeth's kidnapping. His efforts had been wasted. The men, all faced with life sentences, had had no motivation to share anything. As a result the details were sketchy.

Until now. The relief that coursed through him was enormous. He looked down and realized his hands were shaking. Slowly, so as not to draw her attention, he put them under the table, effectively hiding his show of nerves. With deliberate lightness he made the kind of innocuous comment her revelation would merit in a world where kidnappers and their victims were merely obscure news stories. "Are you sure it was just once, honey?" he asked, forcing a teasing note into his voice. "The woman I made love with upstairs didn't seem to be saddled with the . . . shyness one might associate with almost-virgins."

"Just once," she said firmly, her face brightening to a soft pink. "Although after what happened this afternoon, I guess that first time really didn't count for much, if anything." She looked at him, a sudden shyness apparent in her gaze. "It *was* good, wasn't it, Luke? Tell me I'm not imagining you felt what I did."

He reached across the table and captured her hand, relieved that his own was steady again. "It was perfect."

She curled her hands inside his. "I'm not sure that I'm not falling in love with you. I'll let you know when I'm certain."

Her startling words filled him with panic. He'd never imagined she'd love him, never even hoped for such a thing to happen. Wanted, yes, but knew better than to hope, even though it seemed he'd loved her forever. Coming to Quincy Island was a risk he'd been willing to take with his emotions, not hers. He'd considered the beating his heart would take as essentially irrelevant. As her lover, a man she cared for, he'd known he could walk away, leave her to find a man someday who was what he couldn't be.

As the man she loved, Luke knew he would still have to walk away. But the mess he'd be leaving behind would be his fault, his responsibility. He'd wanted her to care, but even in his wildest dreams, he'd never once fantasized that she might come to love him.

Her heart wasn't supposed to be his to break.

"Perhaps that's not such a good idea, Elisabeth." He blanked his expression, not wanting her to see into his soul and know how hard it was to give back to her the one thing he wanted more than anything in the world. The one thing he couldn't have. "I told you earlier that falling in love with me would be a mistake."

"You want me to keep it a secret? You didn't." Her eyes clouded with confusion. "What did you imagine would happen? That I would jump into bed with you without feeling anything?"

"I didn't plan for you to fall in love. I didn't think—"

She cut him off, her voice filled with fury. "No, Sinclair. You *didn't* think! You *still* aren't. It might be reasonable for you to fall into bed and climb out again without expecting your partner to care if you ever came back, but *I'm not like that*. I wouldn't have gone to bed in the first place without knowing I felt something for you."

"You said you didn't love me."

"*I said I didn't know!*" She snatched back her hand and wiped her eyes, catching the tears before they fell. "Well, now I know. Sorry I didn't obey orders and all that, but you're the one who said love is something you can't control."

"I was talking about myself," he said, shaking his head in disbelief at how the situation had gotten out of hand. "I wouldn't have made love to you if I had known this would happen."

"Then you made a bad choice," she muttered. Her tears started to fall and she swiped her hand across the wet paths they made on her cheeks. "Although I suppose it would have happened even if we hadn't made love."

He tried to reason with her. "There hasn't been enough time, Elisabeth. Use some common sense. I've been here just one day You're confusing love with caring. Why, only this morning you admitted you're not used to being around men."

"But you love me—"

He interrupted, using her same argument. "I've had four years to lose my heart to you, honey. You hardly know me at all."

"You don't believe me."

"I don't *want* to believe you." He raked his fingers

through his hair. "I knew I shouldn't have made love to you. . . ." He hesitated, then softened his words with an apology for having been so incredibly stupid. "I shouldn't have come here at all."

Her expression was mutinous. "I fail to understand why this is such a disaster, Sinclair."

"Dammit, Elisabeth. Don't you see it's going to make everything that much harder?"

"Make what harder?"

"Leaving you." He shuttered his heart against the terrible hurt he saw in her eyes, knowing that she had to understand the realities of their situation. "I'll have to leave sooner or later. There's no use pretending anything else."

"Of course you'll leave Quincy Island," she said, speaking slowly as though she were feeling her way along an uncertain path. "I didn't expect you to stay forever. But I don't see why you can't come back once in a while."

"It wouldn't be a good idea. If I'd known how complicated it was going to get—"

"Loving you is complicated?"

"Loving me is impossible." He gritted his teeth against the urge to pull her into his arms and kiss away her questions. "You need to get that through your head before it's too late."

"What are you talking about?" she whispered.

"It's the one thing Wyatt and I agree on. I can't be the man you need me to be, and nothing can change that."

"I was under the impression things went pretty well upstairs." It didn't come out as the joke he knew she intended, but he gave her a half smile for the effort.

"This has nothing to do with the physical side of

things," he said softly. "I told you it was perfect, and I meant it."

"But obviously not perfect enough to keep you interested, is that it?" Her lower lip trembled, and he winced as she clamped it between her teeth in a brutal attempt at control.

"I told you, sex isn't the issue here. It's who I am that's the problem. Loving each other is beside the point, too, except that I didn't want for you to be hurt." He waited for another argument, but none was forthcoming. She just stared at him, her confusion clear in her expression.

For something that he and Wyatt understood so well, Luke suddenly discovered it wasn't so easily put into words. Still, he had to try. "My life and my job, they reflect the kind of man I am. While some of what I do is fairly nondescript administrative work, for the most part I'm Wyatt's chief of security because of what I can do to prevent bad things from happening. And when prevention is impossible, I get involved in straightening out the mess. Sometimes it involves hurting people who are trying to hurt those I'm supposed to protect."

As he spoke, he monitored her reaction, waiting for the moment when understanding would make it possible for him to stop. That comprehension hadn't come yet, so he took it a bit farther. "I'm not a gentle man, Elisabeth. To do what I have to do to survive, I have to be harsh and cruel and violent to a degree you wouldn't recognize. I can't change that part of me, even if I wanted to."

"I haven't asked you to," she whispered.

"Not yet, but that's because when you look at me, there's so much that you don't see. I'm not a gentle man, Elisabeth. Wyatt and I both agree I'm too rough for you, too violent."

She suddenly looked as though she was going to laugh.

"Let me get this straight, Sinclair. You and Wyatt—together—have decided I'm too fragile to handle a man like you."

"It's not a question of handling, Elisabeth. It's a matter of knowing that no matter how much I try, I'll never be what you need in a man."

"You're saying you can't be gentle?"

"Not and do my job. The two don't mix."

"But don't you see, Luke? You *are* gentle. With me you've never been anything else." She stared at him as though trying to see what he was hiding. "Are you afraid you'll hurt me? Because if you are, I can set you straight on that. You'd never hurt me. That harsh side of you isn't out of control. You're too strong to let that happen."

"You still don't get it, do you?" Despair filled him as she shook her head, and Luke knew he'd have to hurt her to make her understand. "What you refuse to see is that I'm no different than Curtis. Do you really want to spend your life with a man like that?"

"Well, no. Not really."

Elisabeth spoke the words aloud, wishing someone besides Sneakers was around to hear them. But Luke was gone, outside doing whatever he thought was more important than arguing with her.

And she'd let him go, too stunned from hearing Curtis's name to try to stop him.

Luke would be back after he'd worked through the anger. Knowing she would have to be satisfied with that, Elisabeth began clearing the table, going through the motions of cleaning up as she reflected on the mess at hand. Luke loved her—four years' worth of loving that apparently made his claim more valid by virtue of duration. Her own single day's worth of discovery lacked credibility, or so he believed.

She wondered how he could make such a seemingly logical assumption when he was the one who had fallen in love with a picture. At least she'd had the sense to wait until she had flesh and blood to base her judgment upon.

Only a man would be so arrogant as to argue common sense without using any himself.

She grinned, pushing Sneakers aside with her knee as he tried to dig crab legs out of the trash. The Doberman whined plaintively as she tied the plastic trash bag and carried it out to the garbage can in the garage. Returning to the kitchen, she wiped down the table and wondered how best to approach the subject of Curtis and still maintain the facade of being frightened of "things that go bump in the night."

She wasn't finished with Luke Sinclair yet, not when it came to getting a little revenge for his high-tech intrusion on her peace and quiet. But it wasn't fair to let him think Curtis was anything more than a name from the past.

The porch door slammed, and Sneakers gave a woof of delight as Luke pushed open the kitchen door. He paused and leveled his gaze on her, his jaw so tight, she was afraid it would break. "I didn't mean to do that to you. I'm sorry."

She leaned back against the table, the rag dangling from one hand. "There are a few things we need to clear up. The first is Curtis."

"I shouldn't have—"

She interrupted with a quick shake of her head. "I haven't heard his name out loud in years. You surprised me. That's all."

"You were as white as a sheet, honey. That's a lot more than surprise." He walked to the counter and leaned against it, his gaze thoughtful.

Elisabeth swallowed, and wished explaining could be as easy as living with that explanation. "Curtis terrifies me. I admit it. But I've had a lot of time to deal with that fear. As a mature adult logically I know that he can't hurt me, not anymore." She balled up the rag and threw it into the sink, giving herself more time to get her words organized. "You only startled me because I'm not used to thinking about him. He's part of the past now. I've accepted that."

"But you're still afraid." It was a statement more than a question, but she gave him the reply he wanted.

"I'm still afraid." And she was, but not of the things he imagined. She couldn't share that part with him, though—not until she was through with Mr. Chief of Security. "Not of Curtis, but of the little things."

"Like men who show up when they're not expected," he said, referring to his arrival on the island.

She nodded. "And alarms that go off in the night. It's like you saying Curtis's name. Things that I'm not prepared for bother me." And that, she decided, should be enough to convince him she panicked when the alarms went off.

Just one more night.

His gaze sharpened on her. "So why are you still here on Quincy Island if you're not afraid anymore?"

"Because Curtis took something from me." She sighed, the rush of air as much a sign of frustration as regret. "He took something, and I'm afraid I wouldn't be able to survive out there without it."

"What?" His voice was suddenly harsh, a demand that she answer.

"Instinct, I guess you'd call it. As it has to do with trust." Shivering, she rubbed her hands up and down her arms. The fierce look in Luke's eyes made her wish she'd kept this one secret to herself. "I was so surprised when Curtis did what he did to me. I'd been dating him for several months. . . ." Her voice trailed off as she remembered her audience. "But I guess you'd know that. Anyway what the file probably doesn't say is how I felt about him."

"Did you love him?"

"Not that, thank God." She smiled and shook her head. "But I trusted him. Perhaps not in the complete sense, because I never once considered becoming intimate with him. I don't think I even kissed him very seriously. But I trusted him to be who he said he was. We had fun together." She looked up at Luke and frowned. "It never occurred to me that he would hurt me."

Luke moved away from the counter, coming to stand just inches in front of her. She tilted her head to look up at him, waiting for him to ask the one question she dreaded.

He didn't fail her. "Why do you trust me?"

"Because Wyatt does." She saw the pain in his eyes, even though it was only there for a second. "I'm sorry I can't tell you it's because of my own instincts, but that's the way it is. I trust you and the Sloanes and everyone else on this island because I know Wyatt has already made those judgments. It's as simple as that." She dropped her hands to the table, gripping the edge until her knuckles hurt.

He lifted a hand to her face, stroking her with fingers that were wonderfully gentle and warm. "You shouldn't apologize for coping the only way you know how."

"Even though it hurts?"

"Even though it hurts." He bent down and brushed his lips across her forehead. "I suppose only a cad would point out here that if you're so damned sure you love me, then your trust should be a part of that and not dependent upon someone else's judgment."

"You're right."

"I am?"

She nodded. "Only a cad would point that out." The warm breath of his laughter caressed her cheek, and she rubbed against him in sheer contentment.

"Is that the only reason you stay here, honey?" He lifted his head to look at her. "Because you're afraid you won't know who to trust?"

"It's enough."

He stared at her for a long moment. "Would you leave here, with me, if I asked you to?"

"With you?" The part of her that was frustrated with his male I-can-love-you-but-you-can't-love-me attitude suddenly saw light where there had been only murky confusion before. Had he changed his mind, realized there was more to her than a fragile, frightened woman . . . so much more? Enough, perhaps, to want her with him even though his world was immersed in shadows and hate?

He nodded. "For a week, maybe more. I think it would be good for you to get off this island."

A week. So much for hopes. She gritted her teeth, realizing this man had a will to be reckoned with. It would take more than a day to convince Luke she wanted to spend her life loving him. A smile broke over her as she realized the enormity of the commitment inherent in that thought.

She wanted to spend her life loving him.

The only surprise was that she wasn't surprised. It

seemed almost natural, the depth of feeling she now admitted. What had begun four years ago as a nagging curiosity about a man she'd never met had evolved into love—with all the stages in between a kaleidoscopic blur of pure, uncensored emotion.

She'd made love to a man she loved. The idea pleased her, thrilled her.

She thought perhaps it was a shade too early to share that with Luke, particularly given the fact that her earlier semideclarations had been rebuffed. Still, it didn't hurt to tease. "I thought you were mad at me, and now you're asking me to go away with you?"

"I was angry with myself, not you." His voice was low and scratchy. "Will you come away with me?"

"Where?"

"Seattle, maybe over to Victoria, British Columbia." He slid an arm around her shoulders and brought her close against him, waiting until she put her arms around his waist before continuing. "If you trust me, then you know I'll keep you safe. It could be a first step in getting out into the world again."

"I'll have to think about it." *Such a big step*, she mused, then giggled as a thought came to her. "I don't have anything to wear. All my clothes are too casual for the city."

"Trust a woman to worry about clothes."

"Don't be any more of a sexist than you can help, Sinclair."

He grumbled something about wishing she'd quit bringing sex into every conversation, then added, "You'd be surprised how casual the world has gotten in six years." He rubbed his face in her hair, his hands warm and strong against her back. "And don't argue with me, because you must realize that yourself. That satellite dish

Wyatt put in must keep you in better touch than most people are."

"I said I'll think about it."

"Why have you never traveled with Wyatt? I know he goes crazy thinking of you alone here on the island." Luke gave her a final hug, then pulled her into his side and began walking toward the living room.

"He never asked." She wrinkled her nose as she saw the stacks of material he was heading toward. "Wyatt never mentions anything he thinks might upset me—beginning with Curtis and ending with why I chose to live on this island in the first place."

"I think that perhaps Wyatt has left you alone for too long."

"So have you, Sinclair, but it's going to take you a while longer to admit it." On that note she slipped out from under his arm and left him to his interior decorating.

It was one thing to have to put up with his decision to cover the windows. It was quite another to offer to help.

She wouldn't dream of it. Besides, she had something more important to do that required sneaking out the back door and getting back inside without Luke realizing she'd been gone. She'd planned on taking care of this detail that afternoon while Luke had been meeting the helicopter, but had decided to wait until after dark when the chances of getting away with it were better.

Her errand took her less than a minute. Heading straight for one of the infrared triggers she'd watched Luke fooling with that afternoon, she reached into the bushes and rotated the laser slightly aside. Not much, but enough to make the infrared beam miss the sensor, thus setting off the alarm when Luke activated the system.

Back in the house, she returned to the living room, settling herself on the sofa with her feet on the coffee table, her gaze riveted on the man with the staple gun. He was standing on a chair, his arms high over his head, a fistful of the heavy material in one hand, staple gun in the other, and a different kind of gun nestled in the small of his back.

She thought it was time he faced reality. "You really don't need that, you know."

He glanced over his shoulder, then resumed tacking the material to the top of the window frame. "It's too late, Elisabeth. This will have to do until you get something better to cover these windows."

"I'm talking about the gun snuggled above your butt, Sinclair. Don't you think wearing it inside the house is overkill? Unless you're thinking of using it on Sneakers of course. I realize he's not your idea of a guard dog, but shooting him seems a bit extreme."

Luke affixed a couple more staples before stepping down from the chair and pulling it to the next window. He glanced at her as he gathered up another length of material. "I know you don't like guns. If it bothers you—"

She interrupted before he got the wrong idea. "It's not a matter of liking them—which I don't particularly, but that's not the point. It's just that I don't see why you need one here."

"It's a hard habit to break, honey." Turning his back to her, he continued working. "Is there a specific reason why you don't like guns?"

The question was a soft insert between the firing of the staple gun, so soft, Elisabeth would have thought he was talking to himself if she didn't know him better. But she did know him, well enough to realize this was no more an idle question than his lovemaking had been a half-hearted gesture.

"Maybe I just don't like loud noises."

"Not good enough. Wyatt once told me he taught you to shoot when you were just a teenager. From what he said, you enjoyed the lessons." The steady pounding of metal brackets into wood accented his words. "He also told me you used to be pretty good with a hand gun as long as it was small and the target wasn't too far away."

"Kids are entertained by the strangest things," she murmured, grabbing a pillow and holding it against her stomach. "I liked roller coasters back then too. You wouldn't catch me dead on one now."

"Wyatt said that after he got you back from Curtis, you wouldn't touch a gun." He fired a final staple into the wall, then stepped off the chair and turned to face her. "He assumed the experience in general put you off guns. I think there's more to it."

Nerves she'd thought had become tamed jumped when he said "Curtis," but she eased them with a couple of deep breaths. "Why don't you take a page out of Wyatt's book and quit bringing up Curtis?"

"I thought you said it only bothered you because you hadn't heard his name out loud in a while."

"I said that to make you feel better." There was a sharp edge to her sassy tone that she knew hadn't escaped him.

He shook his head. "Curtis terrifies you."

She stared at him, then drew a shaky breath and said, "I wish you were wrong."

"There's no disgrace in being afraid of a man who once hurt you." His gaze was clear and open. "Still, it surprises me how well you've learned to handle that fear."

"Out of sight, out of mind," she retorted, unable to help the half smile that quibbled with her uneasiness.

Clearly Luke didn't find that any funnier than she did. "I think that talking about him might keep you from almost fainting the next time someone mentions him."

"You're the only one who has the nerve to do that."

Luke crossed to the library table and set the staple gun inside, then sat opposite her in the giant, over-stuffed chair that Wyatt favored. "I told you earlier that I thought Wyatt had left you alone for too long. These are things you should have gotten out of your system a long time ago."

"I bet that if I called Wyatt, he'd tell you to mind your own business." It was a cheap shot she couldn't resist.

"This *is* my business, honey. You made it mine when you made love with me."

He leaned back in the chair, crossing his legs atop the ottoman and looking for all the world as though he intended to stay where he was until she gave him the answers he wanted. For a reason Elisabeth couldn't begin to fathom, her reluctance to talk about Curtis and related events faded.

"I'm not sure that talking about that schmuck would be very useful," she said, smiling wryly. "Except for a reluctance to leave Quincy Island, I've always thought I survived the experience with relatively minor scars."

"I agree. Overall you appear to be emotionally healthy, particularly for someone who went through what you did." His voice was smooth and even, reassuring in its conviction. "But you admit to some pretty major changes in your life. I think those should be addressed."

"Why?"

"Why not?" He yawned, a reflex that made her smile.

There was an ease in his manner that nudged her that final step toward talking about something she rarely even thought about. His gaze drifted past her to the bookshelves. "Come on, Elisabeth. You're the one who said Curtis took something from you. Don't you think it's time to try to get it back?"

Something deep inside her must have been heavily biased toward Luke's argument, because she really wanted to do this. She wanted the freedom to choose her life. Looking up, she found Luke's gaze solidly on her. Gone was the sleepy, almost nonchalant interest he'd exhibited only moments earlier. In its place was a consuming focus that made her finally understand just how much he cared. He needed to know, for reasons she didn't question.

Just as she needed to tell him.

"What do you want to know?" she asked.

EIGHT

"Start with the gun," Luke said.

Satisfaction surged through him, accompanied by a sense of knowing he was doing the right thing. Wyatt's policy of letting Elisabeth bury the past wasn't good enough, not if it kept her a prisoner. Still, Luke couldn't fault Wyatt for letting his love for his sister get in the way of what had to be done. Love often clouded one's judgment.

In this case, though, Wyatt had made a bad decision. Elisabeth would never be free until she faced her fears.

She winced, pulling the pillow more tightly against her. "You really know how to hit the high spots, don't you?"

He gritted his teeth against the distaste he felt at forcing her to do this. "What happened, Elisabeth? Was it because guns were pointed at you by people you knew wouldn't hesitate to use them?"

A bitter laugh parted her lips. "Not even close." She shut her eyes, remembering the moment he was fishing for with a clarity that had never waned, not even after six long years. Tendrils of disgust crept through her, but she'd committed to telling him and not even her dislike for the subject was enough to stop her.

It was just that the thing about the gun was so stupid.

"Tell me about it," he said quietly.

She opened her eyes and sighed. "I'm afraid it's less a case of them pointing guns at me than of me pointing one at them."

"You got hold of a gun?"

"The first day. They weren't watching as well as they should; I was still mad enough to fight back. Curtis had left me with one of his goons. We were still in Singapore, in one of those falling-down hotels on the fringes of the harbor area. Anyway the idiot turned his back, and I grabbed his gun from the holster, simple as that."

Luke's gaze narrowed. "What happened, Elisabeth? Did you shoot and miss?"

This was the worst part, admitting that everything might have turned out so much differently if she'd only made another choice. Swallowing hard, she met his gaze. "No, Sinclair. I didn't shoot and miss. I didn't shoot at all. I couldn't."

"Why?"

"Because I wasn't willing to kill." She took a deep breath and plunged ahead before she lost her nerve. "I couldn't even bring myself to wound him. After he got over being surprised that I'd dared to resist, it didn't take him long to discover I was less of a threat than a nuisance. He took his gun back and knocked me around a little in retaliation. Then Curtis came back and gave the goon what he'd given me."

"Because he'd let you at his gun?" Luke asked, his gaze still even, still assessing.

She shook her head, a wry smile touching her lips.

"Because he'd marked me. It seems that once he'd collected the money from Wyatt, Curtis planned to sell me to an Arab prince who had a fondness for blond virgins. The price was apparently much higher for unblemished . . . *untouched* goods."

"So he never had any intention of returning you to Wyatt." The roughness in Luke's voice sounded like rage. The look in his eyes confirmed it.

Elisabeth didn't see any sense in Luke getting worked up over something that had happened long ago. She told him the rest in the same matter-of-fact, it's-over-with-and-I'm-just-fine manner that she'd learned to see it in her own mind. "I think the secret here is to appreciate that he had other plans. After that first incident Curtis made sure I was left alone—isolated, really. I rarely saw anyone but him, and he never so much as laid a finger on me." Her eyes sought Luke's, and she could share the things she'd always kept to herself. "He threatened all sorts of mayhem of course. I think it made him feel like a big man to scare me."

"How scared were you?" Luke asked quietly.

"Very. Once we left Singapore for Java, I wasn't at all sure Wyatt would be able to find me. And then there was that horrid cabin they locked me in while we were on the boat—which was most of the time. It was tiny and smelled something fierce. I'm willing to bet I spent as much time being disgusted by my living quarters as I was frightened." She shuddered, remembering how she'd initially been too scared to eat . . . then later, when she'd been almost too weak to care. "From what Wyatt told me later, the boat was anchored off Java for most of the time."

Luke just nodded, his silence encouraging her to continue.

"Curtis visited every day, making sure I was alive, I suppose." She swallowed hard. The knowledge that this was all now a story barely won out over the fears that threatened to overwhelm her in the telling. "I think I remember his indifference more than anything else, though. It was as though I was a thing to him—alive and breathing, but otherwise as much an object as a somewhat valuable painting."

Luke stared at her for several minutes before saying anything. The chaos in his mind that passed for thoughts absorbed him, jerking his emotional responses in so many directions, it was all he could do to contain the violence. He wanted to break something, but knew that giving leash to his fury would shatter the intimately trusting mood between them.

He wanted to take Elisabeth in his arms and make her believe her world was safe, when he knew it wasn't. Wyatt's instructions to tell her nothing gained merit as he began to realize just how cruel it would be to tell her the truth.

Cruel, but certainly much safer all around. If she knew the threat, she could help him fight it. He made up his mind to tell her all of it the next day.

"Did you ever wish Wyatt had just killed Curtis instead of throwing him into prison?" he asked.

A surprising smile lit up her face. "That's the one thing I've always been grateful for. Since I was incapable of killing to save myself, I don't think I'd have been at ease knowing someone I loved had to do it for me."

"I think that if Curtis had managed to sell you to that Arab, Wyatt might have made a different choice." Luke tried not to think about how she was going to feel when he or Wyatt had to make that same choice any day now. "The fact that you were found alive and essentially unharmed was all that saved Curtis."

"If Curtis had managed to sell me, Wyatt would have had to wait in line."

"You would have been first?" So there was a point when she'd get mad enough to kill. He was surprised. It didn't click with what he knew about her.

She shook her head. "I rather think the prince would have taken care of things. The one thing Curtis didn't know, you see, was that I wasn't a virgin." She paused until the flashes of remembered terror subsided to the nervous fluttering of butterflies deep inside. "Arab princes don't take kindly to being cheated."

Luke's scowl was feral. "Revenge would have been expensive, considering what you stood to lose. Your own life would have been worth nothing in those circumstances."

"If Curtis had guessed I wasn't a virgin, there would have been no reason to treat me as well as he did." She shivered, chilled by visions of what could have been. The butterflies in her stomach mutated to bat wings that she beat back with the expertise gained from years of practice. Remembering never failed to bother her, but she couldn't afford to let it get out of hand. Those kinds of fears were simply unacceptable, and she'd decided long ago to keep them in perspective.

She'd survived. That was what counted.

It was time to lighten up. There was a trick she'd taught herself to combat the ugliness of those memories: If one didn't want to remember the realities, one simply distorted them.

Absurdly, until the laughter came easily.

She met Luke's intense gaze with the best "frankly sincere" one she could muster. "Knowing Curtis would meet a gruesome death if he sold me as a virgin was the one thing that gave me the will to survive."

"You won't pull the trigger, but you don't mind letting scum do it for you."

She muffled a giggle behind her hand. "You're dreaming if you believe I imagined Curtis would be brought down with a bullet. My fantasies were almost medieval compared with that. I was hoping for something more interesting—like dragging him behind a racing camel or staking him naked on a sand dune with a few scorpions for company. Either of those would have worked. I'm sure the prince would have come up with something suitable for the occasion. With luck he might have even let me watch."

Luke studied her curiously. "You would have wanted to watch a man die?"

"We're talking about Curtis here, remember? I try not to get all moralistic about death when I think about him." Her lips twitched, and she had less luck controlling them than she had the bat wings. Still, she gritted her teeth and tried to think of anything but the outrageous tale she was spinning.

His gaze narrowed on her mouth. "You're teasing me, aren't you, Squirt."

"Mm-hm." She nestled deeper into the couch cushions, smiling lazily. "After the first week I found myself sleeping almost all the time. A self-protective instinct, I guess. I was rarely awake enough to think coherently, much less fantasize about anything more than a shower and clean clothes." She met his intent gaze. "I got off easy, Sinclair. No real scars, no lasting trauma."

"Being terrified of things that go bump in the night isn't what I'd call normal."

"That's because you've never been afraid of anything

in your life." She sighed, shaking her head at his enviable confidence. "Ask Wyatt about what a pest I was to live with back when we shared an apartment after our parents died. I was always making him get up in the middle of the night to investigate noises."

"Maybe when you were twelve," Luke muttered.

She pretended not to have heard. "Those alarms you've rigged tend to exaggerate an already known paranoia that didn't originate with Curtis." Tossing the pillow she was hugging to one side, she stretched and leaned her head back against the sofa. "I was lucky, Sinclair. I've always known that."

"You call being stuck on this island lucky?" he growled.

She wondered if Luke realized he growled as often as not when he spoke, a trait she hadn't noticed before they'd made love. There were advantages to the intimacies between them that she hadn't foreseen, one being that he was no longer handling her with kid gloves.

She rather liked being treated like a normal, functional human being. "I'm happy here. Nice house, fresh air, good neighbors. What more could I ask for?"

He shrugged. "I'd think you'd get bored, especially considering what you left behind in Singapore. For someone with your ambitions, I'm surprised you'd be content with needlepoint and walking the dog."

"What do you know about my ambitions?" she asked before remembering that of course he knew everything. Still, she waited for his answer, struck by the realization that it had been years since anyone had spoken to her of the life she'd left behind.

"I only know what Wyatt told me." He put his feet on the floor and leaned forward, resting his arms on his thighs. "You wanted to help him run the business, to be a part of it. You had him help you design a course of study at high school and college so that you could learn the things you'd need in a hurry. When you weren't studying, you were doing hands-on training at one or the other of his hotels. By the time you turned twenty-one, you were already a year into your MBA program." His expression was enigmatic as he added, "I can't believe all that ambition has been reduced to nothing."

"I had so much energy," she said wistfully. "Back then sleep was a nuisance and eating a necessity that took entirely more time than I felt necessary."

"Do you miss it?"

"Some." Her hand fisted, she tapped a knuckle against her teeth. "It was so exciting, being a part of that world."

"So why don't you go back?" he asked softly. "I know it would relieve Wyatt's mind if you were closer. And there's no reason you couldn't pick up where you left off."

As if she hadn't considered it at least a thousand times! She quickly extinguished the flicker of interest that his suggestion evoked before it could ignite hopes that were doomed to be dashed. "I wouldn't be any good to him. Like I told you before, I can't trust my instincts about people. Without that ability, I'm useless."

"You won't know until you try." He rose from the chair and eased down beside her on the sofa. Taking her chin in his long fingers, he tilted her face so that she would have no choice but to return his gaze. "You can live on this little island forever and accept that Curtis destroyed your ability to trust."

"Or?" The whisper was a thread of sound in an otherwise silent room.

"Or you can prove to yourself that out of the two of

you, Curtis is the only prisoner." Not quite a lie, Luke told himself. Within days Curtis would either be behind bars again or dead.

She lifted a hand and wrapped her fingers around his wrist. "You make it sound so easy."

"Not easy, just possible." He brushed his lips across her forehead. "Come with me to Seattle, Elisabeth. Prove to yourself that you can do it."

A brave smile curved her lips. "Today Seattle, tomorrow the world?"

"How about Wednesday? We can take the ferry across and be back before dinner." Once he got her there, he'd somehow manage to keep her from returning to Quincy Island until Curtis had been run to ground. But he didn't raise that point now, knowing better than to press too hard, too fast. He slid an arm around her shoulders, absorbing the shivers he didn't think she was even aware of. Pulling her close, he held her for a long time, letting his warmth sink into her.

He waited until her shivers had stopped before covering her lips with his, wanting her to know the difference between comfort and need. She opened to his probing tongue, her hands slipping around his neck as he explored anew the honeyed sweetness of her mouth. Her tongue rasped across his, a velvet rub that filled him with an urgency to deepen the intimacy between them. With deliberate insistence, he pressed her against the back of the sofa, leaving a space between their bodies so that he could touch her as he wanted.

Elisabeth resisted at first, not wanting to forgo the seductive warmth of his chest against hers. But when he took her mouth with his aggressive tongue, she lost the ability to think altogether. Instead she simply responded, arching to the heat of his hand as it slid beneath her sweater and skimmed the silk camisole upward until there was nothing to keep skin from touching skin. Her breasts swelled into his palm, their tips almost painfully sensitive to his delicate caress.

Too delicate. She put her hand on top of his, pressing him closer, harder. He obliged her, his touch hard enough to satisfy her without being truly satisfying, his voice soft as he whispered erotic nothings into her ear.

A luscious heat was building between her thighs when she felt Luke drag the camisole back down to cover her breasts. She opened her eyes as he lifted his head and brushed a wisp of hair from her forehead. "What's wrong?"

He shook his head, then kissed her lightly. "Nothing's wrong, honey. I just need to get some work done outside before I turn in for the night."

"It can't wait an hour or two?" she asked, aware of the petulant tone in her voice and quite sure she wanted him to hear it.

"I suspect I won't be able to walk after I make love to you again." He got up and reached down to pull her to her feet. "Why don't you go ahead and go to bed. I'll join you in an hour."

"You're pretty confident I want you to sleep with me." With her fingertips she stroked the hard length of his arousal where it strained against his jeans.

He submitted for a moment, then brushed her hand away with a low growl. "It's not confidence, honey. It's what's right."

"We're right together?"

"In bed, yes." Then, before she could launch into that touchy subject, he added, "You never said if you'd come with me to Seattle."

"Sure you can spare the day off, Sinclair?"

"I'm sure." He cocked his head, his expression curious but nonjudgmental. "Is that a yes or a no?"

"I think it's a yes."

"Good." He didn't let her see the extreme satisfaction her answer brought because he didn't want her to base her decision on whether or not he approved. The trip was for her.

But he was so damned proud of her.

"You're sure you have to work?" She walked over to the makeshift curtains and pulled one aside. "There's no moon out tonight. You won't be able to see a thing."

"All the better for what I have to do." Casually, without drawing attention to what he was doing, he walked over to where she stood in front of the unprotected window. He took her hand and drew her far enough back into the room so that she had to let go of the material. "I have to double-check all the infrared beams before I can activate the system. With the infrared goggles it's much easier to do when it's dark."

"You're going to check them all?" Frustration tugged her mouth into an involuntary grimace.

He nodded and dropped a kiss on her nose. "All of them. It won't take more than an hour."

Unless there were problems of course, she thought. Which there were, thanks to the small effort she'd taken earlier. But it would only be a little problem, one he'd find, since he was going to double-check his own work.

So what was she going to do now, besides hope he'd think a squirrel had moved the reflector? Should she let him fix it and leave well enough alone? Or should she repeat her earlier performance when he was at the other end of the property?

The longer he stayed outside, the longer she'd be

inside . . . and alone. A dilemma to be sure, but she pasted a smile on her face and wagged her fingers in good-bye as he left the room, heading for the kitchen.

For all her efforts to drive Sinclair crazy, he was doing a good job on her in return. Shaking her head, she walked up the stairs to her room. She'd give him ten minutes, she decided as she rooted through her drawers for a dark sweater and the watch cap that she'd need to cover her hair.

Ten minutes, then she'd sneak outside and do again what she'd already done once that night.

This revenge business was getting tiresome.

An hour later Luke was wondering if it was jet lag or carelessness that had made him less precise than usual. One of the receptors had been set at a full quarter turn away from the beam. He couldn't imagine he'd erred so drastically that afternoon, but the proof was right in front of his eyes. Shaking his head, he reset the mechanism and checked that the beam reflected properly.

He decided that perhaps he should kick his own butt instead of indulging in the disciplinary talking-to he'd been rehearsing for McCain.

When he went back inside the house, Sneakers was fast asleep on the kitchen floor. He stepped across the dog and headed down the hall to the front door, hearing noises from upstairs that told him Elisabeth was in her room. A sensual heat filled him as he remembered how soft she'd been to his touch, how incredibly responsive. He flipped open the cover of the security panel and threw the toggle to activate the outside electronics.

The unexpected blast of the alarm almost knocked

him off his feet. Cursing, he flicked the system off, then headed upstairs to reassure Elisabeth.

It would be a while longer before the passionate encounter of that afternoon was reprised, he thought. If at all that night, because Elisabeth would likely be sound asleep by the time he'd finished going over everything again.

He wondered what the hell he'd missed . . . and knew that he hadn't missed anything.

He wondered why Sneakers had chosen that morning to sneak out early when, according to Elisabeth, he normally slept late.

And finally he wondered if he'd maligned McCain for something that wasn't his fault at all.

He kept his suspicions to himself as he comforted a quivering Elisabeth. She clung to him until her fears were calmed, her silken nightgown a powerful lure that almost got between his desires and his job.

By the time he pried himself away, he was sweating with the effort his restraint had cost him.

Elisabeth, safe in her bed, held her giggles until she heard the back door slam shut. Even then she laughed into her pillow until the loudest of her chortles had subsided.

The look on his face had been priceless—confused and irritated and a little angry.

Which was just how she wanted him to feel. After four years of having to lie about, subvert, and otherwise ignore a system that was so sensitive, it beeped every time a tall seagull walked past, she was finally giving Sinclair a dose of his own medicine.

He'd looked ready to chew lead. She couldn't be more tickled.

And then, because it had been so much fun the first time, she decided to get dressed and do it again.

Luke collected his equipment from where he'd dropped it on the back porch and walked quickly to the outer boundaries of the property. Digging into his carry-all, he pulled out a small radio transmitter and clicked it on. When Matt answered, Luke told him what he wanted. Matt said he'd be there in five minutes.

Luke waited until Matt arrived before getting started, his attention fully focused on the environment around him. Logic told him the property hadn't been breached, not by anything or anyone that would threaten Elisabeth. But it didn't hurt to be careful, not with Curtis on the loose.

"Wyatt called an hour ago," Matt said as he walked up to Luke. "They've found nothing in Kuala Lumpur to indicate he's ever been there. Wyatt's beginning to think their informant might have been a deliberate misinformation job by Curtis."

"Where's he going now?"

"The teams are splitting up. One is heading in this general direction just to be on the safe side—that's the one Wyatt's with. The other is angling toward Indochina. He says Curtis might still have some contacts left over there from the old days."

Luke nodded, wishing the news had been better, knowing that Wyatt must be feeling the same frustration. "If you'll keep watch on the house, I can get this work done faster."

"You're expecting trouble?"

The moon had gone behind a cloud, leaving Luke to

judge Matt's reaction by his voice. That was enough to indicate the man was instantly on his guard.

Luke decided that wasn't such a bad thing. "I'd almost bet on it."

"You haven't talked her into leaving yet?" At Luke's rough denial, Matt added, "She still doesn't know anything?"

"Not yet." He pulled the infrared goggles from the bag and adjusted them on his face. The big black plastic frames were reminiscent of the eye-test machine in an optometrist's office, and about as comfortable as one would expect from something that normally sat on a table. "Curtis has had enough time to get here: I want this system up and running before another night goes by."

"I don't understand how McCain messed it up," the other man said as Luke crouched to check a beam. It was a ghostly, green trail linking the small spool-sized laser to the flat coin of a detector. "He's usually quite thorough."

"I'm not so sure it was McCain." The beam was fine. Luke rose and pushed the glasses onto his forehead. "Pay special attention to the back door."

Matt hesitated, then asked, "Why not the front?"

Luke grunted his approval at the man's quick understanding. "Because the front one sticks."

Matt just nodded and melted into the night, leaving Luke to his work, a job that was hard on the back muscles to begin with and no easier the second time around.

The only thing that kept him from wringing her neck was the possibility that he was wrong.

The clouds overhead soon dissipated. Moonlight flooded the area, making the job both easier and harder—walking around was easier, checking the electronics and optics harder. Matt caught up with him just as he was finishing with the last set. "There's one over by the side of the house that you might want to take another look at."

Luke stared at the man for a moment, then followed him around the corner without asking the obvious question. Matt led him to the base of a large oak tree and pointed at the sensor disk hidden in the bushes opposite. Luke put the goggles back on and immediately saw that the beam was skewed at an angle, completely missing the sensor. He fixed the problem and tucked his equipment away, then led Matt out of earshot of the house.

Matt spoke first. "How'd you know?"

"We've already played this game once tonight. Once I'd gotten the alarm turned off, it occurred to me I wasn't getting as sloppy as I felt." He tossed the carryall onto the ground. "Which one was it? Elisabeth or the dog?"

"Elisabeth. She snuck out the back door once you'd finished this side. Since I didn't figure you wanted me to announce I was watching, I decided to follow her." Matt's grin was a white slash in the moonlight. "It was all I could do not to go up to her and ask what the hell she was doing."

"You have more restraint than I do," Luke muttered. "Did she do anything else interesting?"

"She just went back inside." He checked his watch. "That was about thirty minutes ago."

Luke stared at the ground and shook his head. "Kind of wish it had been Sneakers. Give me a good excuse to shoot him."

"Wyatt wouldn't like it if you shot his sister."

"Probably not." Luke stuffed his hands into the back pockets of his jeans. "She's upstairs now, waiting for me to flip that switch and supposedly scare her half out of her mind. I'm wondering now how long she's been messing with my security system."

"Hard to tell. The first couple of months after your upgrades were installed were pretty busy, but McCain and I just thought it was normal. Until everything got adjusted so that every seagull or rabbit didn't set off the alarm." He took off his baseball cap and slapped it against his thigh. "Since then she's only had to call me every six or eight weeks."

"And when you get here, she's terrified?"

Matt shook his head again. "Usually she's too relieved to get out of that priest hole to show how scared she might have been. 'Damned stupid little closets' is what she calls them."

"At least she was inside."

"What do you want to bet she doesn't get inside the priest hole until she hears me coming?"

Luke's suspicions were ricocheting inside his head in forty directions at once. "She didn't even go that far for me. Every time she's had excuses about why she wasn't inside when I came to give her the 'all clear.'"

Both men were silent as they contemplated the ramifications of Elisabeth's behavior. Luke dragged a weary hand through his hair, thinking how much less complicated things had been when he'd had a nine-thousand-mile buffer between himself and the woman who was supposed to be waiting for him in her bed.

He heaved a frustrated sigh, the grin leaving his mouth as he hefted the strap of the carryall over his shoulder. "Little games like this could get her killed."

"You think she's got any more surprises set up for tonight?"

"Damned if I know." He sighed again, wishing he

didn't have to say what he was about to say. "I hate to ask, but with Curtis still on the loose——"

Matt interrupted before he could finish. "I'll stick around tonight, and every night until this is over. Todd can back you up in the daytime while I sleep."

"Curtis probably won't move in daylight, but it won't hurt to be on guard. Tell Todd to stay away unless I call for him, or if you hear from Wyatt."

"I assume you're not going to confront her."

"Not until I figure out why she's screwing with the system. For now I'll just make her wonder why all hell didn't break loose when I switched it on."

Something she'd said earlier came back to him. He'd told her Wyatt had left her alone for too long, and her reply had been cryptic. *So have you, Sinclair, but it's going to take you a while longer to admit it.*

He thought he was beginning to understand what she'd meant.

"If or when the alarm does go off and I'm convinced she did it, I'll hit the bedroom lights. Twice."

"Which room are you in?"

"The front one." Which of course was Elisabeth's, but he couldn't help it if he had to share that piece of information with Matt. It was her own damned fault.

Matt just nodded. Obviously a man who knew when discretion was called for.

Luke continued. "If you don't see any lights, assume it's Curtis. Don't feel you need to wait for me to take the first shot."

"Courtesy isn't something I'm good at when the shooting starts."

Luke didn't think so, not if Wyatt had hired him. "You've seen a photo of him?"

Matt nodded. "Is Elisabeth going to have a problem if we end up having to kill the bastard?"

"Wound him, kill him, I don't care which. Just stop him." In the almost black night Luke found and held the other man's gaze. "If he so much as touches her, I'll kill him first and worry about the emotional fallout afterward."

"Too bad you weren't around six years ago. I suspect I'd be in bed with my wife instead of doing the shadow patrol."

"You don't think Wyatt can stop him?" Luke asked.

"It's smarter to assume that he won't. That way there won't be any surprises."

"Wyatt's not going to like it if Curtis shows up and he's still in the Far East."

"He's going to like it even less when he hears what his little sister has been up to."

Luke smiled. "If we tell him. I'm beginning to suspect that this is a private thing between Elisabeth and me."

Matt's expression was carefully blank, but Luke knew without asking that the other man would follow his lead when it came time to report to Wyatt. With a casual salute Luke turned and threaded a crooked path back to the house.

It was time to get on with the game—whatever it was.

NINE

Moonlight cloaked Elisabeth as she huddled with Sneakers in the middle of the bed. She whispered soothing noises into the dog's ear and stroked his smooth head, preparing him for what was to come. Sinclair was inside now, the barely audible click as he came through the back door her only clue. No other sounds reached her, and she had to rely on her imagination to visualize his progress through the house. He'd go straight to the control panel, and she wondered if his confidence waffled any as he reached inside to flip the switch.

She'd give anything to see his face.

Sneakers wiggled deeper into the covers that she had pulled up to keep the night's chill at bay, then settled across her knees as though slightly bumpy was his preference in berths. She hardly noticed except to push his paws off her nightgown before he snagged the delicate silk.

What was keeping Sinclair? She couldn't believe he'd not gone first to the control panel, but the silence that stretched and ballooned around her was proof in itself. Silence instead of the blare of alarms.

He'd get to it sooner or later. After he finished what-

ever else he'd found to do that was more important.
Then he'd come running upstairs, his face drawn with
frustration, his hands gentle on her as they soothed and
comforted.

She almost regretted that he would be going back
outside again before coming to bed. Only almost, though,
because he would eventually end up in her arms, sharing
with her whatever was left of the night.

Her priorities were clear. Once she'd convinced
Sinclair that his security system was unnecessary, unwant-
ed, and, for most of the time, unused, he'd be able to spend
all of his time with her and not just the hours when he
wasn't working.

She had only a few days to convince him that she
was the woman he needed and that he was the man she
couldn't live without. She didn't intend to spend those
days sharing him with anyone or anything.

She almost wished she hadn't agreed to go to Seattle.
Not because she was afraid, but because she'd rather
spend the time with Luke. Alone, without a few hundred
thousand chaperones.

So where was he and why hadn't he activated the
alarm?

"It's late. I didn't think you'd still be awake."

Had Sneakers not been draped across her legs,
Elisabeth was certain she would have shot straight
through the roof. As it was, her heart thumped madly in
her chest, and shivers of surprise zipped up and down her
spine. She hadn't expected him to come upstairs without
turning on the alarm, and the shock of seeing him in the
doorway to her bedroom rendered her speechless.

He crossed the floor and came to stand at the end
of the bed. "I'm glad you waited, honey. Thinking of
you up here, all warm and soft and exciting in that

sexy little nightgown, made my hands less steady than they should have been. I had to promise myself that I'd soon be touching you, that everything I imagined doing to you would become a reality as soon as I got the job done." He pulled his sweater over his head and tossed it onto a chair.

Elisabeth wet her lips and tried to think of a way to ask if perhaps he hadn't forgotten something. But she couldn't. Couldn't think, that is, because he was unbuckling his belt and pulling it from his pants.

She didn't want him to go outside, not now.

Not even later.

He turned and sat on the bed to pull off his shoes and socks. "Are you awake, Elisabeth? Or did you go to sleep sitting up?"

"I'm awake," she said quickly, her gaze locked on the powerful muscles that corded his back and shoulders. He looked more powerful than she remembered, more beautiful.

She loved looking at him.

He stood up and pushed off his jeans. "The dog is going to have to go."

What dog? She was unashamedly absorbed by the sight of his fully aroused manhood, a potent statement of why he'd come to her room. Memories of the love-making they'd shared that afternoon rushed back in vivid detail, filling her with an urgency to repeat the experience.

She pushed the blanket from her shoulders, suddenly too warm under his steady gaze.

"The dog, honey. I'm afraid if I tell him to leave, he'll bite me."

She stared blankly at Luke before an inkling of reality filtered into her sluggish brain. Then she looked down at

Sneakers, who snoozed peacefully in her lap. "Oh, yeah. The dog."

"If he's used to sleeping with you, we're going to have a problem."

"No problem." She wouldn't dream of letting Sneakers interfere. "He won't even notice if you pick him up and put him on the rug."

"I have to pick him up?"

"Either that or wake him. I just gave you the quicker option."

Luke muttered something rude about dogs in general and Sneakers in particular, then leaned across the bed and slid his arms under the body of the slumbering Doberman. He straightened and asked, "Any rug?"

She shrugged. "I suppose so. The one by the window is his favorite."

Luke clearly had another rug in mind, because he walked out of the bedroom with the dog in his arms and returned moments later without him. He pulled the door shut before returning to the bed. "Now, what were you saying about 'quickly'?" he asked as he knelt beside her.

"Quickly?" She shook her head, aware only of the subtle play of muscles across his chest as he lifted a hand to her face.

"Yes, quickly." He slid his hand down her neck to her shoulder, his fingers edging beneath the lacy strap of her gown. "I'd hoped we could take our time this time."

"I never said 'Quickly.' You must be thinking of some other woman." His hand was hot on her shoulder, a distraction that rattled what few rational thoughts she had left.

"There are no other women, not for me."

She swallowed, lifting her gaze to find the moonlight

bright in his eyes. "Then I guess it must have been your imagination."

"I'd much rather have you than my imagination," he murmured, brushing his mouth against her throat. Then his hand retreated from her shoulder, a disappointment that was forgotten as he covered her mouth with his.

It was a light kiss, so soft that she would have thought she'd dreamed it if she weren't touching him. Her hands skimmed over his shoulders, her fingertips dancing a flirting caress. Yes, he was real, and his kiss deepened to prove it. She opened beneath his mouth, her tongue mating with his as he curled his fist into her hair and tugged her to lie back across the bed.

He followed her down to the sheets, whispering sweet things she'd never wanted to hear from another man, covering her with his body and making her warm like she'd never been warm before.

It was different this time, different because she knew it was love that brought them together. She knew that without understanding how thoughts were possible, not with his mouth against her breast and his hands drawing moans of pleasure from deep inside of her.

Whatever he wanted, whatever he needed, she gave him. It was a magical time in which her only realities were Luke and the moon and the love they made by its light. She learned what pleased him without any awareness of being taught, and discovered that he knew more about her own needs than she could ever have imagined possible. He showed her what was exciting and fun, always insisting that his control was for her pleasure.

She tested that control with a passion that made him understand control wasn't everything.

It wasn't even feasible when she put her mind to breaking it.

Their lovemaking was natural and thorough, an intimate sharing of soul and body. If he told her he loved her, it was because she already knew that and there was nothing he could do, ever, to change how he felt. He whispered praise and encouragement and didn't argue when she insisted that she loved him despite any beliefs he had to the contrary.

It was too late for arguments, too late because he would always love her. As she would always love him. He accepted her vow in a moment of strength, an instant in which anything was possible. He imagined that together they could make it so.

And then, knowing that love wouldn't change anything, he kissed her harder, made love to her with more passion, more desperation than he'd ever known in his life.

The memories they were making would survive in his heart forever.

Share my life, she wanted to say to him. She didn't, though, because it was enough for now that he learn she meant what she said. She loved him, only him.

She couldn't imagine the kind of emptiness his leaving would bring her. So she put it from her mind, discovering the secrets of his body with an enthusiasm that would have brought him to his knees had he been standing. But they weren't standing, although there was a time when he lifted her high into the air, holding her above his supine body, then lowering her . . . impaling her with such controlled precision that it took her breath away.

As she closed around his hard length, she noticed that breathing wasn't an easy trick for him either.

She fell asleep sprawled atop him. She knew that because she awakened in the same position. Feeling him shift beneath her, she opened her eyes to find his cool gray gaze on her.

She said the first thing that came into her mind. "You forgot to set the alarm before you came to bed."

"No, I didn't."

"But . . ." She let the question die before the words left her mouth, words that would incriminate her if he was paying attention.

She could tell he was paying attention by the sudden tensing of his body beneath hers.

"But what, Elisabeth?" he murmured, smoothing his hands down her back with long, even strokes.

"Nothing." She buried her face in his shoulder and wondered if a friendly seagull had nudged the reflector back into line. Lack of sleep caught up with her, and she drifted off without changing position. Her dreams were filled with seagulls flitting through the erotic explosion of light she'd seen more than once that night at Luke's insistence.

Her bed was a man who finally slept, too, saving his questions for a time when he wasn't distracted by her soft, warm weight.

The LED display on her clock told Elisabeth it was nearly five in the morning when she next opened her eyes. She'd slipped off Luke in her sleep, but he hadn't let her go altogether. With one of his arms under her head and the other around her waist, she was tucked fanny-first against him, a position that was warm and comforting and exhilarating, all at the same time.

Too bad she had to move.

Luke's breathing was deep and regular against her neck as she began to inch away from him. The end of the string for the alarm buster she'd rigged the previous afternoon was tied to the leg of her nightstand. All she had to do was reach down and pull, then slip back into his arms before he was awake enough to realize she'd been gone.

It was harder than she'd imagined. Luke's arm was heavy across her waist. She moved, he adjusted. She moved again, and he raised his hand to cup her breast.

Her heartbeat accelerated from excitement and frustration. If he would just let her go, she could get this over with.

Or maybe she should just skip it, save it for another night.

She didn't think so. After last night's extra duty outside, she didn't think she had much leeway before he figured out what she'd been up to.

Taking a shallow breath, she slid the fingers of both hands around his wrist and pulled his arm down and away, just far enough for her to slide out from under it. Carefully.

She glanced over her shoulder and discovered, much to her relief, that he was still sleeping soundly. Reassured, she wiggled over to the side of the bed, reached down, and found the scissors she'd used to cut the string with. Walking past them with her fingers, she finally found the string.

She was just about to give it a solid yank when the breath was knocked out of her as a large masculine body flattened her against the mattress. Fingers that were stronger than hers took control of the string before he lifted his weight off her. Elisabeth had just about decided that her heart was going to be doing double time for the foreseeable future when Luke eased over her to hunker down beside the night table.

It occurred to her that explaining wouldn't serve any useful purpose, so she kept her mouth shut and hoped Luke remembered that he loved her before he murdered her.

Luke visually followed the path of the string, squinting through eyelids that were gravelly from lack of sleep. He'd known the moment Elisabeth had awakened, and had only pretended to be asleep because sleep was something he desperately needed. But when she'd been so determined to slip away, he'd realized she was up to no good.

Once he figured out what that was, he intended to tie her up and get at least six hours of uninterrupted sleep. In the meantime, though, he needed to find the other end of the string.

Careful not to disturb the tension in the line, he stood and followed it to one of the smaller windows in a corner of the bedroom. Gray streaks of early dawn made it easy to see where the string was tied to a branch just outside the window. Upon closer inspection he realized the branch had been severed from the tree.

A solid yank would bring it crashing against the window, which would either set off the alarm or break the window or both. His gaze narrowed on the knot around the branch. It was tied in such a way as to slip off once the pressure had been released, thus eliminating all signs of conspiracy.

Ingenious. He caught himself just before he repeated the assessment out loud, thinking that praising Elisabeth for this little bit of mischief would be counterproductive.

She deserved a good throttling and was lucky that he was too tired to give it to her. But that didn't quell the angry frustration that was reaching the boiling point.

Carefully, so that the string wouldn't slip and do

the job it was intended to do, he tied it to the window latch, then turned to face Elisabeth. She was sitting up and watching his every move. If she was nervous about the impending confrontation, she didn't show it. Instead she appeared to be appreciating his nakedness in a way that made him wish he could just take her in his arms and forget everything he'd ever known about alarms and security and the things in this world that made his job necessary.

"When you look at me like that," he said, "I almost want to forget how much trouble you've caused me since I set foot on Quincy Island. I'm tempted just to come back to bed and make love to you until you're too tired to move until at least noon." He leaned back against the window and folded his arms across his chest. "But that would only cover the next seven or eight hours, after which I wouldn't know what to expect from you next. If I don't make you understand now how much danger you're in, you might pull another stunt like shifting a laser or sending Sneakers to set off an alarm, and I wouldn't know if it was you or Curtis."

At her blank, uncomprehending expression, he continued. "The hesitation of not knowing might get one of us killed. I'd rather that didn't happen."

"What are you talking about?" she whispered, pulling the covers more tightly around her shoulders. "Curtis is in prison."

Luke shook his head. "Was. He escaped three days ago. Wyatt is afraid he'll show up here."

"That's why you came."

"It's why I came." He took a deep breath, hiding his reaction to the sudden pallor of her face. "Wyatt didn't want to frighten you, so he told me not to tell you."

"Given the circumstances, that doesn't sound very

sensible." Her voice was stronger now, her color better, both indications that she'd absorbed the shock and wasn't letting it get the better of her.

His first guess had been correct. Elisabeth was stronger than Wyatt had ever imagined. Pride that was tempered by relief surged through him as he accepted that she was going to be all right.

For the sake of his own need for rest, he wished he'd confronted her last night instead of waiting for the dawn.

"Your brother is under the misapprehension that you're scared of your own shadow. He didn't want to send you cowering under your bed unless it was absolutely necessary." Luke crossed his legs at the ankle, adjusting his shoulders against the sturdy window frame. Elisabeth followed his every movement, no matter how slight. "What Wyatt doesn't know, of course, was that you didn't stop at ruining your guard dog. You've now turned a state-of-the-art security system into your private amusement park."

"When did you figure it out?"

He scowled at the grin she wasn't completely successful in suppressing. "Too late. If I'd known yesterday that you were playing games, right now I wouldn't feel like I've been hit by a truck."

"You're tired?" she asked innocently.

"I'm exhausted. And it's not funny, because I'm not going to be any good at getting between you and Curtis in this shape."

That reminder sobered her in a single blow. "You really think he'll come here?"

Luke nodded. "Wyatt's got two teams trying to pick up his trail, but we have to assume the worst. He'll come here if he can."

"How does he know where I am?"

"You've been here six years, Elisabeth. Curtis would have had feelers out for information from the first day he was locked away. Just because he was behind bars doesn't mean he didn't have contacts. Or the money to pay them." He shrugged. "If he wanted to badly enough, he could have found you."

She grimaced. "I'm surprised he thinks I'm worth the effort."

"It's thanks to you and Wyatt that he spent six years in that hellhole of a prison. He knows he can't get to Wyatt, not easily. But you're a different matter." He thrust his fingers through his hair, wishing he'd just pulled her off the island that first day, any resistance from her or her brother be damned. "He's going to want revenge, honey. A man like Curtis doesn't forget or forgive."

There was a long silence between them as Elisabeth thought about what he'd said. Having Curtis threatening on the horizon was bad, but not something she couldn't handle. She had Luke to keep her safe. Her faith in him was unshakable.

It did seem to her, however, that leaving would be a prudent move. "Why don't we get on that boat of yours and sail off to a place where Curtis can't find us?"

He looked as though he hadn't expected her to be so cooperative. "I knew I should have told you in the beginning."

"But then I wouldn't have had so much fun watching you try to catch your tail as you chased the alarms." A hand flew to her mouth, too late, though, to erase the words that brought up that rather ticklish point.

His gaze hardened. "I didn't come here for your amusement."

She gave him a weak smile. "Sorry about that. If you hadn't treated me with kid gloves, I wouldn't have dared mess with your perfect little prison."

His eyebrows shot up. "Prison? I was under the impression the security system was for your peace of mind, not to mention your safety."

"If I actually turned the damned thing on—which I don't, by the way, unless company is around—every squirrel, seagull, and loose twig would set it off." She was getting into a more combative mood, just what she needed to tell him a thing or two. "And if it was bad before Wyatt hired you, it only got worse afterward. Why, there were days when I couldn't sneeze without triggering one alarm or another."

"You're exaggerating," he said mildly, wondering how she'd gotten Sneakers to go through the door the previous morning when the dog was clearly well trained to sleep long past dawn. He knew that because it was past the time the dog had arisen the day before and he wasn't busting down the door of the guest room where Luke had settled him not so many hours past.

"I'm not exaggerating, Sinclair." She rose to her knees, tugging at the covers that slipped to reveal her shoulders. "If it weren't for my not wanting to make Wyatt worry any more than he already does, I'd have told you where to stuff your security system long ago."

"And where is that, Squirt?" Luke eased away from the window and covered the distance between them in three long strides.

She almost said, "Where the sun don't shine," but that was too rude, particularly as he was unwrapping the covers that surrounded her and pushing her down to lie flat on the bed. She settled for vague references to file cabinets, deep drawers, and billionaires who needed that level of security, then forgot about it altogether as he followed her onto the bed.

He rubbed his chest against her, his gaze hot and demanding as it met hers. "You put on a pretty good 'frightened' act, Squirt. If I hadn't been so worried about scaring you to death, I might have figured it out sooner."

She laughed. "I'm better than you think, Sinclair. If McCain and Matt haven't tumbled to my shenanigans in six years—"

"How long have you known Matt was on Wyatt's payroll?"

"From the beginning. I know my brother better than you think," she said with a slight reprimand in her tone. "Anyway, you shouldn't worry that it took you two days to catch up with me."

"One and a half," he muttered, grazing her mouth with his. "And it would have been sooner if you hadn't distracted me with your sweet little body."

"It wasn't part of the plan." She threaded her fingers into his hair and pulled him close for a series of quick, wet kisses.

"Neither was falling in love."

She stared up at his solemn face. "You admit I know what I'm talking about?"

He hesitated, then nodded curtly.

She grinned. "For a man who fell in love with a photo, I'm surprised you didn't even once hope that I might fall in love with you too."

He didn't smile in return. "I dreamed, Elisabeth. But I never dared hope."

'Why not?" she whispered.

"To hope is to recognize the possibility. And because I know there can be nothing permanent between us, I didn't dare to hope. It wouldn't have been fair."

"You're still convinced of that, aren't you?" She took a deep breath, easing the frustration that welled up deep inside.

"I know what can't be." Luke fitted himself between her legs and nudged gently forward, knowing he'd find her ready for him, but surprised nonetheless. He threaded his fingers into the hair at her temples and held her head steady, needing to see the acceptance in her eyes. "We have this, we have now. I can't promise you anything more."

She just smiled sweetly as she wrapped her legs around his hips. "We'll see, Sinclair. Nothing's over until it's done."

He slid into her, gritting his teeth at the sweet, persistent pain of her loving. "Meaning?"

"Meaning you don't make all the rules. The last two days should have taught you that much."

Then she lifted her hips to meet his, and he lost all train of thought as he responded to her aggressive soul.

He didn't hold back the passion, nor the love, nor the joy he felt at being this close to her, this intimate. He reveled in the moment and banished to the farthest corners of his mind the circumstances that would inevitably drive them apart.

He fell asleep needing her as he'd never needed another person. Wanting her.

Loving her.

TEN

This time when Elisabeth slid from Luke's embrace, he didn't awaken. Smiling, she tugged the blanket up to cover his shoulders, then tiptoed to the dresser. She dug out fresh lingerie and went into the bathroom to shower and change, carefully pulling the door shut so as not to disturb the man sleeping in her bed.

She rather liked the sound of that.

She dressed quickly, then snuck out of the room, thinking that she'd better hurry before Sneakers set off one of those blasted alarms. Well trained or not, no dog could withstand indefinitely the call of nature. As it was already past nine o'clock, she felt she'd tried his patience far enough.

She found him behind the closed door of the guest room, still sound asleep but willing to jump and frolic the moment she opened the door. She muzzled his morning yips with her fingers, holding his jaws closed all the way down the steps. Detouring to shut off the alarm, she led him to the kitchen and shooed him out the door.

He didn't wait for a second invitation. In a flash he was through the doggie door and outside, chasing visiting wildlife with a furious burst of energy until the grounds were sufficiently private for him to take care of his business. Elisabeth watched from the kitchen window, then hurried to pour kibble into his bowl. His second most important urge of the morning was for food, and if she didn't get it ready, there was every possibility he'd gnaw on Luke until she provided a better alternative.

She imagined Luke would appreciate sleeping in this morning.

Dog food ready and waiting, she ground fresh-frozen beans for coffee and grabbed the day's newspaper—dated exactly one week earlier—from the pile on the counter. Not long after moving to Quincy Island, she had discovered that one of the disadvantages of island life was the lack of a daily newspaper. She'd solved that problem by having a week's worth of Seattle and New York papers delivered with her groceries.

She'd figured that she was enough out of the mainstream that being a week behind wouldn't bother her. Naturally it drove Wyatt crazy when he visited. He couldn't find out what was going on in the world without sitting in front of the television off and on all day. But for Elisabeth it was the perfect solution to a perfect life.

A life that would be lacking when Luke Sinclair went out of it.

She shrugged off those negative thoughts and concentrated on the business section, noticing that the British pound had dipped nearly a penny against the dollar and that a genetics firm she'd invested in had plunged by nearly seventy-five percent.

So much for business. She got up to pour herself a cup of coffee, then flipped to the comics. She was giggling over *Sally Forth* when Sneakers came crashing through the doggie door. He went straight to his food bowl and was half finished when a knock sounded at the door.

A pang of nervousness swept through her until she reminded herself of two things. First, Sneakers hadn't so much as lifted his head from his bowl. Now while Luke's opinion of the dog was less than flattering, Elisabeth knew the animal was alert enough to weed out strangers from friends. An unexpected visit by Old Harry a few months back—he'd been selling fresh salmon—had sent Sneakers into a frenzy. While Harry wasn't exactly a stranger, neither was it normal for him to visit this side of the island.

Sneakers' opinion aside, Elisabeth knew the person on the other side of the door was no one to be alarmed about. Simple logic told her that Curtis wouldn't knock.

Qualms set aside, she opened the door to find Todd. "What brings you out this morning?"

His gaze quartered the kitchen, then returned to meet hers. "Nothing important. Is Sinclair somewhere around?"

"He's sleeping." From Todd's expression Elisabeth was convinced the boy was there with a message from Wyatt. "Do you want me to get him?"

He shook his head. "Dad told me not to wake you, but when I saw Sneakers outside, I figured someone was up."

"Sinclair's had a couple of long nights. I thought it was best to let him catch up on his sleep." She stepped aside to invite Todd in. "Why don't you tell me what you need and I'll let him know when he gets up."

Todd looked reluctant, and she realized he wouldn't know Wyatt's order to keep her in the dark had been overridden. "It's okay, Todd. Luke told me about Curtis."

A single brow inched up his forehead. "Curtis?"

"Mm-hm. Coffee?" she offered. When he hesitated, she decided he didn't really believe her about Curtis. "It's the truth. Sinclair told me about Curtis's escape. Trust me, Todd, I won't pass out at your feet if you tell me he's been tracked to Annacortes."

Todd still looked both baffled and surprised, but managed to say, "He hasn't."

She grinned. "Good."

"I doubt you'd pass out if he had." Todd walked across the kitchen and poured himself a cup of coffee before taking the chair opposite her at the table. "I told Dad that Wyatt was being overprotective. You're a lot stronger than he realizes."

"Too bad you weren't making the decisions," she muttered.

"Obviously you know Dad works for Wyatt. Did Sinclair tell you that too?"

She shook her head, the grin a little lopsided now. "I figured that out a long time ago. It was just more fun to pretend I didn't know."

They laughed together, then she asked about the message he'd brought for Luke.

"Wyatt called early this morning. He thinks they've got Curtis cornered in Hawaii. With the local cops watching the airports, he's pretty certain Curtis won't be able to get off the island."

"That's good news."

"It wouldn't be smart to let down your guard until Curtis is behind bars." Todd sipped his coffee and looked at her with the eyes of a man who knew what he was talking about. Elisabeth was surprised, because this show of maturity exceeded anything she'd ever seen in him. But her surprise was replaced with a feeling of intense admiration for his parents, who'd given Todd the security, responsibility, and love that formed the basis for the self-assurance he'd developed.

She liked knowing he'd go into the world understanding who he was and what he wanted out of life.

"Luke and I talked about getting off the island for a few days," she said. "If the weather holds, I imagine we'll head out on his boat this afternoon."

"You're leaving Quincy Island?" His eyebrows inched up his forehead as he stared at her in disbelief.

"Mm-hm. Luke thinks it's a good idea, and I'm getting a little excited about it too." She stretched her arms high over her head, then let them fall to her sides. "Don't look so surprised, Todd. Did you imagine I'd stay here forever?"

His shrug spoke volumes. "You haven't left here in six years."

"No one ever asked me before," she said smartly, then got up and topped off their cups with hot coffee. She didn't explain that there was no way she would have left the island alone. That might prompt Todd to wonder why she'd never asked anyone to go with her, and she didn't want to confess to the small streak of cowardice running through her. With Luke, though, she knew she could face her fears.

Todd grinned his approval at her. "I suppose I can watch Sneakers for you if you're determined to go."

Hearing his name, the Doberman rose from where he'd been licking his bowl clean and wagged his tail in obvious anticipation. Elisabeth sighed and got up too. "I suppose we'd better go for your romp, dog. Just don't expect me to throw any sticks today. I'm almost as tired as Luke."

Todd stood with her. "I'll take him, Elisabeth. Why don't you stay here and get to work on that new needlepoint?"

She wrinkled her nose. "Because I need some fresh air. You can come along with us, though."

Todd cleared his throat with obvious discomfort. "Actually I think it would be better if I went alone. I don't think Sinclair wants you out on the beach without him."

"But you just said Curtis was in Hawaii." Impatience swelled in her, the same kind of feeling she got when some animal tripped through one of the infrared beams and set off the alarm.

"I said Wyatt *thinks* he's there. Until he's caught, you should assume he could still show up here."

"Why can't I go with you? Between you and Sneakers, Curtis wouldn't dare try anything." If he was already there, which she doubted, because she had faith in her brother's tracking instincts. If he thought Curtis was in Hawaii, then that's precisely where he was.

"You can't come with me because I'm not Sinclair." Todd snapped his fingers at Sneakers and headed toward the door. "If Curtis did decide to try something, Sinclair would know how to stop him."

Elisabeth folded her arms across her chest. "I'm not so sure you wouldn't know what to do," she murmured, taking stock once again of the boy who was more of a man than most men she'd known.

Todd grinned. "I just don't want to have to learn the things Sinclair already knows with you hanging out in the middle, waiting for me to catch up."

He was through the door and outside before she could think of a suitable response. Shaking her head, Elisabeth did something that surprised even her. She went to work on her needlepoint, after pulling aside the long panels of cloth so that she could sew in natural light. Delighted with the first nice day they'd had in a week, she waited somewhat impatiently for Luke to wake up so that she could go outside. When Todd brought Sneakers back to the house, she even turned the alarms back on when he suggested she do so.

As she got back to work with Sneakers curled up in a patch of sunlight, it occurred to her that she'd never been so amenable to following orders. But then, for the first time in six years she admitted they actually made sense.

Luke slept until lunchtime, by which time the sparkling day had unfortunately deteriorated. Sharp gusts rattled the windows, and the sun hid behind clouds that were pregnant with rain. He stood at her bedroom window, studying the white-tipped waves. Alone he'd chance the crossing. But he wouldn't risk Elisabeth in a small boat on such rough waters. Matt Sloane's boat wasn't any bigger or safer. And with the winds gusting so erratically, a helicopter was out of the question.

Unless the weather broke, they'd have to wait until the next day. He swore in the silent room, then went in to shower. While logic told him that Curtis's ability to get onto the island was as limited as their chances of getting off, Luke was still uncomfortable with the delay.

Every instinct he had was screaming at him to get Elisabeth off the island. He dressed and went downstairs to find her putting the final touches on a lunch of grilled-chicken sandwiches and onion rings.

She relayed Wyatt's message, adding her own insert about how relieved she was that it wasn't necessary to attempt to sail in such lousy weather. Besides the probability that she'd be thoroughly seasick, she wasn't at all sure she wanted to spend multiple hours on a small boat when the ferry would be faster and more comfortable.

At which point she admitted to being a rotten sailor in the best of weather, not to mention having a general distaste for small boats ever since her captivity. "I'll go if you think we should," she offered as they sat down to eat. "But I'd really rather not embarrass myself."

He didn't tell her he wouldn't have taken her out in any case. "That's all right, honey. Even if Curtis isn't where Wyatt thinks he is, the chances of his getting through this storm are minimal. We'll take the ferry tomorrow morning."

Her relief was obvious, and she dug into her food with the enthusiasm of a person whose life had just been extended. In between bites she outlined a list of things she wanted to do while they were away. After shopping, shopping, and shopping, she said that if she had any energy left, she'd like to go to the thoroughbred races at Longacres—if it was the season, and she wasn't sure about that.

She also wanted to get a list of the best restaurants in town, because eating out was one of her favorite things. When Luke asked how she'd survived so long without all these pleasures she was so clearly excited about, she admitted to having experienced terrible cravings for the life she'd once led.

"Being here on Quincy Island was safe. Leaving it wasn't. But as black and white as that was, I never stopped missing what I was giving up."

He reached across the table and took her hand,

threading his fingers through hers. "I should have come out here four years ago to take you off this island."

"I wasn't ready then," she returned, taking strength and comfort from his hand warm and hard against hers. "But I am now and I'm excited about going. I can't imagine sleeping tonight, I'm so excited."

He grinned. "Trust me to take care of those things that I can control. You concentrate on filling in that list."

"What more is there?" She returned his grin, remembering with vivid recall how she'd fallen asleep—exhausted—the night before.

"Maybe after a few days we'll head down the coast to Portland or even San Francisco." He smiled at her startled expression. "There's no sense in hurrying back, and I'm due a vacation anyway."

"San Francisco." She licked her lips in anticipation. "I've never been there. Can we walk across the Golden Gate Bridge?"

He didn't answer, asking instead, "You're sure about all this, Squirt?"

"I'm sure." Without taking her hand from his, she got up and circled the table, sliding onto his lap as though it was the most natural thing in the world. "I trust you to keep me out of trouble."

"It's yourself you need to trust." He slipped his arms around her and pulled her to rest against his chest. "I can run interference, but you'll never be able to function out there if you don't take responsibility for yourself."

"One thing at a time, Sinclair," she murmured, her lips moving up his throat. "Wyatt's going to have enough of a shock when he realizes I've flown the coop. Let's allow him to get used to my freedom before we test its boundaries."

Luke tilted her face to meet his, his eyes glowing with

something she imagined was approval. Then he kissed her, a long, hard, open-mouthed kiss that sent her head reeling. When it was over and he lifted her from his lap to stand—unsteadily, she admitted—her lips were wet and just a little swollen.

"I need to check the grounds, honey. Think you can stay inside a little longer?" He got to his feet and went to the door, pausing there for her answer.

"I'll get dinner organized," she said, grinning as she remembered the habanero rice recipe. "Do you have anything against hamburgers and rice?"

He shook his head, his gaze narrowing on her mouth. "Why do I get the feeling you're up to something again?"

She batted her eyes in innocent denial. "I'm not going to mess with your precious security system, Sinclair. Speaking of which, don't you think you should turn it off before you go outside?"

"It's on?" He didn't sound as though he believed her.

"Todd told me to switch it on when he left."

"And you did it?"

She shot him a disparaging scowl. "The way you were sleeping, I didn't figure you'd hear if Curtis shot his way through the front door."

He walked down the hall muttering something about people who couldn't take responsibility for things that were essentially their own fault. Elisabeth let him go without further comment, but avoided getting to work on cleaning the peppers until he'd passed back through the kitchen and gone outside.

Not that he would have protested, she knew, but the recipe was kind of a surprise.

❧————————————❧

Dinner was pretty much as Luke had expected: hot.

He finished the last bit of rice and took a small sip of water, hoping Elisabeth didn't notice the steam billowing out of his ears. When she got up from the table moments later, he was confident she was disappointed in not getting a rise out of him.

Like the games she'd played with the security system, this was a battle of wills he was determined to win. Unlike the other battle, he'd have to win this one by pretending he didn't notice anything was amiss. As he waited for his scorched throat to recover, he sorted through different plans for revenge.

They all involved sneak attacks, a necessary tactic because her tolerance for hot, spicy food was probably grounded in expectation: If she didn't know something was hot, her defenses would be down.

Getting up to help her with the dishes, he found himself looking forward to winning a round in this silent battle. A shudder shook him as he realized he'd better win soon, before she fried his taste buds permanently.

They spent the evening listening to music, Elisabeth working on the needlepoint canvas, Luke reading a book he'd found on Northwest Indian tribes. By mutual agreement they went up to bed early, using the excuse that they had a full day ahead but knowing it was because they wanted the comfort—and the thrill—of each other's arms. Elisabeth took a bath before coming to bed, which was why Luke rather than she answered the phone when it rang.

It was Wyatt, disgruntled at having found out from Matt that Luke had done what he'd been ordered not to do, edgy because Curtis hadn't so much as shown his nose, and worried they'd missed him after all. If nothing happened by morning, he'd bring the team straight to the island. They wouldn't arrive until late afternoon, as they had to transfer from plane to helicopter for the hop across the water.

The fact that Elisabeth wouldn't be there any longer was a plus as far as Wyatt was concerned. Luke, too, but he refused to explain just how he'd convinced her to leave. Instead he cut the conversation short, deciding before he put down the phone that he wouldn't tell Elisabeth that the situation had reverted to full red alert. It made no sense to frighten her more, not when they were leaving the island the next day.

When she came into the bedroom, all soft and rosy from her bath, he deflected her questions about the phone call with the news that while Wyatt wasn't thrilled that Luke had told her about Curtis, he hadn't fired him.

She came into his arms with laughter and teasing, and in the next few minutes she made him forget the phone had rung at all.

That escape was only temporary, though. Later that night, when Elisabeth finally lay deeply asleep, he slipped from her arms and went outside to check on Matt. The winds had calmed a bit, but sporadic rain pelted down from above. Luke spelled Matt for an hour, sending the man inside for hot coffee. Despite the slicker he wore over his clothes, Luke was thoroughly wet when he came back indoors. By the time he'd showered and returned to Elisabeth's bed, he was tired enough to sleep but too wired to do a very good job of it.

It was as though by staying awake he could keep her safe. There were only a few hours left before dawn before he convinced himself that he wouldn't be much good to anyone if he didn't get the rest he needed.

He went to sleep grateful that this was the last

night, for a while, that he'd have to sleep with one eye open.

Dawn came early, bringing with it a day so beautiful, it was as though the rains had scrubbed clean the skies. They arose early. Elisabeth scurried about packing and getting Sneakers ready for the move next door, the grin on her face telling Luke she was a lot more excited than she was nervous. Together, they shut up the house, setting the outside alarms with a remote transmitter before driving away. Matt had an identical transmitter that would allow him to come and go as needed.

The interisland ferry stopped at Quincy Island just a few minutes past ten-thirty, more or less on time and proud of it. The deep bellow of the ship's horn sounded triumphantly as it edged close to the dock. The island's dozen or so residents were gathered near a rickety shack as Harry did his thing with the gangplank. None of them hurried forward when it was finally secured, because they were reluctant to end their weekly session of "howdy" and "how's it going."

It was a social event not to be hurried.

The loading process itself was short and to the point. Elisabeth and Luke were the only embarking passengers, which meant the ferry was free to sail away as soon as all groceries and supplies had been unloaded. Todd was there with his dad to claim their own supplies along with those Elisabeth had ordered. They'd left Sneakers back at the house, figuring it would be less traumatic for the Doberman. Even so, when she had hugged him goodbye, the dog had been a little frantic, his eyes shifting nervously from Elisabeth to Luke as though one of them owed him an explanation.

She felt like a heel for leaving him.

Vetoing Elisabeth's suggestion, Luke had decided to leave her truck behind. It would be simple to rent a vehicle in Seattle, he assured her. They'd get something sleek and fast, maybe with a convertible top. What he didn't tell her was that changing their profile made it necessary to leave her vehicle on Quincy Island. They'd be harder to track with a rental, particularly as he intended to use a fake ID to acquire it.

They stood together at the rail, the full skirt of Elisabeth's summer dress flaring around her knees in the warm breeze. She pointed out Miss Eleanor Croome and Old Harry, telling Luke about the one-sided romance, which that day looked even less likely to flower. Miss Eleanor, apparently not having any luck in ignoring Harry, had decided on a less subtle approach. She bashed the persistent ferry man across the shoulders with her umbrella, then stalked off to collect her supplies, her spine rigid and her expression satisfied.

Which was probably why Old Harry took his sweet time in finishing unloading the supplies. Most of the islanders had departed by that time, leaving only Elisabeth and Luke to watch as Old Harry argued with the ferry's crew, insisting they help him carry his supplies all the way to the shack at the end of the dock. After a few minutes Luke said he might as well go get them some coffee, hoping that by the time he was back, Quincy Island would be a distant shoreline. Elisabeth let him go, and she was so engrossed with Old Harry's shenanigans that she didn't see Sneakers until the dog was nearly on the dock, a dust cloud rising in a long, narrow thread along the road behind him.

"Who on earth told you I'd be here?" she muttered to no one, and sighed gustily as the Doberman spotted her and charged onto the ferry. She turned and dashed for the stairs, meeting Sneakers halfway down, the dog ecstatic, her own mood a bit more subdued.

She grabbed his collar and hauled him toward the gangplank. "You can't come, Sneakers. Seattle would make you nuts with all that noise and traffic."

He yipped in disagreement. She shook her head sternly, then told him to sit. He sat. She backed away. He followed her, his butt never leaving the dock as he closed the distance between them.

She glared at him. "You have to stay here, Sneakers. Todd will be worried when he can't find you."

Sneakers glared back and inched forward. Elisabeth was beginning to worry about having to pull splinters from doggie flesh, not to mention that she was probably running out of time. The ferry would be leaving any minute now.

She heaved another huge sigh and grabbed Sneakers' collar again. She'd have to ask Old Harry to keep the dog until Todd came looking for him. A glance over her shoulder told her the ferry was still dockside, so she hurried over to the shack, dreading having to owe Harry for this very big favor.

Miss Eleanor was nowhere to be seen, although her car was still parked nearby. While Elisabeth would have rather asked the woman for help than go begging to Old Harry, she didn't have time to look for her. So she squared her shoulders and prepared herself to ward off Harry's inevitable proposition.

The shack's door was propped open by a piece of wood. Elisabeth stuck her head inside the unlit room, wasting precious seconds as her eyes became accustomed to the gloom. She was just about to open her mouth and ask Harry if he would please keep Sneakers until the ferry went, when she saw not one, but two bodies inside the shack.

Two bodies that were entwined in an embrace so passionate, it made her blush. It was a beautifully intimate scene, and she would have backed away without making a noise were it not for a singular inconsistency that drove any thought of discretion from her mind: The passionate couple was none other than Miss Eleanor Croome and Old Harry.

Not a combination she'd have imagined in a million years.

Two million.

She must have made a noise, or maybe Sneakers did, because Old Harry suddenly pulled back from Miss Eleanor. He glared at Elisabeth and snapped, "You don't know how to knock, young lady?"

"The door was open?" She phrased it as a question, not sure why she felt in the wrong.

Miss Eleanor smoothed the front of her dress and beamed at Elisabeth. "Not to worry, dear. I'm sure it's my fault the door wasn't closed." To Elisabeth's amazement the older woman stroked Harry's shoulder. "It's just that I was a little eager."

Elisabeth almost asked for what, but bit off the question in the nick of time.

Harry wasn't finished glaring at her. "If you tell anyone about . . ." He stuttered for a few moments, then started over, his glare as emphatic as before. "You keep your mouth shut about Miss Eleanor and me. It's no one's business."

No kidding. "I wouldn't dream of saying anything, promise." Not that anyone would believe her.

"She's got her reputation to think of. I won't have people talking about her."

"Honest, Harry, I won't say a thing."

"Better not." Harry looked down at Sneakers as though he was deciding whether he needed to get a similar pledge from the dog.

Which reminded Elisabeth of why she was there. "Sneakers somehow got away from Todd. Could you possibly keep him until the ferry leaves?" She addressed the question to Miss Eleanor, thinking that the woman would benefit from having a Doberman between herself and Old Harry.

Then again, she hadn't looked as though Harry's passionate kiss had been unwelcome. In fact Elisabeth could have sworn the woman positively glowed—something not easy to tell, given the sparse lighting and her own disinclination to look directly at either Harry or Miss Eleanor.

Harry turned to look out the shed's single window, tucking a ragged shirttail into his trousers. "Too late for that, young lady. The ferry's done gone."

"No, it's not," she said quickly, denying the disaster even as she knew Harry spoke the truth. "It can't leave without me." She stepped out of the shed and saw that the ferry was several hundred yards from the dock. Shielding her eyes with her hand, she studied the open deck, but found no sign of Sinclair.

Which meant he was probably circling the deck, looking for her, a cup of coffee in either hand, his temper fraying as the hot liquid slopped onto his hands.

Her imagination stopped before it got to the part where Luke realized she was no longer on board. There was only so much she could handle, missing the boat being just one part of it. Having to explain to Luke what had happened . . . No, she wasn't up for that yet. Perhaps she would be by the time Luke managed to disembark at Orcas—the ferry's next port of call—borrow a boat from the marina, and head back to Quincy Island. Three or four hours minimum, if he didn't run into any snags. Perhaps by then she'd be able to explain without sounding as stupid as she felt.

She groaned and let go of Sneakers' collar. The Doberman, obviously no longer worried about being the only one left behind, went to lie down in the shade of Elisabeth's truck.

Miss Eleanor slid her arm across her shoulders. "No need to fret, dear. You can go next week, although I have to admit I was surprised to see you going at all. Why, you haven't been off the island for as long as I've lived here, now, have you?"

"Today was to be the first time," Elisabeth said quietly.

"Today was a first in both our books," Miss Eleanor said brightly, then turned to Harry, who was still a little red around the ears. "Now that Elisabeth has missed the boat, you should radio the captain to tell her young man. He'll be thinking she fell overboard."

"Can't. Radio's broke," Harry muttered, rubbing a hand over his beard. "Parts just came in. That Sloane boy is coming over tomorrow to put it together for me."

Miss Eleanor gave Elisabeth a consolation squeeze. "Never mind, Elisabeth. That young man looked as though he had a good head on his shoulders. He'll figure it out and be back in no time."

"Three or four hours at least," Elisabeth groaned, digging her sandal into the sandy soil at her feet.

"Can't be helped," Miss Eleanor said, then turned

back to Harry. "I'm taking Elisabeth home with me for lunch. Why don't you come over later, Harry. For dinner. And put on a clean shirt. That one looks like you've been wearing it all week."

All month was more likely, but Elisabeth kept her opinion to herself as Miss Eleanor urged her in the direction of their vehicles, chattering all the way about what a beautiful day it was and what a shame Elisabeth missed going to Seattle with her young man. Elisabeth helped Miss Eleanor finish loading her supplies. Lunch with the elderly woman sounded infinitely better than waiting alone at the house for Luke. Besides, Miss Eleanor might give her some hint as to why she'd bashed Old Harry with her umbrella one minute and melted in his arms the next.

Then again, maybe she didn't want to know. After the games she herself had played with Sinclair—beginning with siccing her dog on him and ending with her attempt to drive him crazy with the alarm system—she knew appearances of malice weren't anything to go by.

She loved Luke, but that hadn't stopped her from making him a little miserable. Elisabeth wasn't sure she was ready to hear a parallel confession from Miss Eleanor Croome.

Some mysteries in life were better left unexplored. The relationship between Old Harry and Miss Eleanor Croome was one of them.

ELEVEN

It was after two o'clock when Elisabeth finally returned to her own home. Though the lunch with Miss Eleanor had been entertaining, the strain of wondering when Luke would get back had kept her from enjoying herself as much as she would have, given the circumstances.

Miss Eleanor had been positively bursting with enthusiasm, taking Elisabeth into the bedroom of the tiny cottage so that she could help her choose what to wear. Then it was on to the kitchen, where Miss Eleanor fretted over what to cook for dinner and whether she should serve hors d'oeuvres on the patio or in the sitting room.

Miss Eleanor was still in a tizzy when Elisabeth left. Even Sneakers appeared relieved to arrive at their own side of the island, his nerves obviously stretched by the near-miss at the ferry and Miss Eleanor's frenzy.

Elisabeth remembered to switch off the alarm only after it nearly blasted her from behind the wheel of the truck, holding the vehicle steady as she leaned over to grab the transmitter from the glove box. It took her several tries to get the proper sequence of numbers punched into the mechanism. Sneakers looked ready to bite her by the time she finally got it right and the noise abruptly ended.

All of which reminded her of why she never turned it on in the first place.

She headed indoors, leaving Sneakers outside to release his pent-up energies with a little game of "chase the rabbit in circles." Considering he'd already run the length of the island that morning, she was surprised at his enthusiasm for the game. Going to the living-room windows, she pulled each of the heavy black cloths aside and tied them back with a piece of wool from her needlepoint bag. Just as she finished, she saw the Doberman fairly fly down the path in hot pursuit of said rabbit. He was out of sight before she could blink, most likely racing through the trees that fringed the beach. She wondered how long the rabbit would deign to play, not in the least worried that Sneakers would catch it.

The game was strictly a friendly one, the rules of long standing. As long as Sneakers didn't seriously try to catch anything, the little animals of the forest were willing to indulge him in a game of hide-and-seek. Elisabeth figured Sneakers' lack of hunting instincts had something to do with having been trained not to take food from anyone besides his master.

Either that or he didn't recognize the furry creatures as food.

She left the windows and headed into the kitchen, recognizing how empty the house felt without Luke. It would only be a matter of another hour or so, she figured. Meanwhile, she would just have to keep busy.

But she couldn't think of anything to do that would take her mind off the man she'd come so close to in such a short space of time. Opening the refrigerator, she was reminded that she'd told Matt to keep her fresh supplies and freeze what they could. All they'd left her was an assortment of soft drinks and beer, none of which sounded appealing.

Thinking of the Sloanes reminded her that she needed to let them know Sneakers had found his way to the ferry. She didn't want them searching for the dog when he didn't report for dinner that night. She was reaching for the telephone when she heard the kitchen door squeak open behind her. Thinking it was Todd come looking for the dog, she dropped her hand and turned toward the opening door. "Sorry, Todd. I should have realized—"

Her smile of greeting faded. The man standing there was holding a small gun that was aimed directly at her stomach. It wasn't the gun, though, that made her blood drain from her face.

It was the cold, empty look in Curtis's eyes that frightened her—a look of death that she recognized even though she'd never seen it before.

He motioned for her to back up. She did so, wishing her jangling nerves would calm so that she could think. It wasn't possible, though, not yet. She settled for taking deep, even breaths, an attempt to balance herself, to prepare for whatever lay ahead.

"You act surprised to see me, Elisabeth." Curtis leaned against the counter, resting his gun hand in the crook of his other elbow. "Didn't big brother tell you I was coming?"

Another deep breath and she thought she had a handle on herself. "Wyatt had hoped you wouldn't make it this far. I told him I didn't think you'd be stupid enough to come after me." She took confidence from the easy flow of her own words. "I guess you're more stupid than I remember."

His eyes brimmed with rage. "It's your brother who's the stupid one. For someone he pretends to care about, he didn't hide your whereabouts very well. I've known where to find you for over two years now."

"And I've known where to find you for six, but you didn't see me knocking on prison doors, did you?" He looked surprised that she would talk back to him. Remembering the mostly silent, frightened girl she'd been during her captivity, she couldn't blame him.

He wouldn't find her so easily intimidated this time around, she decided, a fury rushing through her that gave her strength. *How dare he come into her home and wave that gun at her!*

"I'd be careful how you speak to me," he snarled. "I don't like it when people aren't respectful."

"I'll bet the prison guards were really respectful, Curtis," she mocked, edging back toward the kitchen table where she'd left her purse. If she could only get to it, she'd have a weapon of sorts—although throwing it at him probably wouldn't match the effectiveness of that gun he held.

She wondered where Todd and Matt were, and if they'd missed Sneakers.

The smile that drew his lips into a taut curve was vicious. "Yes, Elisabeth. The guards learned to be respectful. I had a lot of friends on the outside, friends who could threaten their families if I wished it."

Her stomach turned at his arrogant assertion. "Since the only people who talk to you get paid for it, I wouldn't brag about how well they treat you."

The gibe that had been meant to irritate rebounded on her. His mouth softened as his gaze flitted over her. "It used to be that you were eager to talk to me, to be with me. And you called me Timothy back then, not Curtis."

"Yes, well, I guess I have to admit to being stupid when I was twenty-one. Luckily *I've* outgrown it." She pretended to ignore the knuckles that whitened as he clutched the gun tighter, paying attention instead to how much weight he'd lost over the last six years. His hair had thinned, too, and there were deep creases around his mouth that hadn't been there before.

It felt good to know the six years hadn't been easy on him, especially since it looked as though he was determined to make definite changes in her life. The bundle of nerves that weighed heavily in her stomach lurched as she began to worry about all the variables of what could happen next. Did Curtis know about Luke? Would Sneakers come busting through the door and attack him? She doubted that one, but didn't entirely discount the possibility.

Miracles weren't predictable.

She worried again about Matt and Todd. And Jenny. Had Curtis already been over to their place? She gritted her teeth in frustration, wishing she'd thought to call Matt from Miss Eleanor's.

"I haven't asked you how your trip was." She smiled politely. "Any chance jet lag is getting to you?"

"Not enough to concern you. Your brother pushed me faster than I really wanted to travel—"

"Didn't give you time to catch up on old times with your friends?" She hesitated, as if suddenly realizing she'd spoken out of turn. "What am I thinking? Snakes don't have friends."

"You've got a mouth on you that I don't find at all attractive."

She lifted a shoulder in a careless shrug. "You can't really believe that bothers me."

He straightened from the counter. "Enough! I didn't come here to waste words on you."

"But, Timothy, I was just getting warmed up." She didn't like the way he was waving that gun at her. Remembering that it had been six years since he'd held one didn't reassure her.

"Let's go to your bedroom, Elisabeth. There's someone up there I know you'll want to see."

"Who?" Her stomach heaved in reaction. Had Luke arrived faster than she imagined he would? Or was it one of the Sloanes? It made her sick to imagine what Curtis would do to anyone who got in his way. "Who is it, Curtis?"

He shrugged and wagged that damned gun at her again, his grin a sickly reminder of how evil he really was. "You tell me. He wouldn't even give his name and serial number."

It was all she could do to keep from slugging him. If it hadn't been for the gun, she'd have taken her chances that her willpower would overwhelm his strength. Unfortunately he lacked the confidence in himself that he needed to work without a prop.

She hurried down the hall without worrying if he'd follow, and took the stairs two at a time. Curtis yelled at her to slow down, but she ignored him, racing to find out who else he'd caught in his trap.

It was Matt, stomach down on her bed with his arms and legs pulled behind him and tied in a maze of knots she'd only be able to decipher if she had a map. He was facing away from her, with pieces of cloth knotted behind his head; obviously a gag and blindfold. He was so still that she was suddenly afraid Curtis had done more than hurt him.

She was on her way across the room to the bed when Curtis's hand closed around her arm. She flinched in disgust, shrugging off his hand with a sharp warning.

"If he's dead, you might as well put that little popgun of yours to your head right now. Wyatt values him."

"He's not dead." Curtis backed off enough to let her go to Matt, but not before she noticed the calculating look in his eyes. Good, she thought as she ran the last few steps to the bed. Curtis wouldn't destroy anyone or anything that might bring a profit. She ran the last few steps to the bed, then untied the blindfold and gag without paying any attention whatsoever to Curtis. Matt was oblivious to her presence, making her worry how long he'd been unconscious.

Curtis jerked her back from the bed and asked what the hell she thought she was doing. His grip on her arm was going to leave bruises, she knew, but those she could deal with.

She scowled furiously at him. "Keeping him alive, stupid. He can't possibly breathe like that. Not for long."

"Put the blindfold back on."

The rage that had been building inside of her was suddenly out of control. "So what's he going to see, stupid? Besides the fact that he's out cold, he knows who you are and who I am. Keeping him blindfolded serves no useful purpose."

He raised his hand and whipped it across her face faster than she could duck. As she went down, the only coherent thought she had was that she was glad it hadn't been the hand with the gun.

As it was, she knew her cheek and mouth would be swollen triple-size before the sun set.

She only hoped she was still there to see it.

Without making a big production out of it, she got up from the floor, automatically brushing her skirt back over her thighs as she stood to face him. It was beyond personal between them. This was war.

A war she intended to win. A war she *could* win if she kept her wits about her. All she had to do was stall, keep him from doing anything until Luke had a chance to get there.

"I see you've lost that restraint you so prided yourself on," she said disdainfully, forcing herself not to raise her hand and touch where he'd hurt her. She didn't want to give him the satisfaction.

He just laughed, a loud, cruel sound that made the nerves at the tip of her spine vibrate in disgust. "My restraint was governed by profit, sweet Elisabeth. I'm sure you're not as pure now as you were then. Besides, the market isn't as good for women over twenty-five, although I have to admit, you almost look as young now as you did then."

She met his gaze with a noncommittal one of her own, then touched Matt's shoulder, praying that because Luke hadn't been working for Wyatt six years ago, he hadn't met Curtis face-to-face. If Curtis believed this man was Sinclair, Luke would be an unexpected factor. He'd have the element of surprise on his hands.

"I'd be careful about how many bruises you leave on either one of us, Curtis. Given a lesser excuse, Sinclair here would rather see you dead than back in prison."

"This is Sinclair?" Curtis edged closer to the bed so that he could get a better look, still careful to keep his gun trained on Elisabeth.

She acted upset that she'd let that little fact escape, then brushed off her reaction with a show of irritation. "Who did you think it was? Of course it's Sinclair. Wyatt wouldn't leave me unprotected with you on the loose."

She almost fainted with relief when Curtis accepted her lie.

"No wonder he wouldn't tell me. It's thanks to his efforts that the escape I attempted last year failed." Curtis appeared to relax. "So I've got you *and* Sinclair. This should make your brother doubly amenable to a trade."

Which meant he intended to keep them both alive, for the time being anyway. It was something she'd gambled on when she realized he could as easily have killed Matt as tie him up.

"What on earth do you want from Wyatt now? More money?"

"No, Elisabeth. The money was for causes. I won't waste my time on those anymore." His eyes glimmered in the soft light. "This time I want your brother. Dead."

The madness was in his eyes, and she was almost grateful when he told her to get onto the bed, where he proceeded to hog-tie her as efficiently as he had Matt. By the time he was finished, her fingers and toes had already begun to tingle. She dreaded to think how Matt was faring.

"I won't bother to gag you now," he said, reaching across her to test Matt's bonds. "Wyatt can't possibly get here for another couple of hours. By that time my friends will have returned with the boat and we'll be long gone."

"You're not going to wait for Wyatt here?"

He laughed harshly. "Give me some credit, Elisabeth. I've heard all about that army he's traveling with. I'll pick a time and place when I can control the odds." With that he strode out of the room, leaving her to wonder how much longer Matt would be unconscious, because she wasn't certain they had much time.

Perhaps not even enough to wait for Sinclair to rescue them.

That thought spurred her into action. Not necessarily productive action, however. She spent a fruitless minute or so squirming about on the bed, challenging the integrity of her bonds and losing. Then she remembered the scissors, the ones she'd used to cut the string that she'd tied to the branch a century or so ago.

If only Luke hadn't moved them!

She wriggled over to the edge of the bed and then, taking a deep breath for courage, rolled off the side and onto the thick carpet. The thud she made upon landing was nothing compared with the pounding of her heart, but she didn't stop to assess the effect of either on the man downstairs. There wasn't time.

Rolling over onto her back, she inched her way around the bed, wishing Curtis had at least put her on that side to begin with and ignoring the carpet burns she was getting on her arms as she scooted along. Her hair got in the way more than once, tangling beneath her back, braking her progress so that she had to sit up and shake it forward. By the time she reached the nightstand, she was winded and sore and thinking that she'd cut her bonds first, her hair second.

Only when she had her fingers wrapped around the shears did she begin to believe she could actually pull this off. With hands that were nearly numb from the tight ropes, she sawed and sliced and levered the blades until suddenly the bonds around her wrists slid free. The joy at her victory was tempered by the fact that she was only half done. Getting Matt to safety looked to be equally as challenging, particularly as she hadn't figured that part out yet.

She went to work on her ankles with renewed energy, wishing that Sinclair would get there soon because Matt was still unconscious and she didn't know what to do about that. She was cutting away his bonds when she glanced across the room at the panel that hid the priest hole.

Perfect. Not easy, she told herself as she finished freeing Matt, but doable.

Ignoring the fact that Matt was almost twice her weight, she began the tedious process of rolling him across the bed. She crossed his legs, pulled his far arm toward her so that he wouldn't roll on it, then wiggled beneath his shoulders and levered herself onto her knees, pushing until he rolled over. Then she did it all over again, finding it easier to roll him back to front than the other way around.

A loud banging noise from outside drew her to the window. At first she saw nothing, then Sneakers came into view. The dog was tearing up the beach as though the devil himself was after him. When Curtis burst out of the trees and leveled his shooting arm, she knew what she'd heard had been a gunshot.

Curtis was going to kill her dog. He fired twice more, then headed in the same direction Sneakers had taken. Tears welled in her eyes as Elisabeth turned back to the bed. There was nothing she could do to help her dog. But she could take advantage of Curtis's absence from the house to get Matt into the priest hole. Working quickly, she threw the pillows from the bed onto the floor. Then essentially she threw Matt down after them.

Once everything was on the floor that she intended, she raced across the room, opened the panel to the priest hole, then went back for Matt. He was lying on his side, and there was a lump at his temple that she hoped was Curtis's fault and not hers. Shaking off any misgivings for her rough handling, she began to drag him across the room, feet first, one inch at a time. Her strength against his dead weight.

It took forever.

She'd just gotten him into the priest hole and was brushing away the trail they'd left on the carpet when she heard the kitchen door slam. Beginning to panic, she threw the pillows back onto the bed, then dove inside the priest hole, pulling the door shut behind her.

It was a tight squeeze, particularly as Matt took up most of the floor space, but she was too busy trying to get her breath back to mind. About the time she felt the heat leave her face, she noticed the telephone at Matt's feet.

Not unlike the one in her room. "Dammit, Elisabeth! Why do you always do things the hard way?" she demanded of herself.

She crawled down the length of Matt's body, remembering to keep her mutterings quiet even though Wyatt had assured her the priest hole was soundproof. When she lifted the phone to her ear, she found it was dead.

"Terrific," she grumbled, shoving Matt's feet aside and squeezing to sit beside his knees. "So the phone's dead. Who would you call anyway? Jenny—and scare her to death! Or maybe Miss Eleanor. I'm sure she'd be a tremendous help."

Todd was a variable she couldn't predict. If he knew there was trouble, would he call for help or wade into an already messy situation? She hated to think of Todd getting involved in something that was so dangerous, but knew that if he'd heard the shots Curtis had fired at Sneakers, he would come running.

Straight into Curtis's trap.

And of course there was Luke. Not that she had any doubts that he would read the situation correctly and take care of things in short order, but there was always the chance he wouldn't get there in time. Curtis's cohorts could arrive and take away any chance Luke had of rescuing them.

Suddenly Elisabeth knew she couldn't just sit there. She had to act, even if that meant facing Curtis again.

She was finished with hiding.

The two-mile stretch between the ferry landing and Elisabeth's took Luke about fifteen minutes to run. Old Harry had offered to drive him across the island, but Luke had declined when the man had told him they'd leave as soon as he finished washing his shirt.

The shirt had looked to be more than a ten-minute project.

So he'd run, only partially reassured by Harry's explanation of why Elisabeth had gotten off the ferry. While it was clear she hadn't been in any danger, a prickly feeling at the back of his neck told him something was wrong. That feeling was stronger now, much worse than it had been during what had seemed an interminable three-hour sail from Orcas to Quincy. The boat he'd rented had been the fastest available, the winds strong, but three hours was the best time he'd been able to make and he'd spent the entire time cursing himself for letting Elisabeth out of his sight.

Slowing as he came to the foot of her driveway, he slipped into the bushes at the side. Without knowing why he knew it was necessary, he pulled his gun from the holster and flipped off the safety. He began to thread a path toward the house, grateful that he'd spent so much time with the motion detectors; he was able to avoid them without breaking stride. When he was almost within sight of the house, a stick snapped about ten yards to the right.

Luke pretended not to notice. Instead he changed his direction to lead whoever was nearby away from the house. He hadn't taken two steps when a low-pitched voice stopped him.

"It's me. Todd. There's trouble."

Luke turned to find the boy just a few feet away, gun in one hand, remote phone in the other. "What kind?"

"I'm not sure." He looked over his shoulder toward the trees that sheltered the house, then hunkered down behind a thick bush. He waited until Luke crouched down beside him. "Dad went over to take Elisabeth's groceries about an hour ago. He didn't come back, and I found his truck parked inside Elisabeth's garage."

"Did you go inside the house?"

Todd shook his head. "I went straight back to our place and got Mom out of there; sent her over to Miss Eleanor's. When I got back here, I saw Elisabeth's truck parked outside."

Luke explained briefly about Sneakers. "Have you seen the dog?"

"No, but as I was coming back from our place, I heard three shots fired." He indicated the remote phone. "I was on the phone with Old Harry when that happened. When he told me you were headed this way, I decided to wait."

Luke nodded his approval, his eyes scanning the forest around them. "We have to assume it's Curtis. Do you know what he looks like?" He waited for Todd's nod, then added, "We need to find out how many men he brought with him."

"What do you want me to do?" Todd's voice and expression were calm and confident.

"First, call your mom and tell her to get in touch with authorities—"

"Already taken care of. The sheriff's office said it would take about an hour to get over here from Annacortes."

"Good. Turn off that phone so it doesn't ring, then make your way down to the beach. Stay in the trees, but see if there's anything going on." Luke checked his watch. "Meet me behind the garage in fifteen minutes. If I'm not there, get back to Miss Eleanor's and stay there until the sheriff arrives."

"I check in with Mom every ten minutes. She'll keep me updated on that."

Luke adjusted his sunglasses as Todd rose to move away. He called after him. "Watch out for the motion detectors. I don't know if they're on or not."

Todd just nodded and slipped through the trees, disappearing before he'd gone twenty feet. Luke went in the opposite direction, circling around behind the house until he came to a window at the back of the garage. It took him two minutes to disconnect the alarm wired to the window; then he was inside and easing open the door to Matt's truck. He found the transmitter that controlled the alarm array above the visor.

The detour had been worth the time.

Luke punched in two codes: One to shut down the outside alarms, the other for the inside—just in case Curtis had convinced Elisabeth or Matt to give him the codes. Now he could get inside without alerting anyone. He crawled back out the window, then faded into the woods. With the ten minutes he had left before meeting Todd, he studied the back and sides of the house, searching for any movement inside. After several fruitless minutes during which he didn't see anything, he remembered telling Elisabeth that those windows didn't need to be covered because they weren't that easy to see into from ground level.

He would have given anything to have been proven wrong.

He wasn't, though, so he crawled around to the front of the house to see if the makeshift curtains were still in place. His heart speeded up as he rounded the corner and saw that someone had tied back each and every panel of cloth. Even without rising from the ground, he could see into the room and the hallway beyond. There was no movement, but that didn't mean Curtis and others weren't sitting in chairs facing the other direction. Luke stayed there for several minutes, cutting close the time when he had to leave to meet Todd. He was just getting ready to back away from his vantage point when the figure of a man rose from the large wing chair and crossed to the windows.

Luke could see perfectly the vaguely irritated expression on Curtis's face. He held his breath as Curtis lifted his hand to check the time, knowing the other man couldn't possibly see him but too aware of the risks even to blink.

Curtis stayed at the window for what seemed hours, then abruptly turned on his heel and left the room. Even though he hadn't seen anyone else in the room, Luke left his hiding spot as carefully as he'd approached. By the time he'd made his way to the back of the garage, he was five minutes late and worried that Todd would have headed back to Miss Eleanor's. Luke knew he would need the boy's help if he was going to get inside the house.

Todd was watching the house from behind a stand of trees next to the garage. Breathing a sigh of relief, Luke joined him. "Anything on the beach?"

"No one. No boats, either, although a fast one could come over the horizon or around the island in minutes." His gaze remained on the house, so Luke concentrated on watching the area to the right of it. "I found Sneakers just a few yards from the beach. A bullet grazed his butt, but he should be okay."

The wounded animal worried Luke, because he couldn't predict what Sneakers would do. "I don't suppose you tied him up to keep him out of this."

"Nothing to tie him with." Todd looked down in disgust at the trousers that he wore without a belt and the boots beneath them. "I told him to stay put, but that's not worth a whole lot."

"Never mind. We'll just have to hope he stays where he is." Luke took a moment to think before telling Todd what he wanted him to do.

The boy listened without interrupting, then checked his watch against Luke's and took the alarm-control transmitter as well as Luke's gun, which he dropped into the pocket of his jacket. "This isn't going to work if Curtis isn't the only bad guy in there."

Luke knew that. "Let's just say the odds won't be as favorable. But we don't have time to waste. Curtis looked impatient: I'm worried that if he's alone now, it won't be for long. Waiting isn't going to net us anything." He unclipped the leather holster and dropped it in the leaves.

"Sure you want to do this without a gun?"

"It will confuse him. I'm also hoping he'll equate unarmed with harmless."

Todd almost grinned. "You don't look harmless."

"Curtis's record is devoid of anything that makes me think he understands that a gun is only as smart as the man behind it." He nodded toward the gun Todd held. "Be sure you remember which hand has the gun and which one's got the phone."

Todd allowed a small grin this time, then headed into the woods in the direction of the beach. Luke gave him three minutes before moving out of the shelter of the trees and walking briskly toward the back door.

He'd just raised his hand to knock when the door swung open. Luke found himself looking down the barrel of a gun that resembled the one Matt Sloane carried.

With a look of alarm that he hoped reached his eyes, he lifted his gaze and discovered that not only was Curtis holding the gun, he was also holding Elisabeth. A quick glance told him Curtis had knocked her around, enough to leave marks but not enough to curb her temper.

The woman who claimed to love him looked as though she was mad enough to kill . . . and Luke was pretty sure that all that anger was directed straight at him. It was reassuring in a way, because he knew she wouldn't have room for all that anger if Curtis had hurt her badly.

He could only hope that she would remember who was the bad guy when it came to the crunch.

TWELVE

The situation had veered off in a direction Luke didn't care for. Because he hadn't seen Elisabeth earlier, he'd guessed that Curtis had secured her in another room.

He'd guessed wrong.

"Put your hands up and get in here," Curtis demanded, tightening his forearm across Elisabeth's throat. "And don't do anything foolish. I'll shoot both of you if I have to."

Luke didn't have to pretend to look dismayed, but it took all of his control to keep the rage from showing in his eyes. He followed as Curtis backed into the kitchen, forcing his hands not to curl into fists so that Curtis wouldn't feel threatened. Elisabeth gripped Curtis's forearm with both hands, clearly trying to relieve the pressure on her throat.

"You're hurting her," Luke said, keeping his distance. He knew better than to imagine Curtis had any qualms about shooting.

"Little witch deserves it. She tried to bash me over the head with a book."

Elisabeth clawed at the arm, succeeding in freeing

herself enough to say, "Sinclair got away," before Curtis slammed her on the side of the head with the gun.

Luke watched, enraged, as she sagged against Curtis. He prayed she'd just slide to the floor and get out of the way so that he would be ready when Todd did his thing. But clearly the blow hadn't had enough force to do more than stun her, because in seconds her eyes were open and she was again struggling against Curtis.

Luke was afraid Curtis would kill her if she didn't stop. "Don't fight him, Elisabeth. He's got all the cards." She ceased her struggles, but her eyes were fierce and full of frustration. He nodded his approval as he contemplated what she'd said. *Sinclair got away.*

The double bonus balanced Elisabeth's awkward presence. Not only had Matt escaped, but Curtis didn't know he was standing gun-to-nose with Wyatt's security chief.

"So who are you?" Curtis asked, his eyes flicking over Luke in a manner that suggested he was checking for weapons.

"A neighbor."

"Turn around."

Luke did so, then turned back to face the new questions in Elisabeth's gaze as she obviously noticed the absence of his holster.

Curtis grunted his satisfaction, but didn't lower the gun. He backed against the counter and motioned Luke to walk past him. "Go into the living room where we can all sit down and have a little chat."

Luke went without arguing, wishing he could get a look at his watch. The action was going to start any second now, and he'd rather have the advantage of knowing precisely when.

He was three steps into the living room and just

turning to face Curtis when the alarm went off. Luke didn't wait to see if Curtis reacted. As long as the gun wasn't pointed at Elisabeth, he could take the chance. He dove at Curtis's arm, shoving it downward before the man realized Luke had even moved. With his other hand, Luke grabbed his other arm by the wrist and jerked it away from Elisabeth.

Elisabeth slid out of the way, but not fast enough. As Luke was trying not to crush her between them, Curtis managed to get his gun arm back up. The two men were suddenly still, the tension a near tangible thing as Luke struggled against the reality of a gun pointed in his face.

The alarm abruptly shut off, reminding him there was still hope as long as Todd and perhaps Matt were outside. Then he caught a glimpse of Elisabeth sliding open a drawer—the gun drawer. She reached inside and came out with one of the guns just as Curtis realized she was behind him.

He was too late. Without so much as a moment's hesitation, Elisabeth pressed the gun hard against Curtis's back and snarled, "Put your gun down. *Now*, Timothy. It's my draw."

Luke felt a burst of pride wash through him as he edged away from the business end of Curtis's weapon before Curtis realized he still had a viable hand to play.

Curtis flinched as she ground the thing into his back. Then a look came over his face that made Luke wish Elisabeth had just run when she had the chance.

"You won't fire that, Elisabeth. I seem to remember that you have a certain queasiness when it comes to shooting people."

The only warning Luke had was the fierce hatred he

saw in her eyes. He dove to the side as he heard the hard punch of the trigger, then rolled to his feet and came up behind Curtis, who was already screaming his head off. Luke reached around and disarmed the man before he realized the "bullet" hadn't penetrated that deeply.

Already sick of Curtis's whining, Luke put pressure on the nerve just below Curtis's ear and kept it there until Curtis collapsed in an unconscious heap. At that precise moment Sneakers skated on all four paws around the corner. The Doberman jumped onto Elisabeth, who gave a delighted whoop, tossed the staple gun to the floor, and threw her arms around the animal. They would have both fallen to the ground had Luke not pulled Sneakers off her, but Elisabeth wasn't ready to let go yet. She followed him down to the floor, snuggling her face against his sleek black neck as she murmured words of praise and thankfulness that he was still alive.

Luke waited as Elisabeth inspected the graze on Sneakers' haunches, silently judging that the dog was too rambunctious to be hurting much. Tucking the gun into the small of his back, he figured he'd keep Curtis alive long enough to answer a few questions. For now, though, he trusted Elisabeth would come through with faster answers. Sliding her scarf from around her neck with a flick of his wrist, he tied Curtis's hands behind him and told Sneakers to guard. Luke didn't know who was more surprised—Elisabeth, Sneakers, or himself—when the dog obeyed.

Luke pulled a very reluctant Elisabeth to her feet. "Have you seen anyone besides Curtis?"

She said no, then leaned down yet again to hug Sneakers, who was doing his best to pay attention to the man on the floor. "I thought Curtis killed him."

"I wasn't so sure he hadn't until I found him by the beach."

She jumped as Todd rounded the corner from the hall. "Where did you come from?" she demanded, frowning at the gun in his hand.

"Outside." He looked at Luke. "I decided to slip in when I saw it wasn't working. Sneakers decided the same thing, but he moves a lot faster."

Luke grinned. "It worked just fine. Elisabeth shot Curtis with the staple gun."

She rounded on him, hands on hips and fire spitting from her eyes. "If I'd known you were just going to waltz in here—*unarmed!*—I wouldn't have spent the last hour worrying about you."

Luke shrugged. "It would have worked a little more smoothly if you hadn't popped up."

"I *popped up* because I was afraid that if I waited for you to show, Matt and I would be dead or on some boat to someplace I didn't want to go to." She tossed her hair over her shoulder without taking her eyes off Luke. "Whatever prompted you to come to the door when you must have known something was wrong? Don't you realize you could have gotten killed?"

He lifted a hand to her chin and tilted her face to the light. "The only person who's going to get killed is the one who hurt you."

Her eyes softened, and he felt the fight going out of her as she tried to smile. "You know how I feel about someone I love doing my dirty work."

"You want to do it?" he asked as though he were asking her preference in wines.

She shook her head. "No, but I have to admit to getting a certain satisfaction from nailing him with the staple gun."

"You want him to live?"

"Prison is a good place for him, Luke. He hates it, and knowing he's miserable is enough for me."

It wasn't enough for Luke, but then, it wasn't his choice. "We'll leave him for Wyatt," he said, then glanced at Todd. "Did you see Matt anywhere? Elisabeth said he got away."

"I forgot! Matt didn't get away. He's in the priest hole upstairs." She raced down the hall to the stairs. "He was still unconscious when I put him there."

Luke and Todd passed her on the stairs and had the panel open before she even reached her room. Together they maneuvered Matt out of the closetlike enclosure and lifted him onto the bed. Elisabeth went into the bathroom for a cold cloth, returning just as Matt opened his eyes.

Which was about the same time they heard the fluttering chop of the helicopter as it passed overhead.

The marines had arrived.

The next few hours were pure chaos. Wyatt and his men allied themselves with the deputies from the sheriff's office, the resulting large group having no trouble in snaring Curtis's four accomplices, who arrived on a large cruiser. Matt was rushed by helicopter to a Seattle hospital, where he was to spend the night under observation for concussion. Curtis went to the same hospital where doctors pulled out the half-inch staple, gave him a tetanus shot, then released him to authorities who subsequently awarded Wyatt the pleasure of seeing to his transportation to Singapore.

Miss Eleanor and Jenny hurried over after Todd called them with the all-clear, bringing with them all their fresh grocery supplies so that the extraordinary number of people in Elisabeth's house didn't go hungry. Then Jenny grabbed a few clothes from her own house and boarded the helicopter for what had become a regular shuttle flight between Quincy Island and Seattle.

Even Old Harry showed up, his shirt still a bit wet but cleaner than Elisabeth ever remembered seeing it. While he grumbled a bit about this being no substitute for the quiet dinner for two he'd been looking forward to, he helped Miss Eleanor organize the odds and ends of foodstuffs they'd amassed into something recognizable as a meal.

With Todd's help, Elisabeth bathed the wound on Sneakers' backside, smeared it with antibiotics, and covered it with cotton and tape. Todd volunteered to take the Doberman to the vet and was waiting on the helipad with Sneakers on a leash when the copter returned for the next shuttle flight. Elisabeth helped him coerce the reluctant dog on board, then gave Todd a huge hug that brought a blush to his face.

She hugged him again, more concerned with letting him know how much she cared than she was with his boyish blushes.

Then Elisabeth headed straight down to the beach, ignoring the man Wyatt had assigned to follow her. She'd allowed the small intrusion on her privacy because it was easier than trying to convince her brother that Quincy Island was usually a very safe place to be. Walking at the edge of the surf, she made her way along the same path she'd followed with Luke only a day or so earlier.

Even though she tried to push them aside thoughts of Curtis intruded. Her hands trembled with reaction to all that had happened in the past few hours, and she stared blindly over the waves that rose and fell in a gentle offbeat rhythm.

The fact that it was over was no assurance that it would never happen again, she realized. Curtis had escaped once; he could do it again. She knew that, but the knowledge didn't frighten her as it once had. She was a different person than she'd been six years ago; older, wiser. Stronger.

And if that wasn't enough, she had Luke Sinclair on her side.

Elisabeth took several deep breaths and felt the fears she'd lived with for so long slowly leave her. She was stronger, she repeated to herself. Better. Old enough to know that everyone made mistakes, and her error in trusting Curtis was neither her fault nor her responsibility.

And with that admission Elisabeth knew that Curtis would never again possess the key to the prison she'd inhabited for the last six years.

She was at last free. Free to do anything she wished.

With whomever she wished. Simple, really, now that she'd gotten rid of all that old baggage she'd been carrying around for what seemed like a lifetime or two. If the idea wasn't so entirely repulsive, she'd think she owed Curtis for his brief reappearance into her life.

She buried that thought with a grimace and a laugh. *She was free!*

Now all she had to do was persuade Luke that not only was he the right man for her, he was the *only* man. It was no longer good enough to hope he'd come visit or that she might visit him. She wanted to be with him, in Singapore or Tahiti or wherever he traveled.

He loved her but was convinced he wasn't the right man for her. Too rough, he claimed. Too violent. Because of those reasons he wouldn't ask her to go with him. That much she knew for sure.

Telling him she intended to leave with him was her only choice. She didn't for a second imagine he'd accept her decision with grace. Consumed by her thoughts, she kicked a broken shell out of her path. He'd fight her, she knew, assault her with his own version of why it wouldn't work between them.

He didn't stand a chance. Not now that she'd made up her mind.

She bent over to pick up a tiny pink shell that was still intact. Holding the fragile shell to her ear, she suddenly smiled and wondered if Wyatt had ever mentioned her stubborn streak to his chief of security.

Lifting her face to catch the last rays of a setting sun, she prayed Luke wouldn't take too long to be convinced. Now that she knew what she wanted out of life, she was eager to get on with it.

She wanted Luke and had no intention of taking no for an answer.

Luke watched her from the end of the path that led to the house, her silhouette small and delicate against the spectacular backdrop of the setting sun. The horizon blazed with a bright orange glow that was shot through with purple streaks, the tails of which dipped into the gentle waves. Magnificent as it was, the sunset failed to distract him from the woman who stood facing the display of light and color.

He wanted Elisabeth more than he'd wanted anything or anyone in his entire life. But dreams didn't always come true. Luke knew that better than most. With a dismissing nod to the man who stood guard over her, he crossed the sand and came to stand behind her.

"I wondered if you and Wyatt would ever finish." She spoke without turning.

"We had a lot of business to get out of the way. Doing it all at once was the only way to get rid of him. I didn't think you'd want me in your bed with your brother just down the hall."

"He's gone?"

"On the last shuttle. He wanted to personally escort Curtis back to jail."

"He could have said good-bye."

"I told him I'd do it for him." He rested his hands on her shoulders and pulled her back against him. When she nestled her head in the curve of his shoulder, he folded his arms around her waist. "Wyatt said he'd be back to see you next week."

"I won't be here."

He tensed, then carefully turned her in his arms until she was facing him. "And just where will you be?"

She tilted her head to look up at him, her eyes dark and determined. "Wherever you are, Sinclair. Do you have a problem with that?"

Luke just stared at her, his hands massaging her shoulders in unconscious strokes. He let her question go unanswered, because it was imperative she know something important had changed. "For a little while there on the ferry, right after I discovered you were missing, I was afraid you'd bailed out on me."

"You thought I'd chickened out?" She smiled, shaking her head. "I'd go anywhere with you, Luke Sinclair. Haven't you figured that out yet?"

"I believe it now."

"Why now?" she whispered.

"Because I've figured out you can and do make your own decisions." He brushed his lips across her forehead and tangled the fingers of one hand into her windblown hair.

"Wyatt told you about my stubborn streak," she said, grinning.

He nodded. "That. Mostly, though, it's a matter of realizing that if you want to leave Quincy Island, it's because you're finally ready."

She snuggled her face against his, thinking how easy this was going to be now that he'd come to the same conclusions as she.

He continued before she had a chance to agree. "Besides, Squirt, I don't think I could sleep nights knowing you were here, all alone with only a bunch of gadgets to watch over you."

"They're your gadgets."

"I'm better. And you can't turn me off." He breathed deeply and shut his eyes, then opened them again, meeting her gaze. "I won't leave here without you, and I'm pretty sure I can't be much of a security chief to your brother if I stay."

"Do my needs have anything to do with this?" she teased.

"As long as they coincide with mine." He kissed her nose and sighed heavily. "Are you sure, honey? Can you be happy away from here?"

She nodded. "One hundred percent certain. I'll miss Quincy Island, but I don't *need* to be here. I won't let Curtis dictate my life, not anymore. I've grown beyond that."

His eyes warmed in approval, then he traced the swollen area beside her mouth. "Does it hurt?"

She shook her head, then changed her mind and

nodded. "I think you need to kiss it to make it better."

"You're sure?"

"I've been waiting forever," she said softly.

He touched his lips to her cheek with a delicacy that reminded her of how gentle he really was. She shivered in his arms, then closed her eyes and let him heal her wound. The slight throb vanished, and she sighed in total contentment.

It was magic, she realized. Luke's magic.

Then he claimed her mouth with a real kiss, the kind of kiss she'd been needing all afternoon. By the time he retreated, neither was as calm and relaxed as they'd been only moments before.

"So what's it going to be, Luke?" she whispered, her fingers flexing against the back of his neck. "Are you going to trust that I know what I'm doing when I decide to move in with you?"

"Besides the fact that my apartment's too small . . ."

She shrugged off that argument. "Details, Sinclair. I'm good at those."

"Your brother—"

She interrupted again. "Wyatt will be too happy to have me nearby to care who I'm sleeping with."

He kissed her again, then tucked the unbruised side of her face against his chest. "I tried to quit my job this afternoon. He wouldn't let me."

"Why?" She jerked her head back and stared at him in disbelief.

"He said my contract wasn't up for another two years."

She shook her head impatiently. "You know what I meant. Why do you want to quit? I thought you liked your job."

"I told you before, Elisabeth. It's a rough life, sometimes not a very pretty one." He lifted his hand to stroke the furrows from her brow. "I don't want you exposed to any of that."

"*I'm* the one who shot Curtis in the back." She let go a sigh of relief at his objections. These she could handle.

The only thing she couldn't fight was if he didn't want her.

It looked as though that wasn't going to be an issue.

"A minor wound, Squirt. I've had to do a lot worse when it came to protecting your brother and those around him. The world isn't a safe place for men like Wyatt who wield the kind of power a lot of money brings."

"All the more reason that you should have someone to come home to, someone who will remind you that your soul can be gentle." She lifted high on her toes and urged his head down with her hands. "I'm giving up this beautiful island for you, Sinclair. The least you can do is be a little more gracious about it."

"Despite what you believe, Wyatt won't like it if you live with me without a ring on your finger."

"Wyatt doesn't have a vote in this," she returned, her heart speeding up as she realized he'd already decided to marry her. A good thing, too, because having children was a topic she had intended to raise before too many weeks passed. "But, yes, I'll marry you if you think it will please your boss." She could have sworn that the hand he lifted to her face was trembling.

"I love you, Elisabeth Conner."

"That's why I'm marrying you," she whispered.

"Because I love you?"

She shook her head. "No, because I love you. I've

been waiting my whole life for you, Luke Sinclair. Letting you walk away was never an option."

Holding her gaze, he lowered his head until his lips were brushing hers. He couldn't help the grin that tugged at his mouth. "At least I won't have to worry about quitting. Wyatt will fire me for this."

"Wyatt's already pointed out you've got two years left in your contract. By the time that's over, he'll be an uncle and won't dare fire you." She ran the tip of her tongue across his bottom lip. "It's either you go back to work or we starve. My needlepoint won't even begin to support the two of us."

"You could teach me." He nibbled at the unhurt corner of her mouth, then slid his tongue inside. "I'm good with my hands." To prove his point, his palms drifted down her back to her fanny, where they began a slow massage.

"Needlepoint would be good for you," she said, taking a breath. She caught his tongue with her teeth, then let it slide back between her lips. "Though I doubt if you'll get good fast enough to buy Sneakers' food, much less ours."

"Sneakers will hate Singapore."

"Not if we get a place near the water."

He took a deep breath, then rested his hands on her hips and forced her to lean back. "It's settled, then?"

"It's settled. I'm going to marry you and make you a happy man. In return you will make love to me as frequently as possible."

"We could start now." He brought her hips hard against his and rubbed against her.

Excitement flared in her eyes. "Everyone's gone?"

"Except for a couple of men Wyatt insisted on leaving, but they're bunking over at the Sloanes. Todd called and said he'd stay with his mother in Seattle, then pick up Sneakers from the vet in the morning." He dipped his head to kiss her, then put his arm around her shoulders and began walking in the direction of the house, away from the sun that had finally disappeared beyond the horizon. "Miss Eleanor and Old Harry looked relieved to be getting back to their tête-à-tête."

She laughed softly, then snuggled closer into Luke's side. "I wonder if they've left anything for dinner."

"Not to worry, love. I'll cook."

"You cook?" She sounded surprised.

He grinned into the twilight and urged her toward the house. "You won't believe what I can do with a couple of eggs." Not to mention the habanero sauce he'd found hidden behind the mustard in the refrigerator. "I'll toss something together while you go upstairs and have a good soak."

"I thought we were going to make love before we ate." Her hand slid under the waistband of his jeans.

He lengthened his stride. "Before *and* after. Let's get to it."

Contrarily she came to an abrupt stop, forcing him to swing around to face her. "I think, Sinclair—"

"It's Luke." He slid his arms around her waist and brought her close, where she belonged. "Say it."

Elisabeth studied the man who towered over her. She saw a face filled with character and life and happiness, and gray eyes that unashamedly reflected the emotions of his heart.

He had so much love to give, she mused. She knew she'd never tire of it. "I think, Luke, that falling in love with you is the easiest thing I've ever done."

"Dreams come true," he murmured. "I didn't know that before I met you."

"Then you didn't know anything at all, Sinclair." She smiled up at him, her heart overflowing with love for the man who had set her free. "We live in a world where dreams come true."

"I dreamed you would love me."

"I do."

"No doubts, no hesitation." He shook his head in wonder at her total confidence. "I wish I'd come to you four years ago."

"I wasn't ready for you then. I am now." Her eyes sparkled as she took his hand to lead him into the house. "The question is, are you ready for me?"

"Worried I won't be able to keep up?" he teased, swinging her up into his arms to cross the kitchen in long strides.

She giggled, then put her lips to his ear to tell him exactly how she planned to keep him interested.

For the next fifty years, maybe more.

THE EDITOR'S CORNER

Along with the May flowers come six fabulous Love-swepts that will dazzle you with humor, excitement, and, above all, love. Touching, tender, packed with emotion and wonderfully happy endings, our six upcoming romances are real treasures.

The ever-popular Charlotte Hughes leads things off with **THE DEVIL AND MISS GOODY TWO-SHOES**, LOVESWEPT #684. Kane Stoddard had never answered the dozens of letters Melanie Abercrombie had written him in prison, but her words had kept his spirit alive during the three years he'd been jailed in error—and now he wants nothing more than a new start, and a chance to meet the woman who touched his angry soul. Stunned by the sizzling attraction she feels for Kane, Mel struggles to deny the passionate emotions Kane's touch awakens. No one had ever believed in Kane until Mel's sweet caring makes him dare to taste her innocent lips, makes him hunger to hold her until the sun rises. He can only hope that his fierce loving will vanquish her fear of losing him. Touching and intense, **THE DEVIL AND MISS GOODY TWO-SHOES** is the kind of love story that Charlotte is known and loved for.

This month Terry Lawrence delivers some **CLOSE ENCOUNTERS**, LOVESWEPT #685—but of the romantic kind. Alone in the elevator with his soon-to-be ex-wife, Tony Paretti decides he isn't giving Sara Cohen up without a fight! But when fate sends the elevator plunging ten floors and tosses her into his arms, he seizes his chance—and with breath-stealing abandon embraces the woman he's never stopped loving. Kissing Sara with a savage passion that transcends pain, Tony insists that what they had was too good to let go, that together they are strong enough to face the grief that shattered their marriage. Sara aches to rebuild the bonds of their love but doesn't know if she can trust him with her sorrow, even after Tony confesses the secret hopes that he's never dared to tell another soul. Terry will have you crying and cheering as these two people discover the courage to love again.

Get ready for a case of mistaken identity in **THE ONE FOR ME**, LOVESWEPT #686, by Mary Kay McComas. It was a ridiculous masquerade, pretending to be his twin brother at a business dinner, but Peter Wesley grows utterly confused when his guest returns from the powder room—and promptly steals his heart! She looks astonishingly like the woman he'd dined with earlier, but he's convinced that the cool fire and passionate longing in her bright blue eyes is new and dangerously irresistible. Katherine Asher hates impersonating her look-alike sisters, and seeing Peter makes her regret she'd ever agreed. When he kisses her with primitive yearning, she aches to admit her secret—that she wants him for herself! Once the charade is revealed, Peter woos her with fierce pleasure until she surrenders. She has always taken her happiness last, but is she ready to put her love for him first? **THE ONE FOR ME** is humorous and hot—just too good to resist.

Marcia Evanick gives us a hero who is **PLAYING FOR KEEPS**, LOVESWEPT #687. For the past two years detective Reece Carpenter has solved the fake murder-mystery at the Montgomery clan's annual family reunion, infuriating the beautiful—and competitive—Tennessee Montgomery. But when he faces his tempting rival this time, all he wants to win is her heart! Tennie has come prepared to beat her nemesis if it kills her—but the wild flames in his eyes light a fire in her blood that only his lips can satisfy. Tricked into working as a team, Tennie and Reece struggle to prove which is the better sleuth, but the enforced closeness creates a bigger challenge: to keep their minds on the case when they can't keep their hands off each other! Another keeper from Marcia Evanick.

STRANGE BEDFELLOWS, LOVESWEPT #688, is the newest wonderful romance from Patt Bucheister. John Lomax gave up rescuing ladies in distress when he traded his cop's mean streets for the peace of rural Kentucky, but he feels his resolve weaken when he discovers Silver Knight asleep on his couch! Her sea nymph's eyes brimming with delicious humor, her temptress's smile teasingly seductive, Silver pleads with him to probe a mystery in her New York apartment—and her hunk of a hero is hooked! Fascinated by her reluctant knight, an enigmatic warrior whose pain only she can soothe, Silver wonders if a joyous romp might help her free his spirit from the demons of a shadowy past. He is her reckless gamble, the dare she can't refuse—but she needs to make him understand his true home is in her arms. **STRANGE BEDFELLOWS** is Patt Bucheister at her sizzling best.

And last, but certainly not least, is **NO PROMISES MADE**, LOVESWEPT #689, by Maris Soule. Eric Newman is a sleek black panther of a man who holds Ashley Kehler spellbound, mesmerizing her with a look that strips her bare and caresses her senses, but he could also make her lose control, forget the dreams that drive her . . . and Ashley knows she must resist this seducer who ignites a fever in her blood! Drawn to this golden spitfire who is his opposite in every way, Eric feels exhilarated, intrigued against his will—but devastated by the knowledge that she'll soon be leaving. Ashley wavers between ecstasy and guilt, yet Eric knows the only way to keep his love is to let her go, hoping that she is ready to choose the life that will bring her joy. Don't miss this fabulous story!

Happy reading!

With warmest wishes,

Nita Taublib

Nita Taublib

Associate Publisher

P.S. Don't miss the exciting women's novels from Bantam that are coming your way in May—**DECEPTION**, by Amanda Quick, is the paperback edition of her first *New York Times* bestselling hardcover; **RELENTLESS**, by award-winning author Patricia Potter, is a searing tale of revenge and desire, set in Colorado during the 1870's; **SEIZED BY LOVE**, by Susan Johnson, is a novel of savage passions and dangerous pleasures sweeping from fabulous country estates and hunting lodges to the opulent ballrooms and salons of Russian nobility; and **WILD CHILD**, by bestselling author Suzanne Forster, reunites adversaries who share a tangled past—and for whom an old spark of conflict will kindle into a dangerously passionate blaze. We'll be giving you a sneak peek at these terrific books in next month's LOVESWEPTs. And immediately following this page look for a preview of the exciting romances from Bantam that are *available now*!

Don't miss these exciting books by your favorite Bantam authors

On sale in March:

DARK PARADISE
by Tami Hoag

WARRIOR BRIDE
by Tamara Leigh

REBEL IN SILK
by Sandra Chastain

"Ms. Hoag has deservedly become one of the
romance genre's most treasured authors."
—*Rave Reviews*

Look For

DARK PARADISE

by

Tami Hoag

*Here is nationally bestselling author Tami Hoag's most
dangerously erotic novel yet, a story filled with heart-
stopping suspense and shocking passion . . . a story of a
woman drawn to a man as hard and untamable as the
land he loves, and to a town steeped in secrets—where
a killer lurks.*

Night had fallen by the time Mari finally found
her way to Lucy's place with the aid of the map
Lucy had sent in her first letter. Her "hide-out,"
she'd called it. The huge sky was as black as velvet, sewn with the sequins of more stars than she
had ever imagined. The world suddenly seemed a
vast, empty wilderness, and she pulled into the yard
of the small ranch, questioning for the first time
the wisdom of a surprise arrival. There were no
lights glowing a welcome in the windows of the
handsome new log house. The garage doors were
closed.

She climbed out of her Honda and stretched,
feeling exhausted and rumpled. The past two weeks
had sapped her strength, the decisions she had made

taking chunks of it at a time. The drive up from Sacramento had been accomplished in a twenty-four hour marathon with breaks for nothing more than the bathroom and truck stop burritos, and now the physical strain of that weighed her down like an anchor.

It had seemed essential that she get here as quickly as possible, as if she had been afraid her nerve would give out and she would succumb to the endless dissatisfaction of her life in California if she didn't escape immediately. The wild pendulum her emotions had been riding had left her feeling drained and dizzy. She had counted on falling into Lucy's care the instant she got out of her car, but Lucy didn't appear to be home, and disappointment sent the pendulum swinging downward again.

Foolish, really, she told herself, blinking back the threat of tears as she headed for the front porch. She couldn't have expected Lucy to know she was coming. She hadn't been able to bring herself to call ahead. A call would have meant an explanation of everything that had gone on in the past two weeks, and that was better made in person.

A calico cat watched her approach from the porch rail, but jumped down and ran away as she climbed the steps, its claws scratching the wood floor as it darted around the corner of the porch and disappeared. The wind swept down off the mountain and howled around the weathered outbuildings, bringing with it a sense of isolation and a vague feeling of desertion that Mari tried to shrug off as she raised a hand and knocked on the door.

No lights brightened the windows. No voice called out for her to keep her pants on.

She swallowed at the combination of disappointment and uneasiness that crowded at the back of her throat. Against her will, her eyes did a quick scan of the moon-shadowed ranch yard and the hills beyond. The place was in the middle of nowhere. She had driven through the small town of New Eden and gone miles into the wilderness, seeing no more than two other houses on the way—and those from a great distance.

She knocked again, but didn't wait for an answer before trying the door. Lucy had mentioned wildlife in her few letters. The four-legged, flea-scratching kind.

"Bears. I remember something about bears," she muttered, the nerves at the base of her neck wriggling at the possibility that there were a dozen watching her from the cover of darkness, sizing her up with their beady little eyes while their stomachs growled. "If it's all the same to you, Luce, I'd rather not meet one up close and personal while you're off doing the boot scootin' boogie with some cowboy."

Stepping inside, she fumbled along the wall for a light switch, then blinked against the glare of a dozen small bulbs artfully arranged in a chandelier of antlers. Her first thought was that Lucy's abysmal housekeeping talents had deteriorated to a shocking new low. The place was a disaster area, strewn with books, newspapers, note paper, clothing.

She drifted away from the door and into the great room that encompassed most of the first floor of the house, her brain stumbling to make sense of the contradictory information it was getting. The house was barely a year old, a blend of Western tradition and contemporary architectural touches. Lucy had hired a decorator to capture those intertwined feelings in the interior. But the western watercolor prints on the walls hung at drunken angles. The cushions had been torn from the heavy, overstuffed chairs. The seat of the red leather sofa had been slit from end to end. Stuffing rose up from the wound in ragged tufts. Broken lamps and shattered pottery littered the expensive Berber rug. An overgrown pothos had been ripped from its planter and shredded, and was strung across the carpet like strips of tattered green ribbon.

Not even Lucy was this big a slob.

Mari's pulse picked up the rhythm of fear. "Lucy?" she called, the tremor in her voice a vocal extension of the goosebumps that were pebbling her arms. The only answer was an ominous silence that pressed in on her eardrums until they were pounding.

She stepped over a gutted throw pillow, picked her way around a smashed terra cotta urn and peered into the darkened kitchen area. The refrigerator door was ajar, the light within glowing like the promise of gold inside a treasure chest. The smell, however, promised something less pleasant.

She wrinkled her nose and blinked against the sour fumes as she found the light switch on the wall and flicked it upward. Recessed lighting beamed down on a repulsive mess of spoiling food and spilled beer. Milk puddled on the Mexican tile in front of the refrigerator. The carton lay abandoned on its side. Flies hovered over the garbage like tiny vultures.

"Jesus, Lucy," she muttered, "what kind of party did you throw here?"

And where the hell are you?

The pine cupboard doors stood open, their contents spewed out of them. Stoneware and china and flatware lay broken and scattered. Appropriately macabre place settings for the gruesome meal that had been laid out on the floor.

Mari backed away slowly, her hand trembling as she reached out to steady herself with the one ladder-back chair that remained upright at the long pine harvest table. She caught her full lower lip between her teeth and stared through the sheen of tears. She had worked too many criminal cases not to see this for what it was. The house had been ransacked. The motive could have been robbery or the destruction could have been the aftermath of something else, something uglier.

"Lucy?" she called again, her heart sinking like a stone at the sure knowledge that she wouldn't get an answer.

Her gaze drifted to the stairway that led up to the loft where the bedrooms were tucked, then cut to the telephone that had been ripped from the kitchen wall and now hung by slender tendons of wire.

Her heart beat faster. A fine mist of sweat slicked her palms.

"Lucy?"

"She's dead."

The words were like a pair of shotgun blasts in the still of the room. Mari wheeled around, a scream wedged in her throat right behind her heart. He stood at the other end of the table, six feet of hewn granite in faded jeans and a chambray work shirt. How anything that big could have sneaked up on her was beyond reasoning. Her perceptions distorted by fear, she thought his shoulders rivaled the mountains for size. He stood there, staring at her from beneath the low-riding brim of a dusty black Stetson, his gaze narrow, measuring, his mouth set in a grim, compressed line. His right hand—big with blunt-tipped fingers—hung at his side just inches from a holstered revolver that looked big enough to bring down a buffalo.

WARRIOR BRIDE
by
Tamara Leigh

*" . . . a vibrant, passionate love story that captures all
the splendor of the medieval era . . . A sheer delight."*

—bestselling author Teresa Medeiros

*After four years of planning revenge on the highway-
man who'd stolen her future, Lizanne Balmaine had
the blackguard at the point of her sword. Yet something about the onyx-eyed man she'd abducted and
taken to her family estate was different—something
that made her hesitate at her moment of triumph.
Now she was his prisoner . . . and even more than
her handsome captor she feared her own treacherous
desires.*

"Welcome, my Lord Ranulf," she said. " 'Tis a fine
day for a duel."

He stared unblinkingly at her, then let a frown
settle between his eyes. "Forsooth, I did not expect
you to attend this bloodletting," he said. "I must
needs remember you are not a lady."

Her jaw hardened. "I assure you I would not
miss this for anything," she tossed back.

He looked at the weapons she carried. "And
where is this man who would champion your ill-
fated cause?" he asked, looking past her.

"Man?" She shook her head. "There is no man."

Ranulf considered this, one eyebrow arched.
"You were unable to find a single man willing to
die for you, my lady? Not one?"

Refusing to rise to the bait, Lizanne leaned forward, smiling faintly. "Alas, I fear I am so uncomely that none would offer."

"And what of our bargain?" Ranulf asked, suspicion cast upon his voice.

"It stands."

"You think to hold me till your brother returns?" He shifted more of his weight onto his uninjured leg. "Do you forget that I am an unwilling captive, my lady? 'Tis not likely you will return me to that foul-smelling cell." He took a step toward her.

At his sudden movement, the mare shied away, snorting loudly as it pranced sideways. Lizanne brought the animal under control with an imperceptible tightening of her legs.

"Nay," she said, her eyes never wavering. "Your opponent is here before you now."

Ranulf took some moments to digest this, then burst out laughing. As preposterous as it was, a mere woman challenging an accomplished knight to a duel of swords, her proposal truly did not surprise him, though it certainly amused him.

And she was not jesting! he acknowledged. Amazingly, it fit the conclusions he had wrestled with, and finally accepted, regarding her character.

Had she a death wish, then? Even if that spineless brother of hers had shown her how to swing a sword, it was inconceivable she could have any proficiency with such a heavy, awkward weapon. A sling, perhaps, and he mustn't forget a dagger, but a sword?

Slowly, he sobered, blinking back tears of mirth and drawing deep, ragged breaths of air.

She edged her horse nearer, her indignation evident in her stiffly erect bearing. "I find no humor in the situation. Mayhap you would care to enlighten me, Lord Ranulf?"

"Doubtless, you would not appreciate my explanation, my lady."

Her chin went up. "Think you I will not make a worthy opponent?"

"With your nasty tongue, perhaps, but—"

"Then let us not prolong the suspense any longer," she snapped. Swiftly, she removed the sword from its scabbard and tossed it, hilt first, to him.

Reflexively, Ranulf pulled it from the air, his hand closing around the cool metal hilt. He was taken aback as he held it aloft, for inasmuch as the weapon appeared perfectly honed on both its edges, it was not the weighty sword he was accustomed to. Indeed, it felt awkward in his grasp.

"And what is this, a child's toy?" he quipped, twisting the sword in his hand.

In one fluid motion, Lizanne dismounted and turned to face him. "'Tis the instrument of your death, my lord." Advancing, she drew her own sword, identical to the one he held.

He lowered his sword's point and narrowed his eyes. "Think you I would fight a woman?"

"'Tis as we agreed."

"I agreed to fight a man—"

"Nay, you agreed to fight the opponent of my choice. I stand before you now ready to fulfill our bargain."

"We have no such bargain," he insisted.

"Would you break your vow? Are you so dishonorable?"

Never before had Ranulf's honor been questioned. For King Henry and, when necessary, himself, he had fought hard and well, and he carried numerous battle scars to attest to his valor. Still, her insult rankled him.

"'Tis honor that compels me to decline," he

said, a decidedly dangerous smile playing about his lips.

"Honor?" She laughed, coming to an abrupt halt a few feet from him. "Methinks 'tis your injury, coward. Surely, you can still wield a sword?"

Coward? A muscle in his jaw jerked. This one was expert at stirring the remote depths of his anger. "Were you a man, you would be dead now."

"Then imagine me a man," she retorted, lifting her sword in challenge.

The very notion was laughable. Even garbed as she was, the Lady Lizanne was wholly a woman.

"Nay, I fear I must decline." Resolutely, he leaned on the sword. "'Twill make a fine walking stick, though," he added, flexing the steel blade beneath his weight.

Ignoring his quip, Lizanne took a step nearer. "You cannot decline!"

"Aye, and I do."

"Then I will gut you like a pig!" she shouted and leaped forward.

REBEL IN SILK
by
Sandra Chastain

"*Sandra Chastain's characters' steamy relationships
are the stuff dreams are made of.*"
—*Romantic Times*

*Dallas Burke had come to Willow Creek, Wyoming,
to find her brother's killer, and she had no intention of being scared off—not by the roughnecks who
trashed her newspaper office, nor by the devilishly
handsome cowboy who warned her of the violence to
come. Yet she couldn't deny that the tall, sunbronzed
rancher had given her something to think about,
namely, what it would be like to be held in his
steel-muscled arms and feel his sensuous mouth on
hers . . . .*

A bunch of liquored-up cowboys were riding past
the station, shooting guns into the air, bearing down
on the startled Miss Banning caught by drifts in the
middle of the street.

From the general store, opposite where Dallas
was standing, came a figure who grabbed her valise
in one hand and scooped her up with the other, flung her over his shoulder, and stepped onto
the wooden sidewalk beneath the roof over the
entrance to the saloon.

Dallas let out a shocked cry as the horses
thundered by. She might have been run over had
it not been for the man's quick action. Now,
hanging upside down, she felt her rescuer's hand

cradling her thigh in much too familiar a manner.

"Sir, what are you doing?"

"Saving your life."

The man lifted her higher, then, as she started to slide, gave her bottom another tight squeeze. Being rescued was one thing, but this was out of line. Gratitude flew out of her mind as he groped her backside.

"Put me down, you . . . you . . . lecher!"

"Gladly!" He leaned forward, loosened his grip and let her slide to the sidewalk where she landed in a puddle of melted snow and ice. The valise followed with a thump.

"Well, you didn't have to try to break my leg!" Dallas scrambled to her feet, her embarrassment tempering her fear and turning it into anger.

"No, I could have let the horses do it!"

Dallas had never heard such cold dispassion in a voice. He wasn't flirting with her. He wasn't concerned about her injuries. She didn't know why he'd bothered to touch her so intimately. One minute he was there, and the next he had turned to walk away.

"Wait, please wait! I'm sorry to appear ungrateful. I was just startled."

As she scurried along behind him, all she could see was the hat covering his face and head, his heavy canvas duster, and boots with silver spurs set with turquoise. He wasn't stopping.

Dallas reached out and caught his arm. "Now, just a minute. Where I come from, a man at least gives a lady the chance to say a proper thank you. What kind of man are you?"

"I'm cold, I'm thirsty, and I'm ready for a woman. Are you volunteering?"

There was a snickering sound that ran through the room they'd entered. Dallas raised her head and glanced around. She wasn't the only woman in the saloon, but she was the only one wearing all her clothes.

Any other woman might have gasped. But Dallas suppressed her surprise. She didn't know the layout of the town yet, and until she did, she wouldn't take a chance of offending anyone, even these ladies of pleasure. "I'm afraid not. I'm a newspaperwoman, not a . . . an entertainer."

He ripped his hat away, shaking off the glistening beads of melting snow that hung in the jet-black hair that touched his shoulders. He was frowning at her, his brow drawn into deep lines of displeasure; his lips, barely visible beneath a bushy mustache, pressed into a thin line.

His eyes, dark and deep, held her. She sensed danger and a hot intensity.

Where the man she'd met on the train seemed polished and well-mannered, her present adversary was anything but a gentleman. He was a man of steel who challenged with every glance. She shivered in response.

"Hello," a woman's voice intruded. "I'm Miranda. You must have come in on the train."

Dallas blinked, breaking the contact between her and her rescuer. With an effort, she turned to the woman.

"Ah, yes. I did. Dallas Banning." She started to hold out her hand, realized that she was clutching her valise, then lowered it. "I'm afraid I've made rather a mess of introducing myself to Green Willow Creek."

"Well, I don't know about what happened in the street, but following Jake in here might give your reputation a bit of a tarnish."

"Jake?" This was the Jake that her brother Jamie had been worried about.

"Why, yes," Miranda said, "I assumed you two knew each other?"

"Not likely," Jake growled and turned to the bar. "She's too skinny and her mouth is too big for my taste."

"Miss Banning?" Elliott Parnell, the gentleman she'd met on the train, rushed in from the street. "I saw what happened. Are you all right?"

Jake looked up, catching Dallas between him and the furious look he cast at Elliott Parnell.

Dallas didn't respond. The moment Jake had spotted Mr. Elliott, everything in the saloon had seemed to stop. All movement. All sound. For a long endless moment it seemed as if everyone in the room were frozen in place.

Jake finally spoke. "If she's with you and your sodbusters, Elliott, you'd better get her out of here."

Elliot took Dallas's arm protectively. "No, Jake. We simply came in on the same train. Miss Banning is James Banning's sister."

"Oh? The troublemaking newspaper editor. Almost as bad as the German immigrants. I've got no use for either one. Take my advice, Miss Banning. Get on the next train back to wherever you came from."

"I don't need your advice, Mr. Silver."

"Suit yourself, but somebody didn't want your brother here, and my guess is that you won't be any more welcome!"

Dallas felt a shiver of pure anger ripple down her backbone. She might as well make her position known right now. She came to find out the truth and she wouldn't be threatened. "Mr. Silver—"

"Jake! Elliott!" Miranda interrupted, a warning in her voice. "Can't you see that Miss Banning is half-frozen? Men! You have to forgive them," she said, turning to Dallas. "At the risk of further staining your reputation, I'd be pleased to have you make use of my room to freshen up and get dry. That is if you don't mind being . . . here."

"I'd be most appreciative, Miss Miranda," Dallas said, following her golden-haired hostess to the stairs.

Dallas felt all the eyes in the room boring holes in her back. She didn't have to be told where she was and what was taking place beyond the doors on either side of the corridor. If being here ruined her reputation, so be it. She wasn't here to make friends anyway. Besides, a lead to Jamie's murderer was a lot more likely to come from these people than those who might be shocked by her actions.

For just a second she wondered what would have happened if Jake had marched straight up the stairs with her. Then she shook off the impossible picture that thought had created.

She wasn't here to be bedded.

She was here to kill a man.

She just had to find out which one.

And don't miss these spectacular
romances from Bantam Books,
on sale in April:

DECEPTION
by the New York Times bestselling author
Amanda Quick
"One of the hottest and most
prolific writers in romance today . . ."
—*USA Today*

RELENTLESS
by the highly acclaimed author
Patricia Potter
"One of the romance genre's
finest talents . . ."
—*Romantic Times*

SEIZED BY LOVE
by the mistress of erotic historical romance
Susan Johnson
"Susan Johnson is one of the best."
—*Romantic Times*

WILD CHILD
by the bestselling author
Suzanne Forster
"(Suzanne Forster) is guaranteed to steam up
your reading glasses."
—*L.A. Daily News*

OFFICIAL RULES

To enter the sweepstakes below carefully follow all instructions found elsewhere in this offer.

The **Winners Classic** will award prizes with the following approximate maximum values: 1 Grand Prize: $26,500 (or $25,000 cash alternate); 1 First Prize: $3,000; 5 Second Prizes: $400 each; 35 Third Prizes: $100 each; 1,000 Fourth Prizes: $7.50 each. Total maximum retail value of Winners Classic Sweepstakes is $42,500. Some presentations of this sweepstakes may contain individual entry numbers corresponding to one or more of the aforementioned prize levels. To determine the Winners, individual entry numbers will first be compared with the winning numbers preselected by computer. For winning numbers not returned, prizes will be awarded in random drawings from among all eligible entries received. Prize choices may be offered at various levels. If a winner chooses an automobile prize, all license and registration fees, taxes, destination charges and, other expenses not offered herein are the responsibility of the winner. If a winner chooses a trip, travel must be complete within one year from the time the prize is awarded. Minors must be accompanied by an adult. Travel companion(s) must also sign release of liability. Trips are subject to space and departure availability. Certain black-out dates may apply.

The following applies to the sweepstakes named above:

No purchase necessary. You can also enter the sweepstakes by sending your name and address to: P.O. Box 508, Gibbstown, N.J. 08027. Mail each entry separately. Sweepstakes begins 6/1/93. Entries must be received by 12/30/94. Not responsible for lost, late, damaged, misdirected, illegible or postage due mail. Mechanically reproduced entries are not eligible. All entries become property of the sponsor and will not be returned.

Prize Selection/Validations: Selection of winners will be conducted no later than 5:00 PM on January 28, 1995, by an independent judging organization whose decisions are final. Random drawings will be held at 1211 Avenue of the Americas, New York, N.Y. 10036. Entrants need not be present to win. Odds of winning are determined by total number of entries received. Circulation of this sweepstakes is estimated not to exceed 200 million. All prizes are guaranteed to be awarded and delivered to winners. Winners will be notified by mail and may be required to complete an affidavit of eligibility and release of liability which must be returned within 14 days of date on notification or alternate winners will be selected in a random drawing. Any prize notification letter or any prize returned to a participating sponsor, Bantam Doubleday Dell Publishing Group, Inc., its participating divisions or subsidiaries, or the independent judging organization as undeliverable will be awarded to an alternate winner. Prizes are not transferable. No substitution for prizes except as offered or as may be necessary due to unavailability, in which case a prize of equal or greater value will be awarded. Prizes will be awarded approximately 90 days after the drawing. All taxes are the sole responsibility of the winners. Entry constitutes permission (except where prohibited by law) to use winners' names, hometowns, and likenesses for publicity purposes without further or other compensation. Prizes won by minors will be awarded in the name of parent or legal guardian.

Participation: Sweepstakes open to residents of the United States and Canada, except for the province of Quebec. Sweepstakes sponsored by Bantam Doubleday Dell Publishing Group, Inc., (BDD), 1540 Broadway, New York, NY 10036. Versions of this sweepstakes with different graphics and prize choices will be offered in conjunction with various solicitations or promotions by different subsidiaries and divisions of BDD. Where applicable, winners will have their choice of any prize offered at level won. Employees of BDD, its divisions, subsidiaries, advertising agencies, independent judging organization, and their immediate family members are not eligible.

Canadian residents, in order to win, must first correctly answer a time limited arithmetical skill testing question. Void in Puerto Rico, Quebec and wherever prohibited or restricted by law. Subject to all federal, state, local and provincial laws and regulations. For a list of major prize winners (available after 1/29/95): send a self-addressed, stamped envelope entirely separate from your entry to: Sweepstakes Winners, P.O. Box 517, Gibbstown, NJ 08027. Requests must be received by 12/30/94. DO NOT SEND ANY OTHER CORRESPONDENCE TO THIS P.O. BOX.

Don't miss these fabulous Bantam women's fiction titles

Now on sale

- ## DARK PARADISE
  by Tami Hoag, national bestselling author of *CRY WOLF*

  "Ms Hoag is...a writer of superlative talent." -Romantic Times

  Enter into a thrilling tale where a murderer lurks and death abounds. And where someone has the power to turn a slice of heaven into a dark paradise. _____56161-8 $5.99/$6.99 in Canada

- ## WARRIOR BRIDE
  by Tamara Leigh

  "Fresh, exciting...wonderfully sensual...sure to be noticed in the romance genre."—New York Times bestselling author Amanda Quick

  Ranulf Wardieu was furious to discover his jailer was a raven-haired maiden garbed in men's clothing and skilled in combat. But he vowed that he would storm her defenses with sweet caresses and make his captivating enemy his.. _____56533-8 $5.50/6.99 in Canada

- ## REBEL IN SILK
  by Sandra Chastain

  "Sandra Chastain's characters' steamy relationships are the stuff dreams are made of."—Romantic Times

  Dallas Burke had come to Willow Creek, Wyoming, to find her brother's killer, and she had no intention of being scared off—not by the roughnecks who trashed her newspaper office, nor by the devilishly handsome cowboy who stole her heart. _____56464-1 $5.50/$6.99 in Canada

Ask for these books at your local bookstore or use this page to order.

❏ Please send me the books I have checked above. I am enclosing $ _____ (add $2.50 to cover postage and handling). Send check or money order, no cash or C. O. D.'s please.

Name _____

Address _____

City/ State/ Zip _____

Send order to: Bantam Books, Dept. FN136, 2451 S. Wolf Rd., Des Plaines, IL 60018 FN136 4/94

Allow four to six weeks for delivery.

Prices and availability subject to change without notice.